I0721780

CHIEF WHITE EAGLE
The last free Abnaki Indian
WORKBOOK PRESS
RECOMMENDED
LITERARY BOOK COMPETITION 2020
L. S. WOOD

WORKBOOK PRESS LLC
187 E Warm Springs Rd,
Suite B285, Las Vegas, NV 89119, USA

Website: https://workbookpress.com/
Hotline: 1-888-818-4856
Email: admin@workbookpress.com

Ordering Information:
Quantity sales. Special discounts are available on quantity purchases by corporations, associations, and others.
For details, contact the publisher at the address above.

ISBN-13:   978-1-954753-32-7 (Paperback Version)
              978-1-954753-33-4 (Digital Version)

REV. DATE: 04/02/2021

Chief White Eagle

The Last Free Abnaki Indian

L. S. WOOD

CONTENTS

CONTENTS

BOOK
COVER

ILLUSTRATED BY

LARRY S. WOOD

I would like to dedicate this and my many books to two wonderful women Simone St. Arnaud and Evangeline Rugg who enjoyed reading my books before they passed away. I would also like to dedicate this and all my works to my beautiful and caring wife Rebecca who unselfishly helps so many others.   To my son Scott, to my daughter Jennifer, and to my grandchildren Amber, Sarah, Stacey, Stephen, and Kendrick.

OTHER WORKS BY L. S. WOOD

EARTH LOST WITHOUT POWER

This is a story about greedy people taking over a nation by force and trying to take over the entire earth by fear. Producing neutron bomb weaponry and placing them aboard a multitude of missiles in orbit around the earth. Faulty equipment aboard the missiles caused them all to return to the earth at once. After entering the earth's atmosphere, the foreign nation responsible for the deadly weaponry pushed the panic destruction button so they would not hit the earth, but it was too late. The neutron weaponry took man's ability to produce electricity for his comfort, and took away the earth's ability to make lightning and thunder. Planes large and small fell from the sky, and everything came to a sudden halt around the planet. The multitude of wild neutrons released by these bombs killed people by the thousands, taking away the body's instinctive heart pumping ability and their breathing signals.

THE HEARTBROKEN LEPRECHAUN

SKIP INTO TROUBLE

The story is about a young leprechaun who ventured out into the unknown world of mortals to save his parents who had gone missing. With only a smidgen of his full leprechaunic powers until he gets older and receives them by crying for them, he gets himself and others into serious trouble until he gains his full powers. He almost sinks a sailing vessel, that he unknowingly ended up on, by passing out from being drunk in a passenger's travel trunk before it sailed. With a little Irish luck, he manages to stay alive and accomplishes the task he set out to do by saving his parents and bringing them back home to Ireland from another land.

L. S. Wood lives in north central Massachusetts in Winchendon Mass with his lovely wife Rebecca Ann Wood of fifty plus years. They have two children, a son Scott and a daughter Jennifer. His son is a single parent with four children--three girls and a boy, and his daughter has one boy.

His grandchildren keep him very busy when they are around which is most of the time. His son lives next door to him, and his daughter lives a couple towns away and visits once or twice a week with her little boy who keeps his grandfather very busy.

He graduated from Mount Wachusett Community College, and attended Fitchburg State University. He worked for a bank for a short time before going to work in industry. He stopped working for others and started a real estate and construction company of his own putting up a multitude of new homes in New England. He also started a home heating oil delivery business, gave it to his wife, and since has retired.

He has written many children's books, science fiction, love stories, and more. Many of the books he has written sit on a shelf or in a file cabinet in his study collecting dust. He writes for the pleasure of putting stories down on paper. Due to family and friend pressure in sharing his works with the world, he is now just longing to publish his works, and hopes the people of the world will enjoy his books as much as he enjoyed writing them.

LARRY S. WOOD.

CHIEF WHITE EAGLE

L. S. WOOD

LARRY S. WOOD at beclarwood@
comcast.net

LARRY S. WOOD
1335 ALGER STREET
WINCHENDON MA 01475

CHAPTER ONE

The New Beginning

Quiet solitude filled the sudden burst of warmth and tingling sensations when the joining of egg and sperm created the one named White Eagle as two life-forming substances embrace one another in his mother's womb. Every new mille-second in time for his new life form felt safe yet wild as many new feelings and sensations in cell division and bone growth developed into the very special person who in time would be known as "CHIEF WHITE EAGLE".

The frivolous vibrations from the outside world never upset the developing child held tight within his mother womb because in there he would be safe for his eternity, or so he thought. Some days felt feverishly hot while others felt cool to him as days slowly melted away into the quiet of night when rest overtook the two attached as one in their union. Some days were ordinarily strange as his proportion in size grew more than other days, experiencing many new bizarre feelings in new life-giving fluids as they flowed freely through his newly developing body, nurturing his very existence.

Life was the way it should be and should never change for him as he lazily lay in the comforts of his mother's amniotic fluid within her womb stretching and growing until death should take his breath away, of which he had yet to take. Oh, the pain from this unforeseen event that took away the fine comforts from within his secure refuge. Some disaster had caused the soft warmth in the water surrounding him to drain quickly away and bring pain to his small frame. The world around him was about to change forever, and would never be the same ever again. He was being twisted into an upside down position as the world around him began squeezing him with such force. He thought he was about to burst from the intense pressure, making his torso stretch out in wild uncontrollable contractions. Finally, the pain subsided to a less severe state, as he again felt the safe security he once felt return to him, but for a mere short period of time.

Suddenly, he felt the calm in his quiet world around him again fade quickly away as a more intense pain came to his solitude of peace. He was again being compressed more than he had been just moments before as his head was sent down between the two tight bones in his mother's birth canal to give him life in yet another world where nothing would be as pure as it once had been or as safe as the world he was about to leave. Pain was a new experience in his existence, and he hoped its mere presence would be short lived and never to be experienced again in his lifetime. Small in frame, he exited out his mother's tight birth canal, aware he had journeyed far away into another world not yet known to him. He experienced his first of many new sounds echoing softly into his tiny ears off his eardrums, and a cloudy dark blurred vision to his now seeing eyes. For the first time in life, he saw blurred objects in colorful streaks, and light as it came shining into his tiny eyes.

A strange new feeling made his outer wet covering in skin wrinkle up into tiny little unknown ripples. Suddenly, a new cool feeling of air traveled down his tiny throat and into his new yearning lungs, which suddenly caused him to make a strange funny noise that scared him at first. It brought with it new sensations of cold chills traveling throughout his tiny body. Soon he grew accustomed to this new substance of oxygen flowing within his little body being absorbed by his own two little lungs and not having to rely on his mother for her nurturing. These creatures around him were busy trying to tear away his outer covering as they wiped away the safe amniotic fluids in which he had once been so comforted. When they were finished, they placed him down on his mother's naked chest for her body heat to protect him from the cold air, and put something new and dry over him to comfort his outer being.

These soft deerskins would be his new womb to live in as he grew into adolescence. He experienced something very strange placed up to his tiny lips and into his now breathing mouth. It was dissimilar to his thumb he had suckled on while in the safe warm womb in his mother's body. A warm soothing liquid flowed freely from out his mother's swelled up breast and out its nipple. The warm liquid from within trickled down his throat, soothing the emptiness he had in his small void with its warmth. When he tried to suckle her at first, he coughed and gagged until he at last formed a rhythm in breathing and suckling, taking in a breath of fresh air between the gulps of warm milk. These were new pleasant experiences for him to encounter. He could only hope this new world with these two lovely beaming globes above staring proudly down at him would be the same if not yet better than the world, he just barely left behind.

Suckling his mother's nipple, he filled his empty void causing him yet another strange feeling to take place within his tiny growing body. His eyelids felt extremely heavy as they shut tight to one another blocking out the beauty of the creature above holding him. This hard new work in suckling and breathing all at the same time had exhausted him. The proud new grandmother took her newborn grandson from her daughter Whispering Winds, laid him down onto an open deerskin lined with moss cloth, and gently wrapped him up in it to keep him warm and safe while he slept. Another new experience of pain from within his anatomy wrenched at him. He felt the fluids he had suckled emerge out from his bowels and penis. He disliked these new discomforting funny feelings, so he began to squeal to make the annoying strange feelings go away. His mother turned to him and quickly cleaned away the impurities he had discharged. She cleaned him and made him feel warm again by wrapping him up in clean moss cloth wrappings and a clean deerskin.

Maybe it was time for this lovely creature to fill his empty void, but how would he tell her what his wants were? It frustrated him by not being able to communicate with her, and he began to cry loudly. Oh, how nice it felt to be cradled softly by her as she took him from his rest into her arms, somehow knowing he wanted to fill his void again. She put the ever-feeding thumb close to his mouth so he might suckle on its bliss. He could now see her for the beautiful being she really was. His new youthful vision had cleared significantly so he could see her clearly in the well-lit teepee. Teea helped her daughter Whispering Winds clean up the teepee after giving birth to her son. She wanted her home to look bright and rich when her husband returned home from foraging for food for the family and the tribe's people. He had become the tribe's leading hunter, best known for outsmarting the brightest deer, rabbit, pheasant, fish, and game of wild to keep their tribe well fed for the long cold winter months and short hot summer days.

Whispering Winds experienced mild pain for half the night before starting hard labor close to morning. It first came to her in short hard soft bursts, making her first feel nauseated. She did not want her husband, her brave Red Feathers, to know just how sick she had been feeling during the long night hours while he slept. She was afraid he might choose not to go out hunting with the rest of the tribe's braves and would choose to stay home by her side knowing she was about to give birth to their new child. The tribe was getting low on food and meat, and she did not want to be the cause of anyone going hungry.

Because it was spring, the braves only hunted the Bull Moose and male whitetail deer, the bucks. They all knew the females would be carrying their young and would soon be giving birth to a new generation of wildlife to carry on mother earth's quest in stabilizing the earth and the tribe's needs. The Indians had great respect for mother earth, her birds, her animals, and for her many fish in her streams and lakes.

It was late afternoon when Red Feathers and the hunting party came back to the village with their catch of wild game as food for the tribe. He was carrying a large rear hindquarter from the white tail buck he had harvested down by a watering hole out in the forest. He first spotted the large deer lazily but cautiously grazing on the new tender shoots of spring's new grasses growing wild alongside the water's edge. Red Feathers quickly placed himself down wind so the deer could not smell his presence in his approach to taking aim on him. The buck became extremely nervous hearing a blue jay squawk above Red Feathers' head, signaling out an alarm in warning of an approaching danger.

Red Feathers froze beside a tree and hoped the deer would think he was a part of its thick trunk, and it worked. Cautiously, he stepped away from the tree's trunk and closer toward the deer to get a better good clear shot at the prized animal. Every time the deer twitched or moved to lift its head, Red Feathers would freeze into a stiff statue bent down toward the ground looking similar to a broken off tree's stump. The young buck was getting more nervous with every step the young brave made toward him. Soon the cautious animal gave up the tender green shoots of nourishment and started off into the woods for refuge, feeling something amiss.   Clever as a hungry mountain lion on the prowl for his prey, the young brave moved in swiftly for his kill. As a returning flock of sparrows took flight from the tree's high canopy above the tall forest, two red squirrels began chattering out a cry about his unwanted presence. Red Feathers had taken out a specially made hunting arrow that he used for big game from his quiver. He took quick careful aim with his bow, pulling the sharp-notched arrow shaft up tight to the bow's strong string. With his long shaft bow bent to its maximum limit in bend and power, he released the arrow to seek out its target. The arrow was fast in flight similar to lightning streaking from cloud to cloud during a mighty storm at lightning speed. The pointed arrow's shaft swiftly made its mark. The big buck jumped in sudden surprise as the arrow penetrated deep into its side and into its heart. The large animal fell dead on the ground without making a quiver, not feeling but a pinch of pain before its life instantly ended on the forest floor. Red Feathers was proud that the deer felt less pain than a sharp slap in the face by a branch while following too close to another deer in front of it. He wanted to be the best he could at everything he did, especially in his hunting skills for his people, and to make every kill as painless as possible for the prey he needed to hunt.

Red Feathers was hoping for a son to be born first to him and Whispering Winds so he might teach him how to hunt the way he did. A healthy little girl would be as welcomed a child in his tent as would be a son because he loved all children. He was a man who loved the earth and every creature that lived there upon it. A daughter would be a blessing for Whispering Winds to have around and to teach the child the ways of the tribe's women.

Returning to his village that afternoon with the hunting

party carrying part the game they had scored, he spotted Whispering Winds sitting next to their tiny campfire by their teepee holding a small bundle in her arms close to her bosom like a small child nursing. Red Feathers ran quickly to her side with high hopes and anxiety about seeing their new child. His great hooting yelp was so loud that it alarmed the entire village, and everyone sprang to their feet. Red Feathers was so proud that he began stomping the ground with his feet as he yelled out to the Great White Spirit thanking him for a wonderful child. He still did not know if it was a son or a daughter Whispering Winds had given birth to and was cradling. He gave song and dance while still holding onto the large hindquarter of the deer he had flung over his shoulder as he kept thanking the Great White Spirit for such a wonderful gift. The extra weight felt more like a mere little rabbit he had taken from a snare in the forest rather than the heavy deer it really was. The excitement mesmerized him. The hunting party he had been hunting with came quickly to Red Feather's teepee thinking something very amiss was taking place at the time. His cry in joyful glee sounded more like a harrowing war cry to them. A war cry meant danger, used when an enemy attacks the village, and not used for joyous reasons.

Chief White Cloud, chief of the tribe and Red Feather's eldest brother, overlooked the sudden outburst of joyful mixed hooting as his younger brother looked overcome with pride. He and the other tribe members stood laughing at him, watching him dance around his teepee with the huge deer's rear quarter still attached to his proud shoulder. Whispering Winds stood up as she watched her proud brave dancing around. She reached out her arms toward him with the precious little bundle. "Here, Red Feathers, hold your son." He instantly stopped his cheerful dancing and dropped the deer's hindquarter from his shoulder to the ground. With a twinkle in his eyes, he took little White

Eagle from his mother's arms Not quite holding his new son's deer hide wrappings aptly, his covering fell to the ground taking the moss-cloth diaper with them, leaving him naked. With a quick chill from the cold afternoon air on him, his little boy wet all over his proud father as Red Feathers laughed. He first held him close to his chest, and then proudly showed him off to his proud brother, the chief. He held him up for his father to see and then way up into the cool spring air for the rest of the villagers to have a good look at his new son, and then held him tight to his bosom once more with great pride. Little White Eagle cried all while his proud father held him in the chilled air. Red Feathers reached down to retrieve his son's wrappings to re-cover him and to keep him warm. Whispering Winds took him from his father to re-cover him and protect him from the cold air, as the approach of night fell quickly upon the village. As soon as his mother took him from his father's arms and rewrapped him, he stopped crying. Little White Eagle did not like being chilled or cold.

The celebration of the new birth in the village lasted late into the night. Around the village by the small lake, several of the late-night campfires were being watched as they lay hidden deep within the vast forest. A pair of unfriendly eyes was watching the celebration take place that night from high on a tall hill not far from the village. They were taking count of the many Indians living there and would soon leave his observation post to bring back others to uproot the friendly tribe's people from their quiet home.

CHAPTER TWO

An Early Morning's Journey

In the bright early morning hours, red amber rays of warm sunlight drew up the morning dew from the moist forest vegetation growing wildly around the small lake into the air as a misty fog. White Eagle's bright blue eyes caught a glimmered ripple on the water's surface as a beaver poked its tiny head up through the quiet lake's surface. He marveled as the many little ripples traveled slowly toward the shore, exciting his young curiosity. He watched the rippling effects the beaver made in the water as it swam along softly bouncing on his mother's back in her back sack. The beaver stayed along the water's surface near the opposite shore leaving a small wake in the water behind it. Suddenly, it disappeared as quickly as it had appeared after slapping its strong flat hard tail firmly against the water's surface. It sounded similar to the sound his mother made when she washed their dirty clothes down by the water's edge. When the bouncing stopped, he again spotted the small head sticking out of the water's surface as the beaver climbed up the far off shoreline and headed up toward a thicket.

Suddenly, his whole world spun around on him. First, he was looking up into a tall oak tree where he had spotted two frisky gray squirrels chasing one another through its many high branches. Then, spinning rapidly around, he felt like an acorn would feel while falling rapidly and soon to hit the ground in a hard thud, as his mother gently placed him down on a blanket she had spread out on the grassy surface. He was now learning more and experiencing more in this new young life. While he was in his mother's womb, everything was mostly quiet and very relaxed for him as he grew. This new world was exciting, and he wanted to absorb everything that was taking place around him all at once. He wanted to learn what the strange sounds meant that were coming out the mouths of the ones taking care of him. He wanted to move around as they did, and to swim with the creature he had seen in the lake floating in the cool waters.

His mother had come to the lake to wash their clothes again as he lay relaxed on the blanket and observed everything going on around him. He lay still in his rabbit fur-lined sack attached to a roped harness that made it easier for his mother to carry him everywhere she went. A sharp hard snap caught his and his mother's attention as a tall tree from across the lake snapped off at its base and fell over into the lake. Standing on his two hind legs and resting on its tail behind the half broken off stump, stood the dark brown beaver who just moments before had climbed out of the lake and disappeared into the wooded thicket. He had acted as a wedge pushing at the tree, forcing it to fall, and watched how it fell and where it had landed in the water.

Satisfied with his work, the beaver gnawed away at the remaining wood fibers that were holding the thinning tree's shaft tight to its trunk, and the tree floated freely away into the water. He next scurried down to the water's edge while gliding on its tummy. Taking the branch in his mouth, he then swam off toward his beaver hut pulling the tall slender tree's branch in tow behind him. The young tender bark from the tree would be part of his food storage for the long cold winter months ahead, along with the many new water lily pads coming to bloom along the edge of the water for his young brood of spring pups living in his hut to eat and grow into maturity. In the far off distance, White Eagle could hear the sound of a cow moose calling out to her young calf while his own mother continued washing their garments out on the beach. She was briskly scrubbing their clothes on a flat protruding rock to get the soil out from them, and then rinsing them out by slapping them hard on the water's surface like the beaver did its tail. He looked again across the lake for the beaver to be there, but it had gone.

With a slight gnawing in the pit of his empty stomach, he began softly whining out for his mother's warm milk. She did not pay immediate attention from his soft call so he screeched out a deathly demanding call to her. She immediately let her washing fall to the ground and attended to her whining papoose. Checking his garments first for need of change, she found them dry. She quickly lay down beside him on the pelt, and presented him one of her breasts to fill his empty void. The warmth of her soft skin up against his cool cold cheeks soothed him into a sleepy stupor. Whispering Winds enjoyed being the young mother she became and the closeness she shared with her son. She lay on the pelt wondering what her wonderful son would turn out to be when he grew to maturity. Would he be a great hunter like his father, or the tribe's chief like his uncle? He was in line to be the tribe's new chief, because his uncle had no sons of his own to be chief. After quenching White Eagle's needs, Whispering Winds returned to her washing lay waiting for her on the washing stone. White Eagle looked around for the beaver to come poking its head up and out the water again, but it did not. Finishing with her laundry, Whispering Winds picked her son up off the soft pelt and spun him around quickly to position him once again on her back for their short walk back to their teepee to dry their clothing in the warm sun.

The new day's sun was just beginning to break its warm rays down through the early morning fog covering the forestland around the several mountains, village, and small lake. Springtime in Vermont is beautiful. Vermont was a name the white people from across the great waters had given the land where White Eagle and his people lived. A new treasure in freshness filled the spring's air after the long hard winter's snow had melted away from the land. Spring brought with it a new freshness of air to breathe, a wonderful time of year when the forest fills itself with plentiful happy music, abounding in new life.

It is a time of year that the many different animals therein give birth to their new young, a new beginning of life for most animals and plants. To smell the many different plant life flourishing, their sweet smells, and the beauty they present in sprouting flowers and blooms as assorted foliage, filled the air with a freshness the Indians love to embrace as a new beginning in life for all. Spring is the time of year when the Great White Spirit from above blesses his land with many new beginnings. Every day turned up new adventures for White Eagle in his new little world.

While making the many trips to the water's edge to wash their clothing, he looked for the little beaver to be out in the water. Every once in a great while, White Eagle's searching eyes would spot the little creature swimming along on the far off shoreline across the lake. Having his own chauffeur was wonderful for him as he watched the world around him, always going backwards on his mother's back. He marveled at the squirrels chasing about in the canopy of tall trees. Every once in a while his mother would take him from her back, quickly spinning him around to show him a little rabbit hopping along or a young fawn with its many spots trotting along quickly after its mother fleeing from being seen.

He was small and loved seeing the many different animals his mother would try pointing out to him as they scooted away into the underbrush in a hurry. The worst part of her showing him all the different animals was when she flung the straps supporting him off her shoulders and spun him around to see them. His world spinning around made him dizzy, and almost brought up the sweet milk. Icky-poi, the dirt in his mouth did not taste so good nor did the stems of green grass he plucked from beside his pelt as he tried to eat the earth and weed. The funny faces White Eagle made when he put the dirt and grass into his mouth made Whispering Winds laugh aloud. She carefully wiped away the dirt and took the long fibers of grass from his mouth. She went quickly to a tall bush, plucked away a few of its ripened berries from its branches, and took them back to White Eagle. He was still trying to rid himself of the awful taste in his mouth. She placed one of the ripened berries in his mouth, and at first, he did not know what to do with it. He rolled it around inside his mouth with his tongue until at last he caught hold of it between his new teeth. It did not seem to have any flavor to it until he ruptured its outer casing allowing the sweet juices to flood his mouth and liven up his taste buds with pleasure. He made an awful funny face at first that quickly turned to joy as he presented a happy face from its deliciousness. How could this little round blueberry taste so delightfully good, and the grass and dirt of the earth so unpleasant?

White Eagle loved traveling along in the soft deerskin backpack on his mother's back watching the other small braves and little girls of the tribe follow along behind their mothers. His mother, along with most the other women of the tribe and their children, would go off into the woods in search of wild berries and herbs for the medicine man's stash that he needed in order to take care of the tribe. They would also gather the special weeds for the medicine man to use in making his special tobacco for the peace pipe and its different ceremonies. He especially enjoyed gathering fruit with his mother as she introduced him to the many different enjoyable large fruits and berries that grew wild in the forest, along the small streams, and by the water's edge near their small lake.

One day while resting on the pelt waiting for Whispering Winds to finish washing their clothes, he spotted some ducks out in the lake. A mother duck and her several little ducklings were frantically paddling out away from the shore on the opposite side of the lake where a gray wolf stood watching them as his dinner swam swiftly away from him. Within a blink of his small eye, the gray wolf had disappeared back into the thicket of the wilderness. It must have gone looking in search of an easier meal as the ducklings were too far away from shore for him to catch easily.

Not far away from him stood a young robin pulling with all its might in desperation to unearth a stubborn earthworm, but it would not let go of the borrow it had in the grass. Determined, the young robin stretched its head back toward the sky above leaning as far backward as it possibly could, lastly freeing the worm from the ground, and ate the worm for his meal. Inquisitive with his new beginning in life and all that was happening around him, White Eagle could not imagine at his young age what these precious memories would mean to him or how they would help him later on in his longevity. Lying on his deerskin blanket not far from his mother, he was resting peacefully when his father Red Feathers came into the teepee. He noticed a different look spread across his father's face, a look of deep concern, and a sound of alarm in his voice. He sat down to talk to his wife about what concerned him. Not liking his being left out of their conversation, or ignored by his parents, White Eagle managed to crawl over to his father's leg. He pulled himself up, took his first step in life, and fell forward into his mother's lap. This was great fun for him as his parents were not as serious after that special moment in time. Whatever it was they were talking about could not have been very serious because now they had smiles on their once-frowning faces.

The strong thick odor in the air was from a different kind of smoke and made White Eagle cough. This smoke was heavily different and not the same ordinary wispy smoke made by any campfire that he was accustomed to smelling. Half walking and half crawling, he went over to the teepee's flap and took a gaze outside. Poking his head outside like the beaver up out the water, he saw the fire making the heavy smelling smoke breezing its way toward their teepee and making him cough. It looked like a bigger fire than he had ever witnessed before, many times bigger and longer than the other fires. He watched as his people covered the hot embers in the fire pit with wet branches, leaves, and moss to make the smoke thick. Above the fire, his people stacked branches woven together as a meshed supporting rack. On the branched mesh, they were laying halves of fish to smoke and dry for winter food. The heavy hot smoke billowed up around the halved fish drifting gently on a breeze toward the teepee making him cough profusely. Whispering Winds quickly took him away from the flap and closed it up tight to keep the stringent smoke outside. Everyday brought something new to his young life as he grew toward adulthood.

The air soon changed with the changing of the seasons in the valley over the village and the lake, as the leaves on the trees changed color. The foliage surrounding the village soon became the many colors of the rainbow, and then the leaves of autumn soon began to fall from their branches. The tribe's people became very busy in their efforts to harvest the vegetables from their several gardens spread out around the village. The fall harvest being plentiful made the season a happy time for the tribe as they all pitched in storing the fruits from their hard work away into their bins dug deep into mother earth for her to keep them safe for the long harsh winter months ahead.

As soon as the first snows of winter began to fall, White Eagle had mastered the art of walking upright without falling over. He picked up a handful of the new snow and threw it all about. This was another new happy experience for him, yet a sad one. Whispering Winds weaned him from drinking the sweet nectar from her breasts. He did not understand why he could not share the love he felt when suckling his mother's milk. It wasn't just the sweetness in her milk he was going to miss, it would be the closeness they shared with his little cheeks pressed firmly up tight against her soft skin that he would miss the most. It did not seem fair to lose the closeness he shared with his mother, and the security it brought him. He soon became accustomed to the wild berry drinks they made for him, and the plentiful clean clear water from the lake. It had to be the fault of the new season's cold air and snows of winter brought to the village by the changing of the new moon that was to blame for his great loss. She would still pick him up to cuddle his need in closeness, yet she would not let him breast feed.

What other curses would the changes of seasons have in store for him later on in his lifetime? His learning the art of talking helped him understand the seriousness of his parents' late night talks with one another. It helped when he stood by his mother or father and listened to the other tribe's member's talk about the good and bad times ahead for them. He understood what they were saying, but did not quite understand the seriousness of it. This confused his young mind, but made him all that much more curious.

The white man was coming and settling closer and closer every day to their village. In the spring of the new season, they would have to move their village further north many miles from the fury these white men brought with them toward the Indians. Their tribe had lost many good brother braves while fighting the white man to protect their land. Listening to lengthy conversations of his elders, White Eagle learned the white man showed no mercy for Indians by the way they lived. He learned the Indians had saved the white man from dying their first winter in the new land, and what the Indians received in return from the white man was nothing but grief. On the land to the south, he said, brother tribes were already living on reservations. They were prisoners in and on their own land the Great White Spirit above gave to all people to live in peace and harmony. There are those in the world who think they own everything, including some Indian tribes across the land. Greed seems to be the cause of all faults in humans' behavior.

Their chief, Chief White Cloud, decided it was better to move his people further north than to face another encounter with the white man ever again. He didn't want to lose any more of his good people by fighting the white man in trying to protect their land. If they had to move their village every ten years or so to save just one life, it would be worth it and would be better off for all especially the young of the tribe. It would be better to move than to become prisoners on their own land.

The winter months were fun playing out in the snow. White Eagle was enjoying the life his parents and the other tribes' people made for him with all the other Indian children. He especially liked playing with Winonah, a young girl his own age just a couple of wigwams away from his, and the other younger braves and squaws in the tribe. Life was good. The days of winter were short. To pass time away, stories of funny hunting parties, great wisdom, and of survival of the Indian were told at the council fire at night when the weather outside was good.

When the air was calm and the fire was warming, different people of the tribe would talk about the happy times of old before the white man appeared upon their land and destroyed their good ways of life. The older braves talked about great hunting trips they had and encounters they had with the wolf, the bear, and some mountain lions. Some of the older braves talked about the encounters they had with the white man, as others wanted to stay in the village and not have to move again. The wise old medicine man told stories about the raven. He talked about how the bobcat lost its tail by not using its head, and how the chief was right in his wanting to move the tribe further northward to a safer place away from the white man's aggression. He told them all how the wise old owl was the wisest of all creatures living in the forest. He told them that the wolf howled at the silvery moon above at night because he had lost his loving mate to another sly wolf by the light of the moon, and he howled in sorrow for her return. When the cold winter winds stopped blowing, the deep snows of winter began melting away from longer days and the warming air of spring.

Chief White Cloud called upon Red Feathers to come to the council meeting tent. It was time to scout out a new location for the tribe's new village location to the north. Red Feathers, along with three other trusted braves that the chief hand picked out for the task, bid farewell to their families and friends before striking out on their long journey north, west, or north northeasterly on their quest to protect the tribe. They found they had to stay away from the Connecticut River Valley where the white man had already settled. This made it hard on the four braves to find a new location for their good people. By keeping to the heavy woods and mountainous terrain made their search for the new village ever the more difficult. The views they encountered from high over the land was beautiful to see, but the rugged ground made it hard on their feet and legs. Red Feathers and his small band of warriors returned to the village after many days and nights away.

At the council fire that night, Red Feathers told the members of the tribe about their long journey north in search of a suitable place for the new village. The white man had already taken claim to the land all along the great river. They had settled east, south, west, and some already cleared land north of them for their farms along its bank, and had many wooden wigwam already built. To the west-northwest was more rough terrain that was too rugged for the frail white man to settle upon. They couldn't survive away from the river, as they needed water to survive. He explained how they had found a good location a few day's journey north of them situated below a big mountain by a small swamp with plenty of water for them to use and an assortment in wild game for them to hunt for meat. The land would be good for planting their many crops for the fall harvest, and would be a good safe place for their women and children to live for many years to come without the bother of the white man finding them. It would be a six or seven-day trip from their village to the new location, maybe even more with so many of them.

Having complete trust in his younger brother, Chief White Cloud gave his order to break up their village in several days' time. In moving the village, they would start by first taking down the large teepee where the tribe's warriors met for council meetings to discuss the safety of their tribe. They would then take down half of the smaller wigwams and make the journey north in two or three moves to make it easier on his people.

CHAPTER THREE

The White Man

The white man had not bothered Chief White Cloud's tribe in several years. Never since the chief had moved his tribe to this new location by the hidden lake from downstream living on the edge of the great river. There the white man came and took their land from them. They had to move to save his people and leave their fallen brothers behind. He didn't want to have another bloody disturbance take place between his tribe and the white man ever again. He had hoped in this new location they would be safe forever from the white man, but he knew down deep in his heart it would not be so.

The white man had turned out to be an aggressive animal toward the Indians' way of life, and eventually one day would take over the land the Indians used that belonged to the Great White Spirit. He knew the Indians being free on their own land would be limited, and wanted to be free from capture as long as he could possibly protect his people.

Over the telegraph wire at the little military outpost located in White River Junction, Vermont came a wired message for the outpost's commander. "Scouting party, four warriors left Abnaki village April first, returned back to village two weeks later, any instructions?" "Commander Flint, sir, this message just came in over the wire for you." The telegraph operator ran into Commander Flint's office and quickly handed him the wired message. "Any response you want me to return, sir?" "Yes, call Major

Bennett in here at once, Private." "Yes, sir, Commander Flint." "Major, what do you make of this telegram we just received from our Indian scout on watch?" "I am not sure, sir. That small tribe of Indians is probably the last of the free Indians in the region not on a reservation. They have no guns or any horses. They have not posed any threat to anyone ever since they left this area several years ago. It could be a hunting party gone out in search of food for them". "Not likely, Major, hunting parties usually return on the same day and never past three days. They were gone for too many days before returning to the village this time. The single scout couldn't follow them and watch over the village at the same time".

"What are you thinking, sir?" "I don't really know, Major. We just do not want any trouble brewing from those savages. We don't need a war party of young crazy savage warriors going out causing trouble in this region for revenge on some innocent farmers in the region, if you know what I mean, Major. If it is a war party of young Indians, it needs stopping immediately before it gets out of hand and before anyone dies. Never did like the orders to leave those savages all alone out there. Not that I have anything against those savages mind you, but if I had my way about it I would put every last one of those savage heathens on a remote reservation somewhere behind bars in jails, or shackles tied to a tree somewhere so they couldn't move or do anything stupid. You know what I mean, don't you, Major?" "Yes, sir, Commander Flint. Everyone knows how you feel about the Indians. Would you like me to make a personal inspection of the village, Commander, and report my findings directly back to you, sir?" "Yes, Major Bennett. Find out what is really going on out there, and report your findings back here to this office at once. Then we will ask for permission to go out and capture those good for nothing heathens and put them all in jail on a reservation somewhere. As soon as possible,

Major Bennett. You hear me Bennett, as soon as possible. We do not want any funny business going on up there. Shoot to kill, shoot to kill. We need it stopped now, before we have another Indian war on our hands. Shoot first and then ask questions afterward. You have my own personal permission to shoot first, Major. We should have made them savages our slaves instead of all those damned black savages we stole from Africa. Then we wouldn't have had to have any reservations to store them away and all the grief they have caused us, right Major Bennett?" "Yes, sir, Commander Flint, right. I will report back to you as soon as I find out what is going on out there." "Shoot to kill first major, remember, and then ask your questions." "Shoot to kill, sir." Major Bennett saluted the commander, and swiftly turned and walked out of his office. Major Bennett had all he could do to not tell Commander Flint just what he thought about him. He thought he was a complete incompetent bigot, a person not fit to hold the position of commander in the cavalry. He seemed to be very prejudice against most men, especially the American Indians. He did not like the blacks of the world either, once told to him by Commander Flint, or anyone else with authority above his rank as commanding officer. He was out for blood against the world and did not care who spilled the blood for him.

With determination, Major Bennett would not be the responsible one takin blood for him if he could help it. He wanted his visit to the Indian village to be a friendly and productive one without any violence. If the village had to move to a reservation, he wanted it to be as peaceful an event as possible for them and everyone involved. Major Bennett was a loving caring family man with deep passion in equality for all mankind.

"Private", Major Bennett called out. "Wire out a message over the telegraph for me at once, please. Wire Lieutenant Morris and tell him we will be arriving in a couple of days to make a visit out to the Indian village. Have him call in the Indian scout from his lookout post. We will need him to lead the battalion of men out to the village for a powwow with the chief of the tribe. We need the number of how many braves live in the village. How many men will be needed if trouble should break out with the tribe? Return message requested immediately."

Lieutenant Morris wired back almost immediately after receiving the wire from Major Bennett. The Indian scout was sitting right there with him in his office getting ready to return to his position back above the Indian village where he had been watching the daily activities take place below. Wire to Major Bennett from Lieutenant Morris. "There are about 180 Indians strong living in the village. 75 braves, and 75 women taking care of about 30 young mixed-age children. No guns visible in camp, only bow and arrows for hunting game for food. Need 20 well-armed soldiers in case trouble should break out with villagers."

Returning to the Indian village with a young spike horned white tail deer in tow for fresh new meat for the tribe to enjoy, Crow reported immediately to Chief White Cloud. He had a serious frown on his very concerned looking face. "Your hunting party did well, Crow. Why take so long to come back with meat?" "Have to follow deer long way before finding it on high rocks. Chief knows Crow will make good hunter like Red Feathers someday." Crow didn't look amused, and explained to him how they had to follow the wounded deer for miles after hitting it with an arrow. It had only been slightly wounded as the shot was a poor one, and they were not going to let the deer suffer for a long time, so they followed it. Good hunters never let an animal suffer long if they can help it. Sometimes a good shot turns sour on an animal, and both the hunter and the animal suffer its consequences in different ways.

"Crow and party follow deer long time," he said. "The young deer lead Crow to campsite on far ridge on hill behind large rock."

"We found scouting party campsite located there. Looks like Indian scouting camp for white man watching down over White Cloud's village. Scout been watching over our village from high on top cliff, but no one is there right now. The scout for the white man had been watching over their village for many, many moons. The fire pit where he sleeps is still hot under the ash where he had his last fire in early morning, now gone from site. Do not know when he will return to watch over Chief's village again, very soon Crow think. Crow no like white man scout watching over our village. Chief call council meeting soon, have powwow. See what braves and Chief want to do about scouting camp on far hill." Chief White Cloud called out for a meeting at once at the fire pit. The entire village assembled around the huge circle encompassing Chief White Cloud and Crow as Crow was adding more firewood to the flaming pit. Everyone was excited to hear what their chief had to say in his calling such a quick meeting of his braves. Was he going to change his mind about moving the village, or did he have different ideas what he was going to do now?

No one in the village knew the seriousness of the meeting called without previous notice. Something very serious was brewing, and everyone in the village wanted to know exactly what was taking place. Chief White Cloud spoke of how Crow and his hunting party had found the scout's campsite high on the adjoining mountain overlooking their village. He explained how he was not very happy about having someone, especially a white man or one of his scouts, watching over their every move. The site had been there for many moons, he told them, and wanted to move their village as soon as possible. He did not want the white man to come storming down on their village, put them on a reservation, and held as prisoners. He wanted his village moved immediately. He didn't want to wait another day, never mind another week or two.

It was time to move to their new location before it was too late for them to move at all. He wanted the great council teepee left standing and the last to come down. He might even leave it behind, and they would have to build another new one. He wanted as many to sleep in the council wigwam that night as were possible while taking down the smaller wigwams. He was going to send Crow back to the scout's camp and warn the villagers when the scout might return to watch over them again. He did not want to, but he would have Crow take the scout's life if need be in order to protect his people from the white man.

White Eagle was small, but he could sense the tension in the air. His mother held him tight in her arms as she listened to the words of wisdom spoken as the chief spoke to his people. Looking up at his father, White Eagle could see great concern spread wide across his face as he looked into his mother's eyes with her grip squeezing him tighter and tighter with her own concern for her little boy's safety. Chief White Cloud talked on and on about the necessary move for his people, and decided they would too leave all the wigwams behind. They would be too heavy a load for them to carry with them. If they did, the tribe would leave tracks on the forest floor easily followed by the white man or by one of his many scouts. He said they should take as many if not all of the animal skins they had in store to make as many new wigwams from them as they could. They would have to share wigwams until enough more pelts could be harvested while hunting food for the tribe, and the rest of the wigwams to be made for them all to live in. He would send a party of braves back to retrieve as many wigwams as possible in the future if it was safe to do so.

The chief was mad as hell at the situation at hand, as no one from his village had caused anyone any harm in the area away from his village. This was the white man's way of treating the Indians. They had to pack up and leave their village before the white man caged them on a reservation like wild animals in a zoo. The scout camp above might be one of a rouge Indian staying his distance or a white man soldier preparing an ambush upon their friendly village. The chief had the final word of what they were going to do next, and now they were to move the next day. The good useful animal skins attached to any teepee would be detached from the newer built wigwams and leave the older ones to stay standing. Half the village looked as if the tribe was building new wigwams for all to have from a distance, as their shiny bare poles stood out in the early morning sun light. As soon as the early birds of morning began to sing, Chief White Cloud's Abnaki village was preparing for their long move further north away from the white man once again. There was no turmoil among any of the villagers, and everything was coming together like clockwork. The chief had planned to leave a few of his braves behind to show activity in the village should the scout return, as the others moved northward. Crow had made his way back to the overlooking scout camp high on the adjacent mountain, and positioned himself on a cliff out of sight of anyone approaching the white man's campsite. He was visible to his villagers below if he stood up and waved his arms together as a warning signal to them. The new morning air was thick with moisture. If the army scout returned during this time of day before the villagers were able to get under way, Crow would have to slay the scout for their safety. Crow was very nervous about having to slay anyone, as he was a kind human being. His wish at the time was time itself. Time for his fellow villagers to move safely north and allow he and the several other braves left behind in the village below to follow their loved ones north to their new location. With a waving motion to follow him, the chief's people were off through the woods on their long journey to a new start and village that they all hoped would be a safe sacred place for them to all remain forever.

Chief White Cloud had put a heavy burden onto his people to bear that day. The move north would be hard on them all without the aid of animals to carry their burdensome loads of skins, food, and belongings with them. Without horses, the journey would be hard on all the villagers especially the older tribe's people and the younger children. Behind the chief and his brother walked the medicine man carrying his peace pipe filled with hot ash and puffing out white smoke. He was using it to chase away any evil spirits that might lay ahead of them in their quested travels. Behind the medicine man walked the rest of the tribe in silence, avoiding any twigs or other small objects on the ground that might make a noise of any consequence if stepped on. As soon as the tribe walked into the woods, the elder tribe members taught the younger ones how to walk flat footed on the fallen leaves on the forest floor in order to not leave a trail behind them that a cavalry Indian scout might follow to track them. Chief White Cloud asked the medicine man to ask for rain to fall on the earth of the forest after they had passed through it. He was hoping the leaves on the forest floor would swell back up from being walked on along with anything else that might leave a trail behind them. Red Feathers sent Red Hawk ahead to scout out the trail. He wanted to make sure there were no dangerous situations lying ahead that might foil their daring effort to reach their new village site. Red Hawk was to return quickly and warn the tribe if any trouble might lay ahead for them. He was to report on anything that looked amiss, even a broken off twig from a tree or bush that looked suspicious to him. The children of the tribe had to be especially quiet during the long trip into the deep woods. The woods were so quiet that any noise created by them would travel great distances.

With almost two hundred members of the tribe walking on the ground at the same time on the wet morning leaves in harmony sounded as if a breeze was blowing softly through the trees. Mid-morning, Red Hawk returned to the tribe with a finding in his scouting travels. It was the first sign of the white man in their travels ahead. It was a road cut into the woods by the white man. They would have to be extremely careful in crossing any roadway and not leave any sign that they had been there noticed by any white man in its near proximity. Chief White Cloud placed guards strategically up and down each side the roads to watch out for the white man should any one come along to foil their quest for their new start in life. Quickly, they quietly scurried across the roadway and into the thick of the forest on the other side. Red Hawk again disappeared into the woods ahead to search out the trail for any more signs that the white man might be up ahead. Red Feathers continued leading the tribe through thickets and groves of the forest ahead, and not leaving any visible sign of their trail behind for any to follow. A couple of his best hunting party braves lagged behind the tribe and covered up any disturbance the tribe had made on the ground for any to follow. The few braves bringing up the rear of the party traveled great distances away from the trail to pick up pine needles and fresh leaves from the ground to place over any disturbed surface in an effort to make the ground restored once more. The several braves left behind by the chief in the old village would create a diversion trail leaving the village for anyone to follow after Crow returned from the white man's campsite above the village. They would make the diversion trail easy to follow leading easterly toward the big river, and then end the fake trail at its riverbank. They would then backtrack on the fictitious trail back through the woods, or use the water of the big river to follow their tribe north to their new village site below the great mountain cliff, inland away from the white man.

The sudden screeching of a great-horned owl scared the daylights out of Crow. It was late afternoon with no sign of any white man, rouge Indian, or cavalry Indian scout anywhere around the campsite. The only sign of life other than the great-horned owl were the several braves left behind in the village below. A couple of the braves had dressed like women of the tribe to create a diversion should the spy of the white man return to watch over them. They were busy doing chores around the village as woman would do, hoping the scout above would think the rest of the tribe was asleep, or doing chores inside their wigwams. Walking from early dawn until late dusk with heavy loads to bear, every member of the tribe stood exhausted from the long hard travels over the tough terrain. More so the elders and very young of the tribe, but there were no complaints from anyone knowing the importance of the move.

Red Hawk returned this time bringing good news for the tribe to hear for a change. There was a good place up ahead a short distance to make camp for the night. The site was a small clearing in the woods they could use to rest for the night. There would be no fires this night. The chief did not want any telltale signs that anyone might be in the woods that night if a white man was in seeing distance anywhere around the small clearing. White Eagle, not truly understanding the importance of the move, was having a grand old time for himself. When he got tired, someone would pick him up and carry him along until he fussed to get back down. Down on the ground was not as much fun for White Eagle as being carried along by his mother, father, or another brave willing to carry an extra burden on his back for a short time along with his own heavy load. Being carried along was the best as he could watch everyone walking along behind. The short ones, the tall ones, the fat, and the skinny ones, but most of all were the squirrels dancing and prancing about in the forest canopy above.

The music in and above the forest fascinated his imagination listening to the birds singing out their songs. The blue jays were scolding the invading party to their land below as the mourning doves cooed their mating calls to their mates. This long walk in the woods was better than sitting by the shoreline while his mother washed their clothes and waiting for the beaver to pop his head up out the water. He spotted a rabbit running away from them and a porcupine clinging to the branches way up in a tree looking as if it was asleep as they passed below. He spotted a couple of young deer feeding on leaves as they crested over a hill while he was being carried on the shoulders of the medicine man for a short distance. White Eagle was having the time of his life in this new adventure he thought he was having. White Eagle didn't really like being quiet. He wanted to know why the porcupine was asleep way up in the tree during the daylight hours. Everyone was supposed to sleep during the night time when it got dark outside and awake when it was light out. Why did the deer run away from them? No one was going to harm the deer, only pass by them.

Whispering Winds asked White Eagle to be quiet and to be big and brave like his father and the chief until the tribe got to their new village in a couple of days. Once there, he could make all the noise he wanted to make along with the other children of the tribe, but not until then, she told him. She explained how he had to be as quiet as a mouse walking around the forest with a hungry hawk flying above it, looking for its next meal.

He understood perfectly what she was saying, but did not want to be quiet until his father looked over at him with a stern face. Instantly, his mouth shut tight as if someone had put a lock on it. Once in a great while, White Eagle could hear another small child around his age talking and asking questions in the cluster of people walking along behind them. The mother caring for the child reprimanded him or her and tried to quiet them down.

Everything was quite peaceful as they walked along in the warm summer's sun except for an occasional scolding from some blue jays aloft and the chattering scolding from some squirrels as they passed along beneath them in the woods. As the air became cooler with the approach of evening, the natural music of the animals in the forest subsided into quietness.

They found the small clearing where they would camp for the short nighttime hours ahead. It seemed only a few minutes when White Eagle was awakened by the music of the forest returning to the morning air. As he opened his eyes, the light of day was breaking over the horizon. The few remaining stars above were quickly fading into the light blue haze of day as everyone began getting ready for another long hard day of journeying through the woods.

From early morning until late into that evening, they traveled along through the dense forest staying away from the big river and the white man, traversing several roads the white man had cut through the wilderness as they pressed on. Chief White Cloud did not realize just how far north the site to their new village would be.

The white man had settled great distances north of their old village and it did not look promising to him that they would be safe anywhere in the land now. Red Hawk returned with new signs of the white man up ahead. On his final return, he came with good news for all who were extremely tired. He had found another safe place for them to camp again for the night.

With a heavy foggy mist floating in the air above them as clouds began forming in the sky, Chief White Cloud allowed his people to have a fire for the night. The tribe huddled close together elbow to elbow beneath a large outcropping of stone ledge for cover to sleep for the night. A couple of the stronger braves stood watch over their people as they slept, putting more wood on the warming fire, and making sure everyone would be safe as they rested for the night.

CHAPTER FOUR

Crow's Safe Return

In the early morning of the third day, Crow returned to the village below. He awoke the others in the village with the hooting call of the great-horned owl. The guard stood by the council teepee in the village ready to fight if necessary and returned his mating call in response. Crow then safely entered the village without alarming anyone that he was coming home to be with them.

The thick cloudy canopy above the village filled with strong mist was to their advantage this day. Not far to their south southeast of their village rested Major Bennett in a camp they had made ready for the night. He had twenty heavily armed men and the Indian scout with him. They had made camp the day before on the opposite side of the mountain when the rain began to fall down hard on them. It was the same mountain Crow had been sitting on above the village looking for the return of the scout to his campsite. In the early morning rains, Crow and his fellow warriors placed their heavy loads on their strong backs for the long journey north to join up with their family and friends. They scraped the surface of the soil and leaves below their feet to make it look as if the whole of the tribe had made the trail leading away from the village toward the great river to their east.

It looked as if two hundred or more Indians had traveled out of the village all at the same time in a hurried rush. The warriors made it look like the tribe had pulled along heavily loaded down canoes and poled drays behind them. The hard rains of the night covered up any signs of their fellow brothers and sisters leaving the village a couple of days earlier. The rain lifted up many flattened down leaves and pine needles back to their original way before the tribe had flattened them down with so many feet hiding any evidence that they had traveled over them. With the warming days of spring came the many new buds in fresh life on the wild plants thriving in the forest. With all the new growth reacting quickly with the warm rains, it made it virtually impossible to follow the quickly disappearing signs of any trail in the woods made by the tribe.

The braves left behind at the village were to make a diversion trail for the tribe's escape. If caught, there would only be a small number of men to lose rather than the whole tribe.

In midmorning, Major Bennett broke up camp and readied his men for their final trek of their mission. Being part Indian himself, he did not share the same feelings toward the Indians as did Commander Flint. At least he thought he was part Indian as his parents had told him.

Major Bennett was not a man of prejudice toward anyone, and felt the same way toward men as did the late President Abraham Lincoln. Equality to all humanity, no matter what color skin they had or religion they all believed in. He felt all men should be free to travel the lands of the world. No man should be a slave to others, only to himself and to his family for their wellbeing.

The rain had finally stopped, and the clouds above were fleeing the forest with traces of blue sky poking down through them. Beams of sunlight began shining down through the trees as Major Bennett and his men prepared to leave their camp. He was not in a rush to tramp through the forest and get his men soaked. Major Bennett had many young feisty soldiers with him in his detail of men. They, hearing about the Indian wars and the Civil War, were thirsty for blood themselves, hungry for a confrontation with an enemy, the Indians, to prove their manhood. They looked forward to being able to brag to others and tell stories to family about the battles they had with the Indians when they returned home from this detail.

Most of the men with him had no compassion for life, especially an Indian's life. Major Bennett had to reprimand a couple of the hardliners twice that night at camp about their yearning for a battle with these Indians. He almost yelled out at them with hostility in his voice when he heard such nonsense coming out their young mouths.

"There shall be no shooting unless I give the orders to, if I give one." "They are human beings as you are supposed to be yourselves." "They have family among themselves as you all have family back home." "Think of them as brothers, sisters, parents, and grandparents." "Our orders here are to have a powwow with the Indians, and see what, if anything, they are up to." "Is that all perfectly clear men?"

Several men did not share the same feelings toward the Indian as Major Bennett did. Some of their relatives including women and children had died at the hands of Indians years ago, by being scalped or were burned to death at a stake. These few men specifically wanted revenge on the Indians. They were going to cause an uprising when they had the chance. Why should they show any mercy for these heathens when they were in shooting range of them? The Indians were going to pay one way or another, and they did not care what Major Bennett said.

They, along with Commander Flint, merely wanted some sweet revenge, and the more Indians killed by them the better. The few renegade men had been hand selected to serve with Major Bennett by the commander himself.

Cresting the Indian scout's lookout post on top the mountain across from the Indian village, the village below looked deserted. There stood not a single Indian roaming around anywhere outside any teepee including the large council teepee.

"What do you make of that, Corporal," asked Major Bennett looking down on the quiet village below. "I don't really know, sir." "They have never left the village totally deserted before." Their chief may have died or something as drastic. They could all be down by the water performing a burial ritual and the medicine man performing his magic with his pipe chasing away any evil spirits, sir." "I don't really know."

Major Bennett gave a direct order. He ordered Sergeant Bursey to take the Indian scout along with him down to the Indian village below. He ordered him to find the Indians and report back to him as soon as possible. His orders were specific to stay out of sight of the Indians and not to make any contact with them. He did not want to raise any suspicion among them or let them know anyone was around.

Major Bennett did not know Sergeant Bursey was one of the worst renegade soldiers Commander Flint had handpicked and sent along with him to cause an uprising among the Indians. If the major had suspected this to be the case, he would have gone to his superiors and reported the matter to higher authorities. He didn't want to be any part of such a dastardly task.

There was not a cloud anywhere in the sky by high noon, as the sky was turning dark all around them. The sun was disappearing behind a darkness that was beginning to cover its illumination. Chief White Cloud turned to his medicine man for an answer. "What causes sun to disappear and bring night to fall over Great White Spirit's land, great one?"

A full eclipse of the sun was taking place as the moon passed between the earth and the sun making the earth turn dark in shadow. The medicine man explained how the moon was a good spirit. It was a good sign for them indicating they were almost to their new village and it would be a good life for them there. The Indians passed down the story about the meaning of the eclipse from generation to generation. It represented a new beginning for all life watched over by the Great Moon Spirit. It was the Great White Spirit's way in cleansing away any evil spirits among them. It would protect them for many moons to come and go over the land and their village. This is what he had been calling for ever since they left the old village, and it finally came after smoking the pipe with its special herbs.

White Eagle and the members of his tribe peered with eyes almost shut as they all looked up into the bright ring in the sky at the eclipse of the sun. It looked like a big black round rock had covered over most of the roundness of the sun, as a big round red ring shown bright around the blackness of the moon covering the sun's middle sphere. The eclipse lasted only a short time as the light of day soon returned to the earth.

The tribe's people, hearing the eclipse of the sun was a good sign from the Great White Spirit, breathed a sigh of relief. The good spirit was on their side, so the move requested by their chief was a good thing. They quietly cheered as they continued in their crusade. The magical sign of the eclipse gave the tribe more strength. The heavy loads on their backs seemed to get lighter with time, as they knew the end of their travels was nearing. It would only take another day or two before they were to reach their new village site below the mountain to the north.

White Eagle was sick and tired of walking and walking and walking, and tired of riding along on his mother's back or carried along by his father and others. The newness and excitement of this new adventure had long worn off. He wanted to stop and play with his little friends from back in the village who were traveling along behind him. This new adventure was not fun anymore, and he wanted it to be over with right then.

He wondered what the beavers in the pond were doing. He wanted to sleep on his deer pelt in his father's teepee. Why were they moving? He liked living near the lake and watching his animal friends play along its shoreline and watch the birds fly.

Crow led his party of braves easterly toward the Connecticut River as planned. It took them a full day and a half's journey to divert the white man off the trail of the others heading north. They came across several roads and open fields made by the hands of the white man in their travels easterly. Carefully, the braves crossed the road without leaving any marks on the road or nearby in the woods. When they reached the opposite side of the road, they would start making their false trail all over again.

The braves purposely left a small beaten down trail near the roadways as if everyone had crossed single file trying not to make much of a trail to follow, but one good scout would be able to follow by its markings. Each brave in

Crow's small group dragged a long crotched branch with sharp points on their ends behind them. Those weighted down poles left grooved travel marks in and on the ground as the poles turned over leaf after leaf in their weary travels of diversion. The deep marks made their trail look as if the whole tribe had left in a hurry.

The trail looked like the tribe had dragged heavy loaded-down drays, slings, and war canoes behind them filled with supplies to support them in their travels. Reaching the river's edge, the men scattered left and right dragging their poles behind them and swinging them sideways shaking them about disturbing the riverbank and water's edge making it look as if the whole tribe had gathered at the river's edge before scrambling into the large war canoes in their quick departure.

The landing for their fake quick departure was located just below a large set of falls and rapids located in the river. The white man called these falls Macondo Falls. The river to the south looked quite like a mirror away from the large falls. No one could possibly paddle a canoe up through the rapids to the north or portage their canoes through the woods anywhere near the falls without a white man seeing them unless it was in the middle of the darkest of nights.

There were several wooden wigwams within shouting distance from where they ended their baffling trail. To confuse the white man even more, Crow threw down a broken canoe paddle on the river bank to make the diversion site look more real.

"Well, Sergeant, what did the two of you find down there? Are the Indians down by the lake burying their chief, or what? What is taking place down there?" "No, sir, Major Bennett, there is no one down there. They have all packed up their belongings and left the village. They have all moved on, sir, gone." "What do you mean gone and left the village, Sergeant?" "Well, they have picked up and moved out, sir. They left half of their wigwams standing along with the larger council teepee and a couple of their smaller canoes down by the water's edge. They must have taken all the larger war canoes with them as they are missing, sir. Well at least I think they have all left, but they could be coming back I guess. I do not really know, sir. It really looks deserted down there. There is absolutely nothing left in any of the wigwams, and there is a large trail leading out of the village heading east, sir. It looks to me as if the Indians left their village in one hell of a hurry. Maybe one of the village scouts or braves out hunting spotted us coming earlier in the day, and the tribe vamoosed like the wind out of the area. They have not been gone very long, sir. The ash beneath the council fire pit is still hot at its base. They have not been away from the village more than a few short hours, maybe early this morning or late last evening during the rainstorm. The trail leading away from the village has not been rained on it yet. It had to have been early this morning, sir. Without any moonlight, traveling along at night in the dark woods would be almost impossible for a trained scout never mind an entire tribe." "Pack it up men, we are moving out." "Is it an easy trail to follow, Sergeant?" "Yes, it is Major. You cannot move an entire village of a couple hundred people through the woods without leaving some sort of visible trail to follow. It looks like the Indians were pulling along some very heavy loads behind them, sir. Probably the several war canoes they had down by the lake along with a couple of hand-pulled drays. It will be an easy trail to follow, sir."

With the dark of night nearing, Crow led his small party of warriors up the shoreline of the river near the massive rapids and up beside the thunderous waterfalls. Carefully in their travels, they passed real close to a couple of the white man's wooden wigwams. They traveled along staying hidden in the water as much as possible except for once or twice in order to traverse the falls so as not to make any sign of them being there.

Reaching a small tributary flowing into the Connecticut River several miles up the big river, they followed the small stream inland. They pursued the water flowing easterly toward them well into the deep woods. Crow used the water flowing toward them as their trail. The watery stream trail led Crow and his men forward into the safety of the deep woods in the black of night using the darkness of it as cover. The darkness was to their advantage as they slipped quietly past a small town and a farm or two.

The heavy pungent fragrance from a skunk spraying stopped a hound dog dead in its tracks. The dog had picked up the scent of Crow and his party of braves as they passed close by a small farmhouse while wading up the stream. The dog came bounding across an open field barking at them when it suddenly surprised a skunk that was digging up and eating grubs from the ground. The skunk in its defense peppered the dog with its spray, sending the dog bounding back toward the farmhouse crying from the burning liquid that it had sprayed into his eyes.

As soon as the door to the wooden teepee opened up, the braves heard the farmer and his wife yelling at the dog to get back outdoors. Crow and his warriors quietly laughed at seeing and hearing the frantic uproar taking place at the farmhouse. They slipped quietly unnoticed past the homestead and further into the wilderness.

"Make camp, Sergeant." "We cannot follow them any further in the darkness." "Yes, sir, Major." "Company halt, make camp." Talk around the campfire for the men that night was all about the Indians they were following. Where were the Indians going? What were they really up to? Why had they left their village so soon and why were they heading east toward the river? Were they going to try to settle near the Connecticut River or just past it and settle somewhere in the state of New Hampshire to live?

Major Bennett knew if Commander Flint had his way about it, he would have them all shot or put into shackles and chains, including all of their children. He would have all the ones that he caught put into prison, and the other ones would have been shot while trying to escape capture. He had told Major Bennett that he was not prejudice against the Indians, but everyone knew better. He seemed a heartless man with a grudge against the world.

This put Major Bennett at odds against himself for not knowing what to do when they caught up with the Indians. Would one of the trigger-happy men sent with him start shooting the Indians the second they caught up to them, or would they listen to his commands. He did not really know. If this tribe of Indians was waiting for them with guns drawn as they passed, it would be a slaughter.

Major Bennett figured it out after leaving the Indian village. Commander Flint had sent along a couple of his trigger-happy soldiers to do something foolish for him. They were going to shoot first and ask questions afterward just like the commander had suggested. These were the men getting the younger ones all fired up about how savage the Indians were, but he knew better. If the Indians were what these men said they were, they would have been out killing innocent farmers around the area already, but they were not.

The older soldiers who got the younger ones aside one

by one instilled horrific images in their young minds of how these Indians killed young children before raping their mothers and molesting the women in many different ways before killing them. It was not a pretty picture for anyone to form in their mind while out on a peace-seeking mission. The Indians must have sensed some harm coming to their village, so they up and left. He didn't know what else to make of the matter, and he did not know what was going to happen next.

By late day, Major Bennett and his company of men came upon the Connecticut River where the trail leading from the village suddenly ended on its banks. "Look, Major, a broken canoe paddle, sir." "They must have been dragging all of their war canoes along with them to help them escape." "How many canoes were left at the village, Sergeant?" "I do not really remember, sir. Two, two-man canoes I think. One or two four-man canoes, but there weren't any war canoes on the shoreline that I remember, sir." "Do any of you men remember any large war canoes back by the village?" Not a one could remember any on the shoreline near the village.

"That is it then" he said. "They all loaded into the larger war canoes and headed south on the river. There just isn't any other explanation." "Sergeant Bursey, where is the nearest telegraph wiring office located where I might wire a message to Commander Flint?" "Just up the road a ways from here. A couple of miles or so is one according to our guide here, sir."

"Good, go send a telegraph to Commander Flint at once, and tell him the Indians have left their village. No, tell him they have abandoned their village and taken their war canoes with them to the Connecticut River and could be headed south toward them. Tell him they could have used the war canoes to cross the river and are planning to set up a new village somewhere in the state of New Hampshire. Tell him we are waiting further instructions of what to do next, Major Bennett."

Neither Major Bennett nor any of the others realized Chief White Cloud, Crow, and Red Feathers had the braves staying behind taking the war canoes and others out into the middle of the lake to scuttle them. This was their first step in trying to confuse the white man in his search. They hoped this diversion of using the canoes as bait would lead the white man away from where they were trying to locate their new village north, and the white man would leave them alone forever. Chief White Cloud feared for his people's welfare, and only wished he had had more time to move them more peacefully and not in such a hurry. The sudden move would give Crow and the other warriors with him time to cover any tracks the tribe had first left in the woods just outside the village. It would allow the small party of warriors to catch up to the tribe up north in their new village later on if they were successful in avoiding capture. If captured, they would die first rather than tell their enemy where their people were.

CHAPTER FIVE

A New Village - A New Life

In the dawning of the new day, Red Hawk told Chief White Cloud they should arrive at their new village by day's end. The location of the new village was out in the far stretching wilderness not easily assessable by the white man as the other village had been. The chief knew the day would come when they would no longer be safe anywhere in their land because of the white man.

When camped for the last night before reaching their new village below a small cliff, White Eagle played with his little girl friend Winonah for a short while. They held onto each other's hands while jumping up and down as two children would in a world all their own without worry.

When they finally reached their destination, Red Feathers pointed out to his brother the chief why he and the other warriors had chosen this particular location for their new village. Behind them stood an enormous sheer cliff for protection from attack from the west. It was a good location for a lookout atop the sheer cliff because a brave could climb to its highest point and stand guard over the village below.

To the east lay a massive swamp made by their friend, the beaver. There was a natural spring by its edge feeding the swamp, a good source of water for the tribe. He pointed out the many signs of wildlife living in the area. It would be a good place to hunt for food, have pelts for their clothing, and furs for their wigwams. "Good choice,

Red Feathers, good choice. We will make the new village here. No white man will want to come take village away from Abnaki Indian here. Good fish in swamp water, tell by fish breaking water by tree catching silly fly too close to water's surface. Look, it makes big splash atop water." Red Feathers looked toward the large ripples made by the fish with a smile on his face, as Chief White Cloud pointed toward the broken calmness of the water to his right.

"No white man going to come and take village away from us here. Good for Indian live far away from white man with good fish in swamp for food and good protection of cliff behind village. Good soil in ground to plant crops for food and plenty of water for the tribe to drink and bathe. Red Feathers make big brother White Cloud very proud of him and make good choice in location for new village. Now is time to put up new village for our people."

The rigorous task in rebuilding the new village was at hand. Cutting down the new poles for the wigwams' skeletal frames and several larger poles for the new council teepee took most of the daylight hours to accomplish. By day's end, the tribe had several wigwams erected in accordance with the old village layout.

White Eagle would not have to live out under the stars or the bright light of the new moon tonight, nor would many of the tribe's people face the dark of night outside. The women and children would be able to sleep inside a teepee while their fathers and other braves would face the creatures of the night outside again.

The mosquitoes, black flies, deer flies, and other bugs of the night would take their toll biting and sucking the blood from the ones outside without mercy if they did not wipe their exposed skin area down with the oil from the fern plants growing wild by the swamp. The Indians living in the western world had many remedies for most situations that arose in the wild, except for the invasion of the white man into their land.

Early the next morning, Whispering Winds arose to face another work-filled day. White Eagle was sleeping comfortably on a soft dear skin, and didn't want to wake when his mother tried hard to wake him. It was the first night in the long week of traveling that he had slept this well. He didn't want to go with her to help strip the bark from the teepee poles needed for the other wigwams. Stripping the bark off the poles would keep the annoying bugs from eating their way into the bark and bothering the occupants in the wigwams at night. The tribe's men worked feverishly hard cutting down the poles and placing them beside the large flat rock. The women of the village just after dawn gathered the hot ash from the fire the day before in its base along with some dried leaves to start a fire. With the fire ablaze, they stripped the remaining poles of their bark and cured the slender poles in the open fire by rotating them until they were fully dry.

Drying the poles gave the poles strength and prolonged their life by giving them longer life to carry heavy loads of snow during the winter months. When the process was complete, they wiped down the poles with hot pitch they had gathered from cutting open the bark from the pine tree as well as boiling down many of its green needles into a thick paste. The laborious process preserved the wood and gave it a longer lifespan.

They would have to strip the back covered poles from off the wigwams they first erected the day before, one teepee at a time, to cure the poles inside them as they did not have time to cure them all the first day when they first put them up for shelter for the night. It made the work twice as hard, but it would be worth every minute it took to treat every pole in every teepee.

While helping as much as a small brave could help, White Eagle spotted an eagle soaring high above the cliff when its shadow zoomed over him and landed high beside him. The flicker of light and shadow made him look up as the eagle zoomed out from in front of the sun. His eyes began to hurt and sting from the bright light as he watched the eagle soar. He remembered the eclipse of the sun from a couple of days past, but knew this was a very large bird instead. Its massive wingspan looked bigger than he was as he imagined soaring high above his people like the big bird above.

If only his people had wings like the eagle, they would be able to be free, not chased away from their old village by the aggressive white man. He was young but had the wisdom of the old owl. He watched as the eagle soared higher and higher on the warm wind currents rising up over the mountaintop. He remembered seeing live turkeys and very big snowy owls at his old village, but never had he seen a bird of this magnitude. He continued watching as it soared higher up into the sky turning into a tiny speck before it disappeared into the never-ending heights in the heavens above.

The sound made by several poles clashing together brought White Eagle back to reality. His father, Red Feathers, along with several of the other braves, had returned to the village carrying long slender poles for the erection of the council teepee. He did not want to work; he wanted to run and play. His age was taking over the duties of the situation. He was yet a child at heart as he rose to his feet to go chasing after the elusive squirrel. He was a small boy, but had to stay to help as much as a little boy could in serving his people in preparing their new village. He needed to stay by his mother's side to help strip the bark from the council teepee poles as all the other children in camp were doing as best they could along with their mothers. He was not much help, but it was a good lesson in life that he needed to learn to be a great leader one day.

He was mad at his mother. It would take forever to prepare all the poles. Why his father and the other braves could not put up the new poles the same way they had the several wigwams the day before? One day he would understand and thank his mother for her persistence in making him stay and help as well as learn the many traits in life's important lessons. Never to be told again to get the important work done first before he went to play. He realized the importance of working together like playing with the other children.

Having stayed inside the newly erected teepee the first night, and not having to cope with the many annoying mosquitoes outside biting him as he had the past several nights, triggered his need inside his mind of what was right. He was very young and realized life's survival requirements at a very early age. It was a necessity that all the tribe's people work together to make a better life for them.

On the tenth day at the new village as darkness approached, there came a mating call from a great horned owl. White Eagle looked up from where he was sitting on his mother's lap by the big fire at the base of the sheer cliff. He watched and listened as his father returned the great horned owl mating call.

It was Crow and the other braves who had stayed behind in the old village to make a diversion for the tribe in their escape. They had found their way northward to the new village and to their loved ones. While sitting around the council campfire that evening, every brave who had stayed behind in the old village told stories of their adventures in their daring travel to the new village.

Red Feathers asked Crow if they had seen or encountered the army scout or rouge Indian at the overlooking campsite or whomever it was that had camped out there. Crow told them he had not and was glad he had not, for he did not want to have anyone's blood on his hands. It was bad enough he had to take the life of the deer, the bear, and all the other creatures of the forest they hunted for food. He felt bad for the many animals he had taken for food, a gift from the Great White Spirit.

It was not the Great White Spirit's wish that one man should take the blood of another man. To take another's blood in protecting himself or a loved one would not be a friendly thought, but he would do it if he had to. Crow told them how they stayed behind only two days instead of the three or four days they planned on because of the rains that came. They wanted to make the trail left behind an easy one for anyone to follow, and the rain would help cover up the tracks the tribe had made only two days prior.

Everything back at the old village went as planned. They took the several war canoes out into the middle of the lake the first night under the cover of darkness so no one would see them do it. They took out two two-man canoes in tow so they could return to shore. They then took out all the other canoes and returned with just a couple. They punched holes in the bottoms of them so no one would be able to use them to discover the others out in the lake.

It was so foggy the morning they left the village that no one would have been able to see them go from the camp site high on the hill. Crow had not yet seen any sign of whoever it was in the camp above when he was up there. He wondered if whoever it had been had moved on. Crow had not seen anything dangerous lurking in the forest or near the lake from high on the mountain.

He asked Chief White Cloud if he had acted too quickly in making the move from the old village. The medicine man instantly stood up standing tall, mad, and glaring over at Crow as he yelled out at him. "Did you not see the sign from the Great White Spirit above?" He spoke with purpose in his voice. "When our people passed through from the dangers in our old village and into the light of a new beginning for our new lives, and when the new sun was born into day for the better of our tribe. The old village is not safe to go back to. The chief must forget about sending braves back to the old village for pelts from the old wigwams. It is not safe to return there anymore. Many bad spirits live in the old village and would harm our people if anyone returns there. The Great White Spirit told Chief White Cloud it was time to move the village. The chief has good strength given to him by the Great White Spirit. Don't make the Great White Spirit mad at you, Crow, for doubting your chief. The chief did not make the move too soon. Chief White Cloud listened to the Great White Spirit's wishes, and moved the village the way he was supposed to move it. Crow had better ask Great White Spirit to forgive him for thinking such nonsense."

Crow bowed in shame to Chief White Cloud as he left the council fire after realizing what he had said sounded insubordinate to his leader. He didn't mean to offend his chief or the Great White Spirit above. He returned to the council ring after sitting by himself and asking for forgiveness from all in silence.

Chief White Cloud welcomed Crow back into the council ring with a smile. He knew what Crow meant and had second thoughts about moving the village himself.

The chief was not the type of individual to hold a grudge against anyone who doubted him as everyone makes mistakes, and was glad when Crow returned to the council fire.

The other braves that stayed behind with Crow talked at the fire about their good and bad experiences after the medicine man sat back down beside Chief White Cloud. They talked about how Crow had safely led them north through the great river and how they stayed hidden like shadows of fish traveling in the water to escape being followed by the white man. They told how they only stepped out of the water to the shore allowing them to traverse the high falls stepping onto stones and roots of trees growing to hide their trail. One brave explained how they all had to hold onto one another in battling the strong currents and rapids trying to push them down the fast moving waters as they fought their way northward.

One of the braves mentioned their good friend the skunk. The braves sitting next to him including Crow all laughed a joyous snicker as he spoke. They all quietly chuckled as he told the chief how a farmer's dog had come bounding down at them from across a field. The dog didn't see the skunk eating the grubs when it sprayed the intrusive beast. The dog went back twice as fast toward the white man's wooden teepee going inside the wooden flap before the farmer's squaw could shut it tight. The braves could hear the farmer and his squaw screaming at the dog for many minutes after they passed a safe distance up through the small stream.

The brave telling the story acted out the part of the farmer's squaw yelling at the dog all while holding his nose as she did and waving his arms in disarray to the matter. The entire village broke out into cheerful laughter while watching and listening to the young brave tell his story in such a funny way.

Another of the braves told how they all became very concerned when the eclipse of the sun took place as none had ever witnessed it before. Not a cloud in the sky, and a big black ball appeared over the sun blocking out its bright yellow rays. They were afraid the Great White Spirit was mad at them for doing something very wrong, and were now very happy to have listened to the medicine man explain how they had all entered into a new day in life.

They told of how they had witnessed the new blossoming in undergrowth taking place on the forest floor covering up the trail the tribe had taken just a few safe days before. Along with all the rain, everything in the forest had instantly changed. In their travels north in the forest, Crow wondered if the tribe had not been detained by the white man, as the trail was so well covered over by nature's natural beauty. They wondered at times if they were going in the right direction. They had to follow Crow as he was the only member in the party that knew the way. At times he was unsure of himself except for the outlining terrain he had followed both north and south with Red Feathers.

CHAPTER SIX

The Disappearance

When word came in over the telegraph line that the Indians had disappeared from their village, Commander Flint was beside himself. He instantly slammed his fist hard down on his desk as he rose from his chair, stomping his feet in a mad rage like a spoiled rotten child throwing a temper tantrum.

"I should have put all the damn savages in prison when I first got here. Why in the hell did I have to listen to those damn fools and idiots in Washington D.C. anyway? I should have been the one making all my own decisions around this region and not those idiots in Washington. I should have never listened to those damn fools, and should have gone with my own gut feelings about those good-for-nothing beasts out there. Those Indians are nothing but a bunch of dirty heathens, murderers, and good-for-nothing peasants since I have been here.

"Sergeant, send this return reply to Major Bennett immediately. Tell him I am sending more troops on tomorrow's train to help him track down those damn stupid Indians. We must stop those savages at any expense. This time I am giving the damn orders around here to shoot first and then ask questions afterward. They are probably all out looking for scalps as we communicate with one another. Remember to give your soldiers their orders. Shoot first. I will send additional orders with the troops in the morning."

"I knew he would do that," Major Bennett said. "I don't know what he has against the poor Indians, but wish I knew. He hates them all with an inner passion as he does most everyone else, especially the Indians. Okay troops, let us find a suitable place to set up camp for the night, and in the morning we will meet up with the train and get our new orders. It looks like we might be here for a long time to come, maybe even longer."

Commander Flint's wire to General Whitmore requested more troops sent immediately for an Indian uprising taking place in his region right now. He needed horse-mounted Calvary and foot soldiers, two battalions each along with four Gatlin guns immediately.

Commander Flint knew General Whitmore had fought several battles with the Indians in the past when he was a younger man and had served in the war. The country had been so quiet for such a long time that he could not believe what his sergeant in charge of the telegraph was reading to him in the wire from Commander Flint. The last report of any trouble with an Indian tribe was from up in Maine over thirty years ago, and most of them were sent to a reservation in upstate New York to live. The rest of the tribe was now living on a reservation in Maine.

The uprising erupted over the distraught Indians not wanting the government to place them on a reservation as prisoners on their own land and not just an Indian uprising over nothing. The battle was a bloody one. It cost the Indians many innocent lives including many women and children. It also cost the army many lives as well. He figured it was time to put this small tribe of Indians, who had not caused any trouble around until now, on their own private reservation so his troops could watch over the savages carefully for everyone's safety.

"Sergeant, send Commander Flint this reply immediately." "Request granted. Will send horse Calvary and foot soldiers per your request, along with four Gatlin guns from Fort Ayer!   Hold the Indian village at all costs. We do not want or need another costly uprising. Protect all Indian women and children. Do not shoot if they are in the way unless necessary General Whitmore"

Commander Flint was ecstatic with pleasure when he received the reply from General Whitmore. He would now be in charge of a real army of men. He would literally squash this tribe of Indians like an ant under his boot heel on a rock and spit upon the corpses before scalping a few of them for his own pleasure. When the troops arrived in the morning, he sent half the troops north to be with Major Bennett. The other half he held in the south with him to search for the missing Indians as they headed north on foot to find them. He was going to surround the tribe by squeezing them into a small opening before shooting them like sitting ducks on an open pond. With Major Bennett driving the Indians south and him driving them north, it was going to be an easy slaughter.

He wanted to become known as the greatest of commanders who saved the western world from the last savage Indians living in the wild. They were sure to meet up with the savages somewhere in the middle of the state between St. Johnsbury and White River Junction, Vermont. With a little luck, he might get one of those bloody red devil savages in his sites with his old "Betsy" sitting tight in his grip, and do one of them in with a single shot to start the fight that would put an end to all Indians' freedom in the land. For some strange reason, Commander Flint possessed a certain madness about him of wanting to kill an Indian, any Indian.

He did not have any just reason in doing what he desired to do, he just wanted to kill an Indian because he was a mentally disturbed individual. Now he would be able to fulfill his dream with authority. He had permission from his superior to go after the Indians with any means to subdue them. This would be his chance to pursue them like a game animal in a sporting hunt. They are no more than a turkey in a turkey shoot or a deer in his sights when he would be able to shoot the first bullet at them. What a wonderful situation to be in, he thought.

Two days had passed before the troops were in place to start the Indian drive south. Major Bennett had orders to send half his men along with one Gatlin gun down into the state of New Hampshire. He would keep the other half with him as they all headed south along the river together searching for the Indian tribe that had disappeared into thin air. In the south, Commander Flint was taking his men north on both sides of the river as planned. If Major Bennett was to find the tribe first, he was to strip them of any weaponry they might have with them and round them up into a tight round circle, like horses in a holding stable, until Commander Flint had time to arrive and take over their control.

Major Bennett had strict orders to send a messenger to inform Commander Flint if he had located them first. Commander Flint had his own plans if he was to find them first, and it was not going to be a nice hello. He didn't care how many Indians survived, if any. All he knew or wanted was to kill an Indian. If any were to survive, he would send them to upstate New York after he had them herded into train cars on loading dock platforms up north in St. Johnsbury or take them down south to White River Junction. He would make sure they would all live on an Indian reservation for the rest of their lives, or in prison, which he would prefer.

The many foot soldiers spread out wide along the riverbanks of the Connecticut River. Major Bennett sent the Calvary deep into the woods looking for the trail they might have left behind. When the two units of men from both north and south met in the middle along the river, they had not found a single sign of the Indians anywhere. They had truly disappeared out of sight.

Commander Flint ordered the men to make another search of the riverbanks and into the woods one last time. They must have overlooked something amiss in there somewhere. He made some of the men on both sides wade out deep into the river to see where these inhumane creatures living in his mind may have sunk their canoes in their avoidance of his men. It was as if they were ghost Indians who were once there, and now who had vanished.

Commander Flint ordered the men to separate again into the two states. After a couple days searching, they turned up nothing again. Commander Flint ordered all the men to assemble at the river's edge just below the mighty falls and rapids where the Indians first entered their escape into the river. In his mind, the commander thought the Indians had to have portaged their heavy war canoes up through the frothy rapids and over the tall falls somehow.

He was starting to act like a mad man in his ridiculous orders to find the evasive Indians. All the men with him especially Major Bennett knew he had lost his rightful mind in his last request, as the Indians would show up somewhere someday. No man, not even an Indian, could possibly portage a small canoe up through the mighty falls never mind lifting one up and over the forceful waters. Nor could they carry them through the thick of the woods and underbrush along the river's bank. It would not allow anyone access along the shoreline in the vicinity to portage them up and around the falls without a farmer living nearby seeing or hearing them in their journey. He was proving it to all the men that he had finally lost his mind to these Indians alluding his common good sense.

The fury in his madness began glimmering and showing up in the depths of his wild staring eyes. He ordered his men to go north on both sides of the river until they reached the Canadian border. The troops and Indian scouts swept the land near and far into the woods looking for the elusive Indian tribe. At one point, an army scout was almost within shouting distance to the village before turning back toward the river. He had been on the opposite side of the big swamp from the village.

Was it by fate and fate alone, the small Indian tribe was not found, or was it the Great White Spirit causing the eclipse of the sun that helped them avoid the white man's rule? At one point in time, an army scout had encircled the village only to pass it by above without noticing it below the cliff as he looked out over the valley toward Mt. Washington. Maybe the medicine man was right. The Great White Spirit was looking out for the tribe after all. For the time being, the friendly Indian tribe would be safe from the white man, the mad man Commander Flint.

CHAPTER SEVEN

The New Village

Staring gently up into the bright blue sky above watching the flight of the majestic bald eagle soaring high in the heavens, White Eagle watched the bird in amazement. It drifted on wind currents without flapping its big wings to soar higher and higher up into the sky above. The midmorning air was crisp. The sun was warming the earth gently, and the bright blue sky above became etched with soft puffy clouds from horizon to horizon. In the distance, a mourning dove cooed out a call to its mate.

At first, White Eagle thought the call was that of an owl as they sounded so much alike. Life in the new village was getting back to normal, whatever normal was for them at this time in life. The village was finally complete. The great council teepee was finally up and finished, as were all the smaller wigwams in the village including the ones needing to be taken down from their hurried first night of erection. The poles inside those wigwams were all stripped of their green bark and cured in the hot fire along with being rubbed down with hot pitch to preserve them.

The hectic life style of moving the old village to its new site was over. The new village below the high cliff would take some time to get accustomed to, even though it was laid out quite similar to the old village, but with some small changes to it. There was no lake with a beach to sit upon and watch the friendly beaver work in its water or to watch the otters play. It would take some time to get accustomed to this new way of life for them all. A couple of the new wigwams in the village were located differently now. Winonah's family teepee in the old village had been right next door to White Eagle's teepee. Their teepee in the new village was on the far side of the village, a hard stone's throw away from his old one. He would now get wet if it rained and he wanted to go play with her inside her teepee.

Things in the new village would be different for most. White Eagle, being the nephew to the chief, had its advantages over many others around him as well as many disadvantages for him to face. He was supposed to be the perfect all-around child all of the time, and would have to face being told about how he was to act many times over in the years ahead of him. He was the only child in the several wigwams surrounding the chief's teepee except for the chief's older daughters. They were young adults now and too old for him to play with.

White Eagle's grandfather, the old chief of the tribe, had his teepee erected right next to his son, the chief's teepee. He was the wisest one of the tribe, as Chief White Cloud would ask him for direction in leading his people forward in life. When it was time to move his people to the new village's location up north, the old wise one was in full agreement about the move. He, too, had bad feelings about the scout camp located high above the old village.

His uncle, the chief, would sit for hours discussing the ways in which to act in his father's absence when the time came, and the Great White Spirit above would call him home. Chief White Cloud wanted to be as wise a leader as his father, the old chief, had been. He never believed he could fill the moccasins his father once wore as leader to his tribe. White Eagle would be next in line for chief of the tribe should Chief White Cloud never have any sons of his own. The chief wanted the very best for his small tribe in every decision he ever made. He never wanted his people to be in any danger or to go through life without substance to survive on.

Still staring skyward, White Eagle watched as the bald eagle descended back down toward the earth and landed on her nest high on an adjoining cliff. She stood on the side of the nest flapping her large wingspan rapidly. It looked to him as if she was about to pluck her nest off its perch. Suddenly, she rose above the nest, tucked her wings tightly to her sides, and dove toward the earth below at a tremendous speed. She opened her wings wide and caught the soft warm air currents rising above her as she ascended above her nest again. She returned to her nest only to repeat her actions three more times.

White Eagle wondered what she was up to as he watched her. Suddenly, he spotted a smaller set of wings flapping on the edge of the big nest as she descended one last time. It was a baby bald eagle standing on the rim of the nest getting ready to fly. Spreading and flapping its wings as its mother had done, like a rock falling off a cliff, it plummeted toward the earth below at a tremendous speed. White Eagle thought for sure it was going to be the end for the little bird as he watched.

Down and down and down it fell. All of a sudden, it spread its small wingspan catching the rising wind currents shooting up from the warm mountain as it ascended toward the heavens above to be with its mother. He watched in amazement as the small eagle stopped in midflight and tumbled back toward the earth out of control. He thought it was the end again as the small bird began flapping its wings briskly. The small eagle leveled out in flight in the sky above as its mother came screaming down toward it like a bullet, wanting to help prevent a catastrophe from happening to her baby.

White Eagle developed a strange feeling in the pit of his stomach while watching the troubled eagle trying to fly for the first time. He could only sense in his own mind how falling from a high cliff might feel as he too was falling in his own mind looking at the earth quickly creeping up on him. White Eagle jumped in fright as the voice of his mother broke his deep train of thought. He had been in another world when she spoke to him, and it was time to eat.

The venison cooking on the spit over the open fire delighted his nostrils with its flavor and smell floating in the clean mountain air surrounding them. With hunger in his belly, he quickly joined his mother, father, grandmother, and grandfather at the fire to partake in the feast. Berry root drink was slowly simmering on the open fire beside the spigot of venison. It was a drink similar to the white man's coffee, but made from the roots of the special berry plant harvested in the forest. When boiled, the berry root juices leach out from its roots with sweetness into the boiling water giving it a sweet taste and delightful to drink like eating fresh squeezed berries plucked right from the vine.

In the morning, White Eagle went to go with his mother to wash some of their clothes. She went to the edge of the spacious swamp where a large spring freely flowed out its fresh water from out of the ground. The water was bubbling up from an underground stream flowing smoothly out into the large swamp not far away from the village. As she washed their clothes, she slapped them hard on the water's surface to dislodge any dirt from within them. It was a familiar sound as the noise came echoing back at them from across the swamp, or was it from behind them. He at first had thought it was a friendly beaver making the familiar noise, but it was not.

One could make noises loud or soft just to hear them come echoing back to them from off the sheer cliff. He was not sure he liked this new village because at the old village he could ride with his father in one of the many canoes resting on the beach by its waters edge, and the land at the old village would not talk back to him. He first heard the echo from the cliff when the bald eagle screeched above the village, and thought it was another eagle at first answering the call from the one above the village.

He missed playing with Winonah on the beach when his mother and her mother would be there together washing their clothes. He didn't like her not living right next door to him now as when it rained he could not run right next door to play with her inside her tepee. Everything seemed so different in the new village, and it was not a good difference either. He would have to adjust to not seeing the friendly beaver working or the happy otters playing in the lake the way he used to.

Horrible deathly screams from a small girl crying sent chills up and down White Eagle's spine. He was out picking fresh new wild berries with his grandmother, grandfather, and several of the other smaller children from the village. The girl had stepped onto the entrance to a yellow jacket's nest, and the ground wasps were all over her stinging her profusely. The old chief ran to her aid and began wiping away as many bees as he possibly could from her as he carried her away from the nest opening in the ground.

He was too old to carry her all the way back to the village by himself. She began instantly screaming covered from head to toe with so many large welts from all the bee stings. He sent a couple of the older children back to the village by themselves for help, and to bring back the medicine man with them and his special potion to take away the pain and venom from the many poisonous bee stings.

The young Indians were off and running toward the village as fast as their little legs would go. The little girl was crying from the pain she had. The old chief, not doing so good himself from all of the stings he received while running to her aid, took her to a small muddy water hole.

There, he instructed White Eagle and his grandmother to dig as big a hole in the muddy water hole as possible, as he stripped the young girl and himself down almost naked. He then covered the little girl with the black mud from the waterhole and then covered himself with the wet cool soggy soil as well. It helped to keep the hurtful stings and venom at bay. The cool wetness of the mud kept the little girl and old chief from both going into shock and possibly dying.

When the medicine man arrived with his special potion for the bee stings, the old chief of the tribe cleaned away the mud from the little girl with clean clear water and then from himself. The medicine man went straight to the old chief first who ordered him to help the young girl. The old chief was in great pain, but knew the little girl had received many more bee stings than he had, and she was the one in need of immediate assistance. The medicine man took out his pouch of potion he had made from bear fat, horseradish root, and several other herbs he had recently taken from the forest floor and used to make this special paste to work effectively on bee stings.

He applied the special paste to the young girl first, and then went to work on the old chief with its effectiveness. Within minutes, the potion did its magic on the young girl who stopped crying, and then the old chief who ceased his grimacing from his own pain and discomfort. The black mud from a watering hole usually stops the pain from a single bee sting, but with so many bee stings, it requires a much stronger remedy.

White Eagle would remember this trick that he would use several times over in the course of his lifetime. Every incident taking place in his life, he would file away in the archives of his mind and use later on in his life. Every herb, berry, fruit, leaf, and other plants he might use to help his people would be stored away as the medicine man had done in his own mind. As he grew every day, he learned how to make special bandages for different wounds, a new word to remember, and a new experience to remember.

He learned by watching the others in and around the village doing good things, even when they made their mistakes. He wanted to make a good leader one day, and filed all these experiences away in his young mind. He was young and eager. His grandfather saw great good things in him, and knew one day he would make a great chief leading his people forward into the future.

His grandfather, the old chief, had made a new ruling for the tribe when he was their chief. His memory was starting to fade the older he grew, and he did not want to endanger his loved ones. He decided it was time to appoint his son as chief of the tribe before he died. This way, by stepping aside, his people would not have to listen to him as a babbling old fool leading them astray in their important future. He felt good about the decision, as did the rest of the tribe.

Everyone, of course, except for his son White Cloud, as he could not think of running the affairs of the tribe while his father was still alive. He wanted to be their chief one day, but not until his father's last gasp of air exhaled and death took him away to his happy hunting ground above.

The old chief served his people for another year before retiring his rule over to his son. He knew when the right time had reached his abilities, and handed the peace pipe, ceremonial headdress, and special feathers he needed to his son to enable him to rule over his people. It was a small ceremony witnessed by the entire tribe, but a very special one.

CHAPTER EIGHT

The First Winter

The tribe stocked their new village with winter food as the cold of winter approached. The many spawning salmon had been conveniently trapped in the swamp by their friend, the beaver, making dams downstream and expanding the swamp. The tribe's men, using branch snares, caught the salmon in their wooden mesh nets and smoked them over hot embers with moss attached to hickory sticks for flavoring. The smoke rose up over the fresh fish, drying them out with the hot smoke, preparing them for their dried winter stores of food.

The area around the village was bountiful with game to hunt for meat for the tribe. The tribe's two big gardens bore large crops of corn, squash, and other vegetables now stored away in food burrows dug deep into Mother Earth.

Commander Flint was licking his harsh reprimanded wounds. His foolish request in calling for extra troops to quell an Indian uprising would follow him for the rest of his time served in the army and in his life. His ability to command his post or to lead a high military position was now in question. General Whitmore was so embarrassed that he wished he had never listened to such nonsense when the request came in over the telegraph wire for the extra troops. He thought for sure an Indian uprising was already underway at the time according to Commander Flynn. He soon learned Commander Flint was an incompetent egotistical officer not worthy of any command in the military. The general had a gut feeling the uprising request was premature, but could not wait around letting innocent people lose their lives if it was not.

The news media around the east called it a hoax. What Indian tribe and where were they? How many scalps had been lost in the uprising, and where were the Indians now? The papers said Commander Flint had probably erected the village by the lake to throw off anyone and everyone in believing a tribe of Indians really lived there. He only wanted to make a name for himself, the story read.

Commander Flint's time in the new U.S. Cavalry's new army was coming to its end. He was old enough to retire, yet wanted to stay on in the army at his outpost in White River Junction, Vermont. It was Flint's fault that the Indian tribe, the ghost Indians, were on the warpath in Vermont. The news media haunted Commander Flint daily with new write ups about the lost ghost Indian tribe.

General Whitmore sent Commander Flint transfer orders before his enlistment in the army had come to its end. He had given him two choices to either resign from his post immediately, or take a transfer to Camp Ayer, in Ayer, Massachusetts. He took the transfer to Camp Ayer for the remainder of his stay in the new army. It would be a long hard stay for him as he had four more years to serve before he was able to retire with full pay from the army.

He would bide his time, and when discharged with pay, he would return to Vermont. He made a promise to himself that he would search the rest of his life until he proved them all wrong. He had a vendetta to prove to all, especially to General Whitmore, for stepping on his toes. He would prove to that son of a so and so that he was an honorable man and fit for a command, and make them all eat their foolish words.

The night sky was brilliantly clear with thousands of bright glimmering stars sparkling down. In the far off distance, the colors of the rainbow danced among the Milky Way filling up the night sky with rolling wave after wave of colorful light reflected up and off the polar cap to the north. Many families for miles around watched the beautiful display of the Aurora Borealis from the north as it danced across the cold night sky of winter. With short cold days and long cold nights, the children in the village stayed up late into the night gazing at the beautiful display of colorful lights. The elders of the tribe enjoyed teaching the children about the mysteries attached to the long cold nights that sparkled with mystery attached to the stars above. In the distance, a lone wolf across the swamp howled out at the full moon as it pressed up over the ridge of the cliff behind the village.

Night after night, White Eagle wanted to stay up and watch the skies glisten above and watch the Northern Lights dance among the stars. At first, he could not understand why the Northern Lights were not out every night. He didn't realize nor did the others in the village that it was the sun's rays reflecting back off the ice caps in the northern hemisphere that caused the brilliance in light to be reflected up off the earth and into the sky that made the colorful lights dance among the stars.

One night after the full moon receded to a sliver in size after many nights shining above, a strange mysterious happening took place in the small village below the cliff. It had snowed a light fluffy snow all day long down onto the village and the surrounding landscape. The sky above was aglow with bright shiny stars as a few scattered snow clouds drifted lazily across the heavens. The Aurora Borealis was out in full force as it danced around the snow clouds and into the dark night sky with its many bright colors of orange, red, blue, green, and sparkling yellow.

The brilliant colors shot down to the ground reflecting off the clouds above and lighting up the village. Little colorful white and rainbow ghost like cloudy figures danced around the wigwams in the village. They danced for a minute and then disappeared into the night. Some would turn the full colors of the rainbow before they disappeared, whilst others just up and disappeared into the night sky.

White Eagle was in awe at their brilliance dancing around the village. They looked almost humanlike as warriors dancing around the harvest fire in fall all painted up honoring the Great Food Spirit for such a wonderful harvest. They came to the village to dance, and then left in just a matter of seconds it seemed to White Eagle. He wanted to watch them dance for a longer time than they did.

In the morning when he awoke from his deep sleep, his father, Red Feathers, was holding his own mother, White Eagle's grandmother tightly in his arms. His grandfather had passed on to his happy hunting ground above during the night. Red Feathers explained to his son how his grandfather had gone on to the land where all good warriors, their squaws, and children go when they die. "When is he coming back?" White Eagle asked his father when told the story about his grandfather. "He is not coming back, White Eagle. He has gone to be with the Great White Spirit". "But why not, Father? I am going to miss him. Doesn't he love or care about me anymore? I want to go with him. I love him."

Running out of the flap to the teepee, White Eagle shot off to his grandfather's teepee before anyone could stop him. Inside the teepee, he found his grandfather, the old chief of the tribe, lying on his sleeping pelt fast asleep, he thought. There had not been a death in the village since he was born. He did not really understand the concept of death because he was so young. "Grandfather! Grandfather, I want to go with you to your happy hunting ground. I knew you would come back for me." There was nothing but silence. He yelled at him again to wake him up in case he did not hear him the first time. "Please grandfather! Please can I go with you?" Reaching down to shake him awake, White Eagle grabbed his hand. It was as cold as the winter snow and ice outside the teepee and stiff with the coldness. He pulled his hand back quickly in fright.

He turned to run from his grandfather's teepee, and ran into his own father's open arms who was waiting for him just inside the teepee. "I am scared, Father. I want to go with him. I love him so." Sad tears of sorrow began to rapidly flow down the cheeks of both White Eagle and his father.

Red Feathers told White Eagle the story about losing his own grandfather to his happy hunting ground when he was a small boy. He at the time also wanted to go with his grandfather to his happy hunting ground above. Red Feathers sat him down in their teepee, and explained what death was all about. "The happy hunting ground is where all good warriors go in the heavens above to be with their loved ones who have gone on before them. It is a place where good spirits live, like the little ghosts that danced around the village last night. He explained how they will take good care of him up there while he watches over us from the heavens."

White Eagle stopped crying and tried to digest what his father had just told him about dying. He was trying to figure out how the little spirits came out of heaven, or why these little spirits had to come to his village and take his grandfather from him. "Have I been bad?" He asked his father. "Is that why they came and took Grandfather away from me?"

"No, son, that is not why. You were not bad at all. You are the best brave your grandfather could have ever asked for. He is happy now. You see, he is with his own mother now whom he missed very dearly. He is with his father, his uncles, and everyone else who went on before him. White Eagle was temporarily satisfied with his father's explanation about death. He would blame the little ghost of night, the spirits sent to the village by the Aurora Borealis for taking his grandfather away from him.

He didn't stay awake that night wanting to watch for the bright waves of colorful light the Aurora Borealis would display to the north, if it shown at all. His fascination with the Northern Lights dwindled into nothingness with the passing of his loving grandfather. He understood he was gone, but why? He was too young to accept his loss.

The winter turned out to be a bad one for White Eagle. Several weeks had passed by since his terrible loss. The winter sky above began dumping another light fluffy snow mixture down on their village. By day's end, the snow had stopped, and the light from the half-full moon sparkled down upon the new snow in the village.

He went to sleep not wanting to witness the little colorful spirits; therefore, they would not come, he thought in his young mind. All the snowstorms after his grandfather passed away seemed very light and fluffy, and it scared him half to death. Who would go next out of the village? Would it be his father, his mother, or his grandmother? Should he stay awake to witness the ghostly figures dancing around the village if they should come? He went to sleep knowing everything would be the same in the morning when he awoke, but his young mindful thinking was wrong.

As he closed his eyes, the storm came back vigorously hard. It would be the last big storm of the season. It dumped another foot of snow all around the village by snowing all night long. Not a star anywhere in the sky above, especially no Aurora Borealis ghosts of night.

In the morning when Red Feathers went to check on his mother, she had passed on to her happy hunting ground, joining his father in the illustrious Great White Spirit's land above. She was with him now, and he could imagine in his mind how happy the two of them must be now.

White Eagle was saddened by the shocking news and even more confused. How could this have happened? He purposely went to bed early to sleep. How could these little ghostlike figures possibly come back when he was fast asleep? Yet they came anyway taking his loving grandmother away from him. Oh, how he hated these little ghostlike spirits, and never wanted to see them ever again in his entire life.

CHAPTER NINE

Commander Flint's Retirement

The retirement ceremony for Commander Flint was a formal event at Fort Ayer in Ayer, Massachusetts. Four years had slowly passed along for him as he took all kinds of grief, just wanting to get to this special day. Commander Flint was finally going to retire his rank as a commanding officer in the new U.S. Army established after the old cavalry disbandment.

His sick mind had been possessed for the last several years to prove that the vanishing Indian tribe was not just a myth. There was an Indian village hidden away somewhere in the foothills between White River Junction, Vermont and the Canadian border and he was bound and determined he was going to find it before he died.

Shortly after his ceremonial retirement commencement, Ex-Commander Flint was off toward the northlands of Vermont. His first stop would be at Macondo Falls along the Connecticut River where the Indians first disappeared into thin air. They had to be somewhere around those parts, and he was going to find them. It would be his last quest in life to find those worthless savages and prove his saneness.

Flint considered himself a much smarter man than anyone else in the world and much better in every way as well. He knew they had to have somehow managed to portage the mighty falls with their heavy canoes. He was not quite sure how, but he knew they did. It was the only sensible explanation of how they disappeared into thin air so quickly that night.

All the tributaries flowing into the Connecticut River to the south of the falls toward White River Junction showed no sign of any war canoes, and turned up nothing else of the Indians in his searching. To the north of the great falls, only the first few tributaries flowing into the big river were searched properly, so he thought. He was going to follow each tributary to their source and to the Canadian border if necessary until he found the hidden tribe of Indians.

The Army gave him his old stead, his horse, as a gift for his retirement. She was too old to serve the Army any longer, and they were getting ready to put her out to pasture. He was pleased, as she was all he had left in life except for his madness.

He had lost his wife and two sons to his bitterness. Without them in his life, he was a lonely old man looking for more power over anyone that he could control. He had this special need in life, searching for any reason to act out his raging power of anger and authority on the weak. He now had a reason, an obsession in his life, to find the savage Indians that made him look like a fool. They were going to pay for all the bad insinuations he had taken in life since leaving his outpost in White River Junction.

They were all going to die, every damn one of them, including the savages' little bratty beasts, so there would be no more. They were the ones responsible for all the misgivings he had ever encountered since the day he was born. It had to be the fault of those damned savage Indians in Vermont who kept him from receiving his well-deserved rank of advancement and becoming the general in the army he deserved to be.

Commander Flint was a man with an evil sick mind who would destroy the innocent people he would meet if he had the chance to. Dressed in his military blues, Ex-Commander Flint set out immediately on his mission to find his enemy, the innocent Indian, and kill them one by one.

White Eagle enjoyed the last several years getting use to the new village and the surrounding woods. He liked to hike away from the village and watch the many wild animals living there, and climb the majestic mountain behind the village. He enjoyed looking out over the river valley and its vast mountain range. He was becoming quite good at tracking wild game and imitating their mating calls to call them near to him. Most mornings when White Eagle went outside the teepee, he would imitate a mourning dove calling to its mate, and quite often would receive an answer back from one. He had the ability to chatter as a chipmunk, make the sounds of a young deer calling to its mother, and sound like the many fowl of the air. He fascinated his parents quite often and most the other tribe's members with his unique abilities.

Being several years older now, White Eagle was very adventurous. He and a couple other boys, small braves from the village, ventured off into the wilderness away from the village. A voice in his head continually yelled out at him that it was wrong to go so far away from his people.

They came upon a large cleft of rock sticking up skyward toward the heavens looking like several large pointed arrowheads gathered in a single clump. They decided to scale one of the steep jagged rocks to its peak. Halfway up to the summit, White Eagle decided it was excessively dangerous to continue climbing up, and he decided to return down to its base to be safe.

The one young brave leading the trio up the cleft of

rock called him afraid and cowardice. White Eagle didn't care. He had made up his mind that climbing to its peak was a fool's game to put himself at risk, and climbed back down. Seeing White Eagle begin his descent toward the ground, the smarter of the two friends with him descended back down. The foolish one ascended to its steep summit.

Just as the two boys reached the safety of the ground below the towering cleft of rocks, they heard a death-harrowing scream echoing down from the rock above. It was loud at first, and then faded away into the far distance as if someone had fallen into a deep well or crevice. White Eagle's keen hearing caught screams come echoing out from the tight opening between the cleft of rocks beside of them. They knew their friend was in trouble. He must have fallen over the other side of the towering mass of jetting stone.

Scurrying swiftly around the cleft, they found a narrow opening between two large masses sticking skyward in its side. White Eagle twisted and turned through the narrow path leading in between the towering masses. In the middle, White Eagle found a flat opening many feet across. The rocks around it were like a fortress wall protecting another opening in the floor of the protected area ahead of him.

Looking down over its edge on the floor below, he saw his friend. His friend looked sprawled out on the rocky floor below. Nervously, he called out to him without any response. He spotted another opening in the floor a short distance away. He went to it and found a pathway leading down to the ground below. It was steep and jagged with stalagmites sticking up from its floor and stalactites sticking down from its curved ceiling.

He was not sure he would be able to get down to his

friend below through the rough opening, but he had to try. Clinging to the sharp pointed rocks, he made his way carefully down through the opening, passing by a large open water pool in the floor of the cave on his way over to his friend's side. An enormous large fish in pursuit of a big dragonfly leaped up out of the water pool and snagged the dragonfly for its lunch and dove back down into the water.

It scared the daylights out of White Eagle, as he thought it was just a puddle of water left by some rain. When White Eagle went over to his friend sprawled out on the ground below, his friend laid perfectly still in a heap upon the rocky surface and not breathing. His friend looked as if he was looking at the stone floor beneath him with his eyes wide open. There was no response from him when he tried communicating with him not when he moved him.

Memories from his past came quickly flashing into his mind. He pictured his grandfather lying dead still and cold on the deer pelt in his teepee. He was scared for his friend that death had taken him away. He remembered going with his father to check on his grandmother, and how he closed her eyes when she had died. He reached down with his fingertips and gently closed his friend's eyes. He knew his friend was dead. A voice was calling out to him as he carried his friend's lifeless body out from between the cleft of rocks. His friend outside the towering monument began to cry profusely when he saw White Eagle struggling as he carried their lifeless friend out the narrow passageway.

It was a very sad time in the village that night. No one had died in the village except for White Eagle's grandparents who most expected to die from old age. There had been a celebration for them, but this was not the same. They all felt grief when an elder died, but this night they all cried for one another like hurting little babies crying out for a dead fallen brother. He was too young to die such a tragic death. The young brave's life cut short gave no one in the village anything to celebrate about it. It was time to grieve a loss for the parents.

CHAPTER TEN

The Search Continued

Commander Flint's life had become a struggle in his search for the lost Indian tribe. The first year and a half in his search was nothing but an unpleasant experience of talking to people and wasting his precious time drinking in bar rooms trying hard to think as an Indian would think. He thought if he began to try to think like that, he would be able to locate the tribe that much sooner and have his sweet revenge on them.

The townspeople in the several small towns along the Connecticut River were of no value to him, and things were just not going well for him. The tribe's warriors never ventured too far from their village. Food of fish, wild game, and vegetables were plentiful nearby, giving them no reason to leave the security of the mountain or the swamp in close proximity to provide for them.

Commander Flint had traveled north one side of the Connecticut River to the Canadian border and back again in his search. He never ventured out too far inland along Connecticut's many tributaries as he had planned his fretful search of the evading tribe. His patience always ran short the first mile or so in land from the big river on every stream or river he came to along. He knew in his own mind that the Indians would be a lazy bunch, a good for nothing bunch of heathens. They would be too lazy to venture too far away from the big river.

Oh, how wrong he was in his sick-thinking mind. There just

had to be something the hired Indian scout and military men had not seen along the water's edges. At every creek along the way, he would tie up his horse and wade waste deep out into the river and search for any scuttled canoes along its banks. He was getting closer in his thinking about how the mighty Indian may have eluded him. If only he had ventured back to their original village and looked out in the middle of the lake on its bottom to see the scuttled canoes. Then would his thoughts about their cleverness be satisfied for him, possibly?

The longer and harder Commander Flint looked for the lost tribe, the more determined he became in his quest. He was determined to find them even if it meant dying in the meantime. It would be better to have died trying than to have given up and died from the humility the savage beasts had caused him. He would not give up until they were all behind bars or on a reservation. He thought they deserved nothing better than to be behind a stockade fence. Death would be his ultimate joy for them all.

The locals referred to Commander Flint as the mad man chasing around ghost Indians in the region. News of his coming traveled fast amongst the townspeople bordering the river. Townspeople would try to hide from him peering deep into their eyes for answers that were never coming. He began to think everyone in the region except for himself knew the whereabouts of the lost tribe, and they were all hiding the Indians away from him. After many long weary days spent mostly in the saddle of his horse looking for the lost Indians, he became sicker in mind about everything.

He was now so determined that he went into the backcountry looking for the Indians. The days there proved to be way too much for his old filly high up in the wooded backcountry. She laid down and died on him way out in the northern backwoods wilderness as she was too old for the commander to ride hard from early daylight until the dark of night. He didn't care anymore, he did not have remorse for himself or his dead horse. The more he hurt from being in the saddle, the more he was determined to find his prey. It was late fall as the first snow of the season began to fall on him and his dead horse. He should have been down near the river looking for the Indians instead of way out in the high backcountry. He hadn't been prepared for such an event stranded out there with his horse dying on him.

Being mad of mind, he tried carrying all of his belongings with him as he made his way toward the Connecticut River many miles to his east. Exhausted, he laid down on the ground and fell fast asleep as the snows fell down upon him. When he awoke, the snow had covered him and the ground with a fluffy blanket of white. Anger built up inside him in a rage, as he laid there shivering and cold. Those damn no good beasts did it to him again, he thought. They were the ones who killed his horse so he would freeze to death out in the forest in no man's land.

Not this night, he said to himself as he pulled a sleeping roll from his belongings to curl up in and sleep the night away. Early the next morning after a good night's rest, he started his quest for the river all over again. After eating some breakfast, he headed easterly toward Mount Washington. He knew if he walked straight toward the highest mountain, that it would lead him to the Connecticut River Valley below and eventually to a town.

To his left, he could see a large flume of smoke rising high up into the cold morning air and to the south several smaller trails of smoky flumes from fires drifting skyward into the heavens. The six inches of fresh new snow on the ground made it extremely hard for him to walk, slipping, and sliding on the many fallen leaves beneath his feet and the snow. At times, he would slide down small hills out of control until he fell over off balance and into a heap. This really upset him. He was so out of shape from riding his horse all the while, that it made him huff and puff with every step he took. He didn't know if he should go toward the several smaller fires billowing up smoke toward the south or toward the north where he had started this last trek in his quest. He chose to go north toward the big billowing flume of smoke not so far away. He knew the river turned back and forth zigzagging across the river valley more to the south than it did to the north, and knew his chances would be better going north in finding a village to buy a fresh horse and stay the winter till spring sprang again in the region.

When the ice melted from the river and all the snow had gone, he would be able to start his hunt for the Indians all over again. With nightfall quickly approaching, he set up camp on a high ridge looking out over the river valley stretching out for miles ahead of him. Silvery stars quickly filled the night sky above him as a new full moon shone bright on the new fallen snows of winter.

The scene was beautiful, almost giving him a sense of tranquility. For a moment, he was almost at peace with himself and the world because he was so tired and relaxed. To his south, he could make out six or seven smaller fires sending spiraling flumes of smoke up into the night sky. To his left, three bigger flumes of smoke were billowing toward the heavens. Looking back toward the south, he began to wonder.

These small flumes of smoke were coming up out of the deep woods. It must have been Major Bennett out on maneuvers with some of his men. No, he meant Colonel Bennett. There were no towns in that region away from the river that he could remember. He was glad Major Bennett at the time took over his position at his old post in White River Junction, Vermont, and his promotion to Colonel. He was jealous and downright evilly mad about the damn situation.

Oh, how he envied Colonel Bennett. The more he thought about it the more he hated him for taking over his post. He began to hate Colonel Bennett as much as he did the Indians, as it was probably he who helped cover up those damn evil beasts in their escape in the first place. He probably helped them get away so he might get his damn promotion and take over his old command. He stewed at it repeatedly over in his mind hating Bennett even more until he fell fast asleep. In the morning when he awoke, smoke was rising up out in front of him. To the south, there was not a cloud in the sky anywhere above or any small fires aglow billowing smoke up into the early morning sky. It must have been Bennett and his damn men out horsing around as usual. He never was a good military man anyway, he thought.

Reaching the source of smoke rising up over the ridge, Commander Flint found a team of lumberjacks clearing and burning brush. They were setting up a camp for their winter timber harvest. The logs were pulp logs for the paper mill to make paper from down the river. Some of the pine logs were being used for framing in building the mill at Gilman.

They were going to haul the logs two and three miles to the river's edge, and there stacked them up in piles. When the ice on the river went out in spring, they would float them all down stream to the new factory. Everyone in the lumber camp had heard about the mad man Commander Flint, except for one. They had been told he had lost his mind, and if he ever showed up in their camp to be careful with what they said to him. Commander Flint proved to be the wild cannon out of control as the Indian scout working for the lumber company almost became Commander Flint's first victim in his quest to kill all the Indians. Just as the Indian scout came out from behind one of the few tents in the lumberjack camp responding to the chow bell, Commander Flint drew out his Colt 45 from its holster, and while screaming at him, demanded the Indian scout to halt. The scared scout froze dead in his tracks not knowing anything about this mad white man. If he had not stopped when he did, Commander Flint would have filled him full of lead from his weapon.

Several of the lumberjacks placed themselves between the mad commander and the Indian scout. The supervisor in the group yelled out at the commander, "What in the hell are you doing, you fool? He is one of our company's mountain scouts working with us up here."

"He is nothing but one of those damn scoundrel savages. One of those beastly savages who wrecked my life." He screamed at the men. "Where are the rest of those red devils? Where did they all get off? Where are they now?" He demanded! The frightened Indian scout stood frozen in disbelief, just staring at the mad man standing in front the rest of the lumberjack crew pointing his gun to their faces. The Indian scout knew the English language fluently, but did not know what the commander was talking about, as he had not heard word about this mad lunatic looking for a tribe of invisible lost ghost Indians. He did not know of any tribe left in the new world that was not on a reservation except for up in Canada. There the Indians were still free to roam the land as they always had. There might still be one or two Indian tribes out west, but none on the east coast.

The camp of angered lumberjacks sent the delusional commander on his way. They didn't want this mad man present in their camp. The camp's cook, hearing the commotion, came outside the cooking tent with his rifle drawn. He walked over to Commander Flint and ordered him to put his weapon away, or he was going to meet his maker. Commander Flint heard the camp cook load, and cocked the trigger on his rifle, as he looked up into the cook's eyes. He knew he would be dead in a second or two if he didn't do what the camp cook told him. They could have made him walk out of the woods alone, but suspected he would soon return if he left on foot to cause more trouble with the Indian scout in their camp. They wanted him gone immediately from here. They had the youngest teamster in their camp, Harold Balch, drive the lunatic commander down the mountain to town. Out from sight and out of mind, they knew this Commander Flint individual was a bad apple, and they did not want him spoiling any of the apples in their crate.

When Harold returned to the lumber camp the following day, he had many wild stories for them about the tales told to him by Commander Flint. The commander figured the entire damn bunch of them were in cahoots and were hiding the rest of the lost Indian tribe somewhere up there with them. He swore the Indian scout was one of the tribe's scoundrel savages and had accidentally come out from hiding in one of the many tents up there with them. The commander had told him as soon as he found another horse to buy, he would be back to claim his prize, whatever that meant. He did not quite understand what the prize meant. He said he was going to bring troops back with him and arrest the entire damn bunch of them. He then said he was going to have us all court-marshaled for helping them hide from justice, and was going to have us all put behind bars along with the savage beasts running wild in our hills. He proved himself a real mad man to all those in the camp, and they would be on the lookout for him to return.

CHAPTER ELEVEN

The Search of Smoke

Chief White Cloud sent Red Feathers and Crow north over the snow-covered mountain to see where the big fire was that was filling up the sky with smoke. Someone was very near the village, and he wanted to make sure it was not the white man coming after them.

Returning to the village a couple of days later, they had several stories to tell the chief and council at the fire. They returned with the saddle and Commander Flint's belongings, who had abandoned them high up in the woods when his horse had died and was unable to carry them out of the woods.

Finding the campsite where Commander Flint left his belongings, they headed east finding many white men in the woods cutting down Great White Spirit's trees. There was a black man among them and an Indian scout. The Indian wore a funny haircut shaved on both sides of his head with his hair sticking straight up in the middle like the crown of an owl, and his clothes were different.

They did not know what tribe the Indian scout represented by his clothing. They then backtracked to where the commander had abandoned his saddle and worldly possessions. They figured the things they found had to have belonged to the Indian scout or military scout who had been watching over them from high on the bordering mountain at their last village.

The scout must have been cooking or having a fire to keep warm after his horse had died. There were ashes beside the saddle, and the frozen horse was only a mile away from the campsite. He was a white man soldier or an Indian scout by the markings on the saddle they brought back with them.

The chief knew this was an alarming situation for his people. The white man had again surrounded them. With winter settling in, it would be impossible to move the entire village to another location further north or west. The white man was everywhere.

"Without any disrespect to you, sir, you are no longer in the military." "Yup, you are right, Bennett. That is because of you, and those no good Indian friends of yours. That is why I am out of the military, Bennett, and you know it. Where did you go and hide the damn Indians?"

"Hide them, sir." "What do you mean hide them? We searched for several weeks without finding a single sign or trace of them anywhere. Why was there not a trace of them all the way up to the Canadian border?"

"By the way, Commander, we received a formal complaint about you just the other day. It seems you threatened an Indian guide working for one of the major lumber companies around these parts." "That is no damn Indian guide up there and you know it. All the lumberjacks are conspiring with you and your men, are they not, Bennett? I saw the several small fires you and your men were making up there billowing smoke into the air the other day over the ridge by the lumberjack camp. You can't hide all those Indians forever from me you know, Bennett."

"Are you out of your mind, commander? What fires?

What ridge, what men are you talking about?" "Don't play squirrel and mouse with me, Bennett". "You know perfectly damn well what fires and men I am talking about, Bennett. The maneuvers you took your men on the other day up in the woods. I saw the smoke from your fires with my own two eyes. Five or six fires or maybe more, I do not remember exactly how many fires were billowing up smoke over the ridge next to the camp after my horse died. I had to leave my saddle out there, too, and am going back to get it as soon as I can when the weather breaks. I flipped the saddle over and covered it up with the saddle blanket. A little saddle soap will take care of any moisture it might pick up before I can return for it. You can't say I didn't know now can you, Bennett?"

"Listen to me, Flint. We have been dispersing men around these parts ever since I took over this assignment. This post and my position in it will be finished by the fall of next year. There will be no more army post in White River Junction. The army is leaving the law around these parts to the locals to handle with appointed sheriffs and deputies. There are only a handful of men left in these parts. Maybe including some scattered scouts there are about ten, but not many more than that in the whole state."

"Those damn lumberjacks were a bunch of liars then. They said there were not any more logging camps around for miles. They must have been hiding those savages up there with them then. I am going to get me some dirty savages real soon, Bennett."

"Hold on there a minute, Commander." "You are not authorized, Flint, to get any savages, I mean Indians or anyone else for that matter. If you mess around with anyone again in these parts, you will be arrested. I will arrest you myself, and place you under a federal court-marshal. You can't go around threatening anyone like you did to that poor Indian scout up in the logging camp."

"I knew it, then. You are hiding them savages up there, aren't you, Bennett?   I am going to prove it to the whole world that you were the one behind the savage Indians disappearing on me. You are the one who made me look like a fool, and got me discharged, isn't that right, Bennett? I should have been a great general by now, but look at me. I am just an old has-been because of you, Bennett. I am just an old discharged relic of a military commander, known around these parts as the mad commander out looking for ghost Indians. I heard that the other day while sitting at a bed and breakfast I stayed at."

"What are you babbling about, Commander?" "You don't have the right to call me anything, Bennett; you are nothing but a no-body yourself. What are you talking about, hidden Indians?" "You know damn well what I am talking about, Bennett. Those damn Indians you and those lumberjacks are hiding up there by the logging camp."

"Where did you say you saw the signs of them, Commander?" "You know very well where I saw them, Bennett. They are just south of Lunenburg, Vermont in the backcountry, not too far from the river, but far enough inland to be out of sight of anyone." "Here, point it out on the map for me, Commander." "Right there, Bennett," the commander pointed to an area west of the Connecticut River.

"Why that is mostly swamp out through that area." "There couldn't be enough game or open land out there to support any sizable tribe.   If they were out there, they surely would have been seen by someone as they tried to fish from the river for their winter stores and fertilizer for their crops. You must have spotted the smoke coming up from the village of Gilman where they are making the big paper mill."

"NO! I know where I saw the smoke coming up from, and it was not from the village of Gilman, Vermont! The smoke was rising up further inland from the river and a little west of Gilman. If it was not any of your men out there on maneuvers or the lumberjacks, it must have been those damn Indians. I swear I am going to go get me one of those damn beasts as a trophy, Bennett. No one around these parts is going to stop me, especially you! I'll show you who is crazy, Mr. Col. Bennett, and it won't be me."

Commander Flint saluted Col. Bennett with his middle finger gesture as he turned and stomped out his office, slamming the door behind him. Flint was gone as Col. Bennett sat back in his chair at his desk mulling over what had just transpired. What if Flint was right and it was the Indians? Flint had gone mad all right, right along with his vocabulary he was using, not in tune to when he was in charge of the post.

The winter was an awful one for everyone. Winter storms came in fearlessly leaving heavy blanket after heavy blanket of deep snow over the region. It made it nearly impossible for walking never mind traveling by horseback out in the backcountry.

Commander Flint came down with a real bad cold that soon turned into pneumonia. It laid him up for several weeks with a high fever, which made him even more delusional. He lost part of his memory for a long while. He came real close to dying twice, but managed to pull through it somehow. His anger toward life gave him strength to go on, it seemed. When he was over his pneumonia, the deep snow prohibited Flint from seeking out the Indian tribe. He knew he would die if he attempted such a foolish trick this soon after being sick.

White Eagle learned many new things in life during the long hard winter. His father, Red Feathers, taught him how to make a good sound bow for hunting. He taught him how to make snares to catch small game in order to feed the tribe, and how to select the right strong wooden branches from the hardwood in order to make good strong arrows to hunt game with.

Together in the woods, they found a good strong sapling without any branches. The young tree's fiber in growth grew fine and close together making it a strong shaft for his bow. It was a young maple tree of the right height and thickness for its shaft. Several other young braves from the tribe joined in with them with the lessons of making bows for their own use. They, too, found small strong trees for them to use.

Red Feathers sat them all down around the campfire and showed them first how to strip the outer bark from the tree's strong stock. Then he showed them the fiber strength of the shaft they picked in their saplings, and how it would make their bows much stronger. He showed them how to whittle away the unneeded wood along their shafts to make them light, and how to taper out the ends leaving the middles of their bows thicker for strength. When they were finished stripping and whittling away the unneeded wood, he showed them how to cure the bows in the fire.

They watched as the bow he was making for himself bubbled out the moisture from the wood fiber in its shaft as he held it out over the hot fire. He slowly passed the bow in and out through the flame of the fire not letting the heat of the fire scorch the wood fibers. If the fibers became scorched in any way during the curing process, the bow would break when it was pulled back to be used. Taking most the day, the curing of the bow correctly was a long, slow process.

In his next lesson, he showed them how to put an outer finish on their bows. They joined in by boiling down some sap from the spruce tree along with some of its green sticky needles and some beeswax. He showed them how to rub them down with it until the mixture on the bow's shaft made them glistened in the sunlight. He then showed them how to rub them all down with ash from the fire pit to dull their shine. This way the animals they were hunting would not see their bows glisten and reflect the light of the sun off the shafts.

The next good weather day, he taught them all how to make good arrows for their bows. They went into the woods trudging through the deep snow looking for straight shafts from hardwood trees and sleek branches from them to make their bow arrows. It was a laborious tiring time searching in the deep snow for the shafts for their arrows, and took most of the day to complete.

The next day, he sat them all down around the campfire in the council teepee again, repeating what they had done with their bows just days before. Several of the young braves burned their arrows by holding them in the fire too long. Red Feathers took the scorched arrows and bent them easily as they snapped in half. He explained how they would blow up in their faces if they used them in their bows. They were very dangerous if not cured properly.

The next lesson was in making bowstrings. Using a pelt from a deer, he carefully removed all the hair from it. Using a very sharp knife, he stripped the outer skin into many small size strands. He then showed them how to rub the strands down with beeswax making them flexible and water resistant. Water along with sunlight would make the rawhide dry out and crack, as would a hot fire if they placed their bows down too close to one.

It was fun and exciting for White Eagle when his father showed him how to set up snare traps to catch small game for food for the tribe. He caught many rabbits, gray squirrels, and even a couple of wild turkeys by mistake. He was turning into quite the hunter for his family and for the tribe.

His father spent many days and nights telling White Eagle stories about hunting, fishing, and other adventures he had had in the forest. Whispering Winds would sit and listen with them by the fire as she repaired or prepared clothing for them to wear. White Eagle watched her hands do the fine work and listened with attentive ears as his father told the many stories of himself and the history of the Indians.

He marveled at his mother's abilities as he did his father's. What history making in his life would he see come to fruition as he grew older, he wondered. It was a good thing he could not see his future or the legacy in life he would lead in the years to come. It would have scared him half to death.

As soon as the snow of winter melted, Chief White Cloud sent forth a scouting party for a new location for his village people. He chose Red Feathers, Crow, and a couple of the other braves who had ventured forth in finding the village where they now lived. The scouting party headed north and then west into the wilderness in search of a new location, but found the white man had settled everywhere they searched. There was not enough land left for them in the near proximity of where they were now. It would take many weeks for them to move far enough north to escape the white man, and it would not leave them enough time to prepare for the new winter months ahead.

In their search, they found that the white man had cleared large parcels of land for farms and had cleaned out the forest of its trees. Large game wildlife around the village was moving further and further away from them, making it necessary to move their village to a new location for food, which seemed near impossible at the time.

It had been but a mere few seasons since they moved from their old village to where they are now by the cliff and the large swamp. The white man had flourished all around them by building towns and erecting farms everywhere over the land. A full moon had almost passed when the scouting party returned to the village.

The chief called for a council meeting that night to discuss the situation and the plight of his people. Hawk would be the first brave to talk as he was the eldest of the scouting party this time. Red Feathers and then Crow would speak next.

Sitting on a rock beside the river near the waterfall where the Indians had disappeared, sat Commander Flint. His bout with pneumonia during the long winter months had clouded his memory, as he was trying to remember where he had last seen the Indian tribe's smoke. Flashbacks would come and go to him where he had last seen the logging camp, and then instantly fade away on him. He knew in his mind it was not far away from the loggers where the Indian village was located. He knew the logging camp was to the north, but could not remember which town he had been in where he had seen their smoke. He just could not remember where he was when he had discovered that damn Indian who was supposed to be their scout.

"Bull crap", he thought. "He was one of those damn savages up there from the village." He went above the falls heading north. "Damn it, why can I not remember," he swore thinking to himself. It was a single mountain, no, twin peaks, he remembered. Twin peaks off in the distance with Mount Washington standing tall behind them. No, it was a single peak to the left and a mountain with twin peaks to the right. That was it, a single peak to the left and a twin peak mountain to the right.

He would travel north until he came upon the mountain with a single peak and a twin one. He would use these landmarks in his finding those damn Indians, and show Bennett and the rest of the world just how smart an individual he really was.

The early spring rainy season cast over the region during the month of April. It rained just about every day, he thought as he rode his mount northward. How in the hell was he going to find those damn mountains in the mist and rain, he thought to himself. He could not see more than a half mile ahead of him, never mind see off into the distance which he needed to do in order to find the peeked mountain tops.

Extreme anger built up in his mind, like a man with a high fever out of control. The townspeople in every town he passed could see the madness in his eyes. The mad man commander was back with his eyes of a wolf looking through people when he stopped to talk or eat with them. They felt uneasy with him as if he was looking through them instead of at them. He scared the people in his presence half to death just by being around them, and they were glad when he moved on. Word of his coming traveled fast to the next town he was about to go through.

White Eagle had seen the bald eagle land many times on the high cliff overlooking the village below. Conferring with his mother, he asked if he might climb the mountain behind the village to sit and converse with the brave at his post who was watching over the village that day.

Climbing the trail along the ridge to the top of the mountain, White Eagle spotted an old tom turkey peeking its head out around a bush at him. He wanted to shoot it with his bow and take it home for dinner that night, but he also wanted to go to the top of the mountain to sit and talk with the brave up there. The turkey would have to be dinner for another day. It took White Eagle over an hour to climb the steep trail to where the brave was watching over the village below. The brave caught several glances of him coming up the trail to be with him. When he finally arrived at the lookout's post, he found Fox sitting and looking out over the safety of the village below.

Fox was slowly moving his head from side to side looking out over the terrain below and every ten or twelve times, he would look behind him to see that no one was there as well. He looked like an owl perched high up in a tree looking for a mouse below to eat. White Eagle watched as Fox moved his head back and forth and then around.

Looking toward the east, White Eagle spotted Mount Washington off in the far distance. It was truly a remarkable sight, he thought. There she was standing majestically tall with a snowcapped summit among the shorter mountains. Fox invited White Eagle to sit and talk for a while. He had been watching him ascend the trail to the post. "Long way out over land and down in the village, right White Eagle, like sitting on a cloud up here?" White Eagle nodded his head in response. He felt as if he was on top of the world way up there. His people looked to him like little tiny ants crawling around on the ground below. He could never remember ever being this high up before. He could see the smoke billowing up from the stack of an iron horse ascending to Mount Washington's summit. He had never seen such a thing before.

"What is that on the far mountain, Fox," White Eagle

asked. "Medicine man calls that an iron horse made by the white man. See the white smoke coming up through trees down in valley below? That is smoke from another white man's iron horse. Fox never see one up close, but has heard its loud screaming noise once in a while in valley. Funny thing iron horse white man makes. Look through the trees in the valley. See snake like path on the ground. You wait. You will see iron horse real soon follow path on the ground." Shortly thereafter, a long train came rolling up over the tracks below. White Eagle was astonished that there was such a thing in the world. An iron horse, he thought. He had only heard stories about real live horses he had never seen before, never mind an iron horse. It doesn't have legs like the deer or moose have, he was told. It did not have legs at all. It looked like a large snake slithering along the ground.

He sat there asking Fox question after question about the valley below, as eagles flew above him and then dove down in front of him to the shelved ledge below the lookout post. White Eagle had never seen a bald eagle up this close before, only one flying high up in the sky above the village. It almost scared him, but for some reason it did not. He felt very comfortable sitting there with Fox and having the eagles fly all around him. White Eagle made his stay with Fox a short one, knowing he was asking too many questions for Fox to answer. They were questions he should have been asking his father instead. When he returns back down to the teepee, he will drive his father wild with question after question after visiting with Fox for the couple of hours he sat with him.

Crow arrived to take over for Fox, so White Eagle started to ask him questions as well. Fox felt relieved when Crow arrived as he was all out of answers for White Eagle. He was smart, but White Eagle seemed to be a little bit smarter. He had so many questions that he was afraid he would not have the right answers for him. He was quite the inquisitive young brave and would make a great leader one day, Fox thought.

Not being quite as helpful as Fox was, White Eagle excused himself and headed back down the mountain trail to the village below. He wanted to get back to the plateau where he had first seen the big tom turkey. With a little luck, he would spot the turkey again if Fox had not already taking it with his bow, and they would have it for their dinner that night.

Coming upon a grove of hemlocks growing a third of the way down the mountain trail, White Eagle spotted a much larger turkey than the first one he had seen a couple of hours before. This tom was twice the size of the first as it fluttered its wings and ran behind the hemlock grove. Oh, if he could only be lucky enough to shoot this one with his bow and bring it back home to his mother. Boy would she be proud of him. He had to try.

Carefully he snuck up to the hemlocks, but the turkey saw him coming and ran again, again, and again away from White Eagle. He was determined to have this turkey as a prize for their meal that evening or the following day. After following the turkey for several hundred yards, it seemed to White Eagle that the turkey stopped atop a large rock. Before it had the chance to turn and see if someone was following it, White Eagle had taken careful aim with his bow and let his arrow fly. The turkey went over the backside of the large rock and landed in heap. It shuffled along the ground bleeding with an arrow stuck in its side for a short distance away. It tried to hide by going in under an overhanging slab of rock protruding out from the side of the mountain. Following its trail, White Eagle came upon the turkey. Bending down, he prepared to go under the slab to get his turkey. Beneath the protruding slab, he found the entrance to a large cave in the side of the mountain. Just inside several feet away lay the dead turkey in the dark shadow of the cave. Letting his eyes adjust, he crawled inside to claim his prize. Once inside the cave, he marveled at the size of it. It was much bigger than the council teepee back in the village.

Suddenly, the sound of an eagle screaming came echoing off its inside sidewalls having traveled down the opening in the large cave. Startled by the loud noise, he jumped quickly back. He grabbed his turkey, not wanting to be attacked by one of the huge eagles he had just witnessed while sitting with Fox, and hurried out of the cave's opening below the slab of rock.

No big old bird was going to take away his prize catch of the day. It was his. Descending the trail to the village below, White Eagle caught a glance of an eagle perched on the cliff's overhang sticking out over the village below. She was screeching like the one just inside the cave. Could it be, he thought, the cave above that he was just in, led out to where that eagle was? No, it was too far away, he thought. Could the big cave be connected to where the eagle was sitting on the ledge shelf? He did not think so.

Whispering Winds carefully plucked the big feathers from the huge turkey as she prepared it to be cooked. She wanted to make a breastplate from the feathers for her son, White Eagle, as she was proud of her son, the great hunter. He was going to make a good provider of food for the tribe, as was his father.

Sitting around the family fire, White Eagle began telling his story about the day he had on the mountain. He told them about the many questions he had asked Fox, and how he had taken the turkey they were eating with his bow and arrow, and how he had plucked it out of the cave. He felt like a real warrior now, he said as he laughed with his mother and father.

His father explained the dangers he could have faced inside the cave or any other cave. Bears, mountain lions, wild boar, and other wild animals such as fisher cats dwell in such openings in the Great White Spirit's land he made for all. If a black bear was to have a small bear cub in the cave, the mother bear would have torn the intruder to threads in protecting her cubs, even if the intruder did not mean any harm to them. The wild boar and the mountain lion were as bad if not worse than the black bear. Next time, he told White Eagle it would be much safer to have left the turkey inside the cave than to have risked his life in fetching it out.

The night was a clear peaceful moonlit night with its canopy of bright stars glistening in the overhead. This would be the last relaxing time the tribe would ever spend in their once quiet village. In the morning when the sun rose up high over the horizon to the east, the Indians would face the invasion of the white man in their village. The lost ghost Indian tribe of the northeast would not be lost anymore.

CHAPTER TWELVE

The Invasion of the White Man

In late April, Col. Bennett received a wired telegram from the Central Northeast Logging Company in Gilman, Vermont. "Attention Col. Bennett. U.S. Army Post Number Six, White River Junction, Vermont. Dear Col. Bennett. Small village of Indians encroaching upon company forest land, would like your immediate attention. Sincerely, Mr. Gilmanton, Company chairperson."

Col. Bennett read over the telegram several times in total disbelief as he just could not believe what he was reading. Could it possibly be the lost Indian tribe that had disappeared several years ago? He could not believe it when he read the special telegram, and wondered if it could really be them.

Commander Flint had been right about one thing. This was exactly where he claimed the Indians were when he pointed to it on the map with his finger in the fall. Col. Bennett wondered what the crazy commander was up to today, and where he was at that moment. Knowing him the way he used to know him, and how he acted the last time he saw him, he knew he was up to no good.

Col. Bennett wished at the time he would not be too late in arriving at the Indian village before Flint arrived there and stirred up a whole bunch of trouble with the Indians. Col. Bennett secured several marshals and army personnel and assembled them in the small city of Lancaster, New Hampshire just across the river from where the Indians were supposed to have settled halfway between Lunenburg and Gilman, Vermont.

Col. Bennett's orders were to move the Indian tribe to a safe reservation out of Commander Flint's way, knowing he was a crazy man with deadly intentions for the Indians. The tribe would have to move just north of Lancaster, New Hampshire to a reservation on land the government would supply for them in Colebrook, New Hampshire. There they would have plenty of land to hunt on, a river to catch fish from, and land to plant their gardens of vegetables for their winter stores.

Traveling up Baptist Hill Road toward Lunenburg, Commander Flint knew he was close to finding the hidden Indian tribe's village. To his west, stood the single peaked mountain he remembered standing on when he was lost in the woods with his dead horse, and to his right stood the twin peaked mountains.

The blood in his veins began to boil with anger, as adrenalin shot through them like a fire hose while menacing delight flowed in them at the same time. It was now time for some savages to pay for all the misery and misfortune they had caused him all his life. He wanted to hang them all one by one, women and children alike. He had no feelings for any of them. They were responsible for all the spankings that he ever received when he was a child. All the reprimands he received during his lifetime, and the loss of his wife who took their two young children away from him when she left. They had also turned Major Bennett against him as he helped them to escape. The major had taken over his post and he was forced out of the army. Everything bad ever happening in his lifetime was entirely their fault. The more he thought about it, the more angered he became. The more angered he became, the more ways in which he would like to torture them passed swiftly through his sick mind.

Crossing over and through the covered bridge connecting Lancaster, New Hampshire and Lunenburg, Vermont, Col. Bennett led his men south along Connecticut River Road. The Indian scout from the logging camp led the way for them. When they reached a small brook flowing out of the forest and into the Connecticut River a few miles from Gilman, the Indian scout stopped them. He pointed westward toward a large mountain behind the big swamp, just off the road behind the trees.

He led the men around the great swamp, stopping just south of the Indian village. By the light of the moon, they came within eyesight of the village with its fires all aglow. In the early morning, Col. Bennett accompanied by the Indian scout, approached the Indian village.

A loud war-crying hoot from the Indian high on the sheer cliff above on his lookout posts came echoing down into the village. Everyone came running out from their wigwams to see what the hooting cry was all about. Col. Bennett held his right hand high up into the air above his head as he walked toward the village.

The Indian scout, using sign language, told his brother Indians they had come in peace. Red Feathers recognized the Indian scout by his funny clothes to be the one who had been with the lumberjacks that they had found when they ventured north in search of where the big smoky fire was coming from a few moons ago. He figured Col. Bennett must have been the scout watching over the village who had left his saddle in the woods near the campfire when his horse had died. He must be the same one who has come looking for the saddle he left behind after not finding it where he had left it. He could also be the one who had been watching over them at their old village from high on the next mountain.

Many things were running through Red Feathers' mind as the two approached the village slowly. Chief White Cloud knew some broken English, as did his brother Red Feathers and the medicine man. The three practiced with one another in case they would ever need to use it someday, and this just might be the day. Several marshals and a few army men stood ready in the bush with their rifles drawn and ready to respond if trouble broke out ahead of them.

After a few very tense moments, Col. Bennett turned toward the men hidden behind him in the bush and raised both hands and arms high toward the sky above, and then let them both slowly drop to his sides. The movement of his hands and arms in this manner was a signal to the men that they could put down their rifles, not away, but just down.

White Eagle stood beside his mother watching what was going on. He had never seen a white man before or another Indian dressed the way the Indian scout was dressed. He marveled at the haircut the Indian scout had. His hair was shaved off both sides of his head and the hair on top his head was pointing toward the heavens. He almost wanted to laugh, but knew the time was not right for it. The white man's skin was truly white. It was not deep red or brownish like the Indians' skin. He had heard about a man being black at one of the talks, and wondered if he might be with them.

Col. Bennett, the Indian scout, Red Feathers, the medicine man, and Chief White Cloud all went to the council fire ring to talk. There, the medicine man took out the peace pipe. From a pouch on a string by his side, he took out what looked like tobacco and stuffed the pipe full. He then lit it with hot ash that he swept up from the fire pit.

White Eagle watched with excitement running wild in his mind to what was going to happen next. The medicine man waved the smoke away from the pipe as he brought it to life and the smoke began to flow. He was chasing away the evil spirits that might be within the village. When he was sure all the evil spirits were out of the village, he handed the peace pipe over to his chief, and sat down at the ring beside him. After taking a couple of puffs of smoke from the peace pipe, Chief White Cloud handed the peace pipe over to the Indian scout sitting to his left. The scout took several puffs and handed it to Col. Bennett who was sitting to his left. He took a few puffs from the pipe, and then handed the pipe to Crow who had just sat down at the council ring along with several other elders of the tribe.

Once the peace pipe had made the entire circle around and returned to the medicine man, they began to talk. Col. Bennett tried explaining to the chief and the tribe's people through the interpretation of the Indian scout, that they were trespassing upon land owned by the Central Northeastern Logging Company. The company who owned the land wanted them to move from their land to another location.

Chief White Cloud and his people were confused about how anyone could own the land of the Great White Spirit. The Great White Spirit from above let all men use his land to live on and bury their dead in during the summer months, or let them return their ashes to it if they died during the winter and had to be cremated by fire.

Col. Bennett told Chief White Cloud he was right. The Great White Spirit did indeed own the land of the world. He agreed everyone on it should be able to use the land freely, but that was not the case anymore. There were greedy men with great power who purchased the land with furs and gold from others who had thought they owned the land. New land laws made ownership of it. It was not right, but he had to obey the laws of the land made by these greedy people from across the mighty waters.

The conversation went on for a couple of hours around the council fire ring. Col. Bennett knew a little Indian language, and could only tell when one of the braves was angered about these new laws made by the white man. Col. Bennett went on to tell them about great armies of white men who would come if they did not agree to move from the land that they were living on.

He said he did not want that to happen as he wanted them to move off the land peacefully. He told them of land to the north where they could live in harmony with the white man, and not have to move ever again. The white man would furnish them with horses, cows, goats, sheep, and chickens for meat and eggs. There would be plenty of land to hunt on, and fish in a nearby river for the long winter months, and possibly for some fertilizer for their crops in spring.

White Eagle wondered what kind of animals they were talking about because he had never seen any of them. He had only heard about the horse, and the only horse he had ever seen was the iron horse slithering along its winding trail along the riverbank in the valley below. He saw another iron horse from high atop the lookout's post over the village. The little iron horse was breathing heavy smoke on its trip up the great mountain across the river and valley.

Suddenly White Eagle jumped from the sound of a large gun firing. A rifle blasted out from atop the cliff and echoed out across the river valley. He had never heard the explosion of a gun before. Next, the sound of an Indian screaming came echoing down from above as the shot brave fell through the air from the lookout post.

He lay dead in a heap on the ground before them after careening off the shelved ledge where the great bald eagle had stood. The men around the council ring all jumped to their feet in total disbelief of what was happening around them.

Suddenly White Eagle's mother, Whispering Winds, pulled him backwards off of his feet, and looked at him with fright in her eyes. He fell over backwards flat on his back staring skyward up toward the cliff. He saw a figure holding a long pole pointing it down toward the tribe below. A puff of smoke came out the end of the long pole in his hands accompanied by a massive explosion.

The Indian scout that the white man in blue had brought with him, let out a scream of pain. The Indian scout that had been shot in the shoulder by the figure above, fell over backwards after the bullet lodged in his shoulder. Col. Bennett pulled the revolver from his holster and fired it toward the figure on top of the cliff.

A volley of rifle fire explosions erupted from the men hiding behind the bushes and trees where Col. Bennett and the Indian scout had come from when they first entered the village.

The figure, standing on top of the mountain, let go of the pole he was holding, and it fell down off the cliff and landed not far away from the dead Indian. Next, the silhouette of the man from the top of the cliff bounced off the extended cliff's overhang like the falling brave had done, and landed dead before them all in a heap. He was dressed in army blues, as was Col. Bennett. As the women and children in the village were scampering back and forth for cover and protection, their warrior braves were busy retrieving their bows and arrows. They were readying themselves for retaliation against the white man.

The colonel and the Indian scout with him must have been decoys for the white man to attack their village. Chief White Cloud stood his ground observing what was taking place around them. He hollered with authority in his voice for his braves to stop. "Do not fight" he said, and told them to leave their bows and arrows alone. "Do not fight" he hollered louder to his braves who were still busy getting ready to fight the white man.

"It is all over" he screamed again at the top of his lungs to his warriors. The situation at hand was nerve racking and very wild. Col. Bennett again raised an arm above his head as he knew all the rifles hidden in the woods were now being aimed at all the Indian braves in the village. He did not want any trouble or bloodshed as there had been enough already.

Chief White Cloud, seeing Col. Bennett raise his arm high above his head, yelled out to his people again. He knew that Col. Bennett raised his arm as a signal to his men. He knew that if the colonel was to be hurt or killed, his people would all suffer the consequences.

To White Eagle, everything seemed to have happened in very slow motion. Everything was over in a matter of seconds, but to him it seemed more like an hour or more. He watched as the colonel fired his revolver at the figure standing high on the cliff above the village. He heard the many rifles all being shot at the very same time, as he watched the figure high above the village come crashing down to the ground below. He saw the women of the tribe grab their papooses and run wildly everywhere.

The braves, all wanting to protect their loved ones, were running off for their bows and arrows as White Eagle's mother tried getting him up off the ground to take him to a place of safety.

Suddenly, everything came to a sudden stop as the chief yelled out to his braves to stop again. White Eagle wondered how Chief White Cloud knew everything was going to be all right when he yelled to the braves to stop. Whispering Winds embraced him as he picked himself up off the ground in amazement of what had just transpired. Seeing everything was quiet and almost back to normal, Col. Bennett raised his second hand high up into the air letting them both fall slowly to his sides signaling his men everything was now all right again, and they could put their rifles down again. Behind the cover of the trees and brush, his men put their rifles down. Col. Bennett turned his immediate attention to the wounded scout lying hurt on the ground. The chief signaled for his medicine man to come help patch him up, and to see to it that he was all right. Whispering Winds sent White Eagle to fetch the medicine man's special satchel, the one he used for fixing up wounds with the special powders the women of the tribe helped him make from the special herbs they had gathered from the forest.

With words of great concern in his voice, Chief White Cloud asked Col. Bennett what had just happened. Why did the white man send him to talk peace, and another soldier to kill them?   Col. Bennett told the tribe council commander that Flint had been a good soldier once, but had gone mad, sick of mind in his head. He told the chief that when they moved from their old village by the lake and disappeared into thin air, it made the man lying dead upon the ground look very bad to his superiors. He was out for revenge against all men, and not just the Indians. He told the chief about their last meeting in his office, but did not think Commander Flint knew anything about their real whereabouts, but he was wrong and very sorry. He should have come to the village back then immediately after following their conversation in his office so none of this would have ever happened. He was sorry for the dead Indian brave and for his Indian friend lying wounded in pain. He was also sorry for Commander Flint, and his family having to put up with such a very sick man. Using what little Indian language he knew, and mostly their sign language, he was able to communicate quite well without his Indian interpreter helping him.

White Eagle reflected back to the old village in his mind where he once played by the lake with his little friend Winonah. He remembered the long journey through the woods, and finally arriving to their new village below the cliff. He remembered also how everyone had to be very quiet along the way, and how everyone had to walk flat-footed on the ground and not make any marks on the leaves below their feet so the white man would not be able to find them. He recalled playing with Winonah below the cliff of rock overlooking the beautiful Connecticut Valley a couple of days before arriving in their new village. He wondered if the new village would be as nice as the old one was for his family and tribe, and now they would have to move again to another location. His life as a child was in turmoil.

CHAPTER THIRTEEN

The Big Move North

During the next several weeks, Col. Bennett visited the Indian village frequently getting them ready for their big move. Chief White Cloud, Red Feathers, Crow, and two other braves went north with Col. Bennett to inspect the land that was promised to them. The reservation land in Colebrook, New Hampshire was as nice as Col. Bennett had promised it would be. On the reservation, there was a small lake with a narrow stream running through it leading out to the Connecticut River a few miles away. There were a couple of large hills, almost mountains, for them to hunt on, fields for their crops, and animals promised by the white man already there. It looked like a very promising place for them to move to, and pleased Chief White Cloud and the others with him.

Upon return from the new reservation, Chief White Cloud called for a council meeting to talk over the land they had just visited. White Eagle stood by his mother just outside the council ring listening intently to what the elders sitting around the fire were talking over. Chief White Cloud told his people about the journey they were about to take north in a few days. The generosity of the white man was going to provide them with horses and wagons for the long journey to their new home.

White Eagle had heard about wagons, but like the horse, he had never seen one before. The journey north would be fun, he thought. To ride in a wagon or on a horse would be different, and whatever else he saw in the move would be fun. In the last move, all he saw was the woods and paths the white man had made in the forest, and never a white man's teepee. He was getting excited.

For the next several days, the tribe dismantled their village. They made drays from the several big poll's they took out from the council wigwam to load their belongings onto with two and three families' belongings per horse-drawn dray.

The big council wigwam was the last wigwam to come down. Looking skyward, White Eagle watched as a large bald eagle soared higher and higher up into the heavens. The bald eagle was drifting on the warming air currents rising up from the mountain. Suddenly, she closed her wings, and held them close to her body. She dropped like a rock thrown from a tree toward the earth below. He watched as the tiny speck in the heavens grew bigger and bigger the closer it came to the ground. Suddenly, she opened her strong wings, and shot over to the mighty cliff overhang just above the village they were leaving. She stood on its edge and let out an awful cry. It was as if she was saying goodbye to the tribe below.

A flashback suddenly came to him as she screeched. He remembered the same cry that came echoing down through the cavern in the big cave where he had retrieved the turkey a few weeks ago. He wished he had searched out the cave back then because it looked big enough to have housed the entire tribe inside its massive walls.

This was home to him as he looked around the village, and he did not really want to leave it. He wanted to stay here where bald eagles soared high above the mountains around him. This is where he learned to hunt and trap prey with his father for food for the tribe and his family. It had been a place of joy for him, playing with his friends, and falling in love with Winonah, his childhood girlfriend. Even though she did not know it at the time, but deep down inside, White Eagle knew she was his princess.

Suddenly a branch slapped White Eagle in the face as he rode along on top a horse dragging one of the heavy drays behind it. He almost fell off the horse backwards as the horse kept up its pace following the white man who was leading her through the dense tree growth. He laid over backwards onto the smooth hair of the horse's back, and reached for something to keep him from falling off. He managed to grab ahold of one of the staves of the dray to right himself back up into a sitting position.

This was another lesson in life for him to pay closer attention to what lay ahead of him in his life. Like the branch of the tree, there would be things in his life that would knock him off his feet even when he was paying close attention. Looking up ahead, he saw Chief White Cloud, the Indian scout with a patch on his shoulder, along with Col. Bennett, Crow, and Hawk leading the way.

Making sure there were no more branches ready to take him off the horse's back, he turned his head around. Behind him, he saw an endless trail of his people snaking their way through the woods, and coming up behind him through the trees. To him they looked like the slithering path the iron horse had made along in front and behind the many horses in the procession.

Turning his attention to the path ahead of him, White Eagle glanced over at Col. Bennett because he admired this tall slender man with good posture sitting tall in his saddle on his horse. Beside him to his right, rode a U. S. Government man looking very funny being so short and round, supporting a big long handlebar mustache that curled around into a circle along with his two big puffy sideburns sticking out in front of his ears. His strange funny looks made White Eagle laugh every time he looked over at him.

As the tribe approached the Connecticut River, they heard the loud whistle of an iron horse making its way up the river valley on its way northward. Most of the tribe had never seen an iron horse before, and the loud noise from its whistle made most of them very nervous. Some of the tribe's members pictured it as a monstrous manmade horse, made from many of their copper arrowheads they had learned to make from some special dirt and ore they had found in the mountains. Some pictured it with long muscular looking legs made from copper, breathing fire from its nostrils, as they saw the smoke rising up into the air from its smokestack. None could picture it as being friendly when it was making such a loud noise.

Coming out from the deep woods into a large grass covered meadow, the tribe met up with a group of white men. The men had wagons and fresh horses for them to use in their long journey northward. A couple of the men had very large buckboards pulled by several workhorses each to carry big loads of supplies. They would now be able to carry their ware loads mounted on several drays in one load, instead of using so many horses to do the same job these special wagons could do.

After getting everyone organized with whom everyone would be traveling along with the next day, the tribe made camp for the night. White Eagle went from family to family helping them to place their worldly belongings on a couple of buckboards and wagons waiting for them for their long journey northward to Colebrook, New Hampshire.

Walking around the campsite that night, White Eagle spotted Winonah sitting with her mother at their family campfire. He asked if he might sit with them for a while, and they invited him to stay. After several minutes, he and Winonah excused themselves from sitting and went for a walk together around the camp area. There they talked and reflected back on the village they had to leave. They were confused as to why they had no choice in the matter, for a white man now owned the land that belonged to the Great White Spirit. They made a promise to one another that one day they would both return to the old village site when they grew up. They would get married by the chief of the tribe and raise a family together there as husband and wife. They would live there on the Great White Spirit's land that no man owns, and would live in peace and harmony with all the animals of the forest.

"The white man who says he owns the Great White Spirit's land must be evil," Winonah said. "Not all white men are evil, Winonah," said White Eagle. "Look at Col. Bennett; he is a good white man. Look at the ones who are trying to help us move from the greedy man's land. They all seem to be good white men." White Eagle sighed a pain of despair from deep within his heart as he had to leave Winonah back at her family's campfire, and it was time for him to return to his own family's site. As he walked along, he daydreamed how nice it would be to have Winonah as his bride one day, but there were other braves she might fall in love with in the future instead of him. He was only a mere number in life now, and could only hope his number in life would not be zero.

In the early morning hours, everyone formed into a big wagon train parade like a circus on the move. Many of the older members of the tribe rode along in the several wagons provided. Some of the elder tribe's people road on horseback for the journey north. The able body ones walked alongside the wagons and horses in military formation. The Indians looked soldier-like in parade up the dirt road toward South Lunenburg, Vermont. From there, they would cross over the Connecticut River through a white man's covered bridge and into Lancaster, New Hampshire on their trek north toward the Colebrook reservation where they would make their home.

As they traveled along the river road, they could see the steel tracks that the iron horse rode on alongside the roadway on the flat valley floor next to the river. As they traveled along, an iron horse came steaming slowly along the tracks beside them as they sauntered along in their tight knit group, most all in discontent for having to move again.

The train's engineer being mischievous, blew the train's loud steam whistle to see their reaction. It scared most of them half to death by its shrilling loud noise making the horses jump and prance around in the roadway. The drivers of the buckboard wagons all yelled out at the engineer for being such a fool. The engineer enjoyed what he was causing and watched the poor Indians and the horses all jump around. He foolishly blew his whistle again and again, as he laughed out the window, and rolled out of sight of the tribe.

White Eagle stared over at the iron horse in awe. It did not look anything like he had imagined it would in his mind. It did not have the long hard copper legs he imagined it would have, nor did it blow smoke and fire from out its flaming nostrils. With its long round cylindrical body like a fallen tree and round wagon wheels for its legs, the iron horse rolled out from his sight.

He had not seen a wagon until yesterday, and now an iron horse today. He wondered what else might lay in store for him the rest of his life. Looking out over the iron horse's railroad tracks and into the Connecticut River, he spotted a large log flow coming down the swift flowing river. There were several men walking back and forth atop the many logs with long poles in their hands yelling out to one another as they floated along. They were using the long poles to push at the logs beneath their feet, and drive them down into the river between the logs.

What a strange world the white man was living in, thought White Eagle to himself. They soon came to a white man's teepee. It was a big square shaped teepee with openings in its skin. It allowed them to see inside their living quarters. He had never seen anything quite as strange before. He could see many things hanging on the walls inside of the tepee.

Out in the field next to the white man's teepee, was a white woman holding onto the reins of a workhorse as she walked along beside it with her husband walking along behind them controlling a plow digging up the soil of earth. It was the job of the women and children of the tribe to be digging up and planting the crops. They were to keep the gardens clear of annoying weeds and bugs that might try to eat their hard labors.

The white man was surely a strange breed to White Eagle. Their ways would be quite different from the Indian's ways he would find out soon in his young life. They soon passed by several more white man wigwams and a couple of very large wooden wigwams made especially for the white man's animals to house their cows, horses, and chickens in.

As they traveled along the road made for the wagons by the white man, many white man families gathered along the pathway standing out in front of their wooden wigwams watching the tribe of Indians pass by. The Indians all felt like they were on display which they were.

After a long time traveling, they came to a large long wooden teepee extending all the way across the big river. To White Eagle, it looked like the white man had interwoven many large trees with one another in making the long span across the flowing river. The horses' hooves echoed as they pranced across the wooden floor of the bridge, and the wagon wheels whispered in soft tone with their movement.

They were now in a different state according to the white man. The bridge connected the state of Vermont with the state of New Hampshire. This would be their new land to live on. White Eagle did not understand because he thought that all the land in the world was owned by the Great White Spirit above, and no wooden teepee crossing a river might ever change that, especially if it was made by a white man. As they traveled along, White Eagle watched as two white boys herded some cows out from their farmer's big wooden teepee out into a field surrounded by wooden fences for the cows to graze. The scene made any feeling of freedom he might have had quickly fade away, when he turned and watched his people being herded along down the roadway as were the cattle.

This made White Eagle want to yell out at the world that his people were not cattle. They did not deserve to be made to move from their quiet village against their will. The white man did not own any of the land where their village was. Could the Great White Spirit hear their cry, and do something about this travesty? The greedy white man came from far across the big waters and took control over the Great White Spirit's land against his will. One day the white man will pay for offending the Great White Spirit. What kind of world is this, he thought.

The two white boys were herding their cattle, and some

white men with rifles were herding his people. He was angered sick inside with the very sight of it all. He looked over at his father and his mother down beside him, and then looked over toward the chief of the tribe, his uncle, White Cloud. They looked too happy as a group being moved along as cattle herded from their old village to another village they did not know anything about. Not him, he knew it was very wrong.

With the confusion too great for his young mind to comprehend, he laid back on the horse, pulling the wagon he was on to relax and gaze up into the bright blue sky above. His mind drifted back to the old village where the bald eagle soared high above it. His mind made him feel as if he was flying like an eagle and able to look down on the mass of his people as they made their way northward toward their new village.

Dark clouds and barren land was all he could see ahead for his people. Behind them, the land in the old village was green with fertility. The land looked plush with blooming flowers and abundant fruit springing up all around. Suddenly, he snapped back into reality when the horse he was on came to a sudden stop. It was time to stop for some rest and for his people to have a bite to eat. They stopped just short of the city of Lancaster, New Hampshire. As the tribe stopped to rest and eat, some of the townspeople from Lancaster and around came out to see them, as if they were a new circus just coming to town.

White Eagle was mesmerized with them as they were with his people. Their clothing was not furs of animals as theirs was, and different colors of the rainbow. None of them had on any sweatbands atop their heads as they did to keep the sweat out of their eyes. He spotted a black man dressed up in bright red. Who and what did this mean? He was nothing like the white man standing beside him. He looked so different to him with his wide nose, his curly hair, and his big white eyes. White Eagle could not help but stare at him. What kind of an Indian was he?

After their rest, they struck out again and entered into the city of Lancaster. White Eagle noticed the white man's wigwams were now made from square red stone stacked one on top one another and very high. Many white people were staring out of the holes in the stone wigwams as they marched through the streets heading north. White Eagle was happy when they exited out of the city on its other side. All the hooting and hollering by the white man, the women, and their children made his people very nervous. They were all glad to leave. Reaching the outskirts of the city allowed everyone to relax again.

The memory of his daydreaming came back to him. Why had his old village been so green and plush? Why did the road ahead of them look so dark and gloomy? Could it have been a signal from the Great White Spirit above to him of things to come? What would their new village look like, and what did it have in store for him and his people when they all got there?

That night White Eagle talked to his mother and father about the dream he had experienced on the horse. No great significance could be made of the dream, only little tricks played on him by his mind. He had not smoked the peace pipe and brought out his inner spirit to interact with him, so it could not mean anything. He was too young to know his inner spirit yet. He didn't know if his inner spirit was the cougar, black bear, eagle, or mountain lion. It must have been some fluke of a daydream.

The talk of the night evolved around the long journey of the day. Why did the white man stare at them as if they were bad people, and what were they saying in their foreign tongue about them? White Eagle said he would learn this foreign tongue of English so he would be able to understand the ways of the white man and be able to protect his people better.

In the morning, the caravan of wagons, horses, and people reassembled in line for another long day's march in their long trek northward. It rained hard all night as they rested, and everyone was soaked to the skin before daybreak. Traveling was harder on them now as the roads beneath their feet turned to mud with every step they took.

Fence posts and wooden rails lined the roadway as they walked along. In their travels, they passed cornfield after cornfield, open field after open field, and big gardens that covered the hillsides and valleys of the hills. The forest as White Eagle remembered it seemed to be disappearing before him. Barbed wire with its metal thorns decorated the landside keeping in the white man's cattle, trapped within its boundaries. The white man had taken down the wonderful forest and taken over land. They had even taken the stone from earth and lined them up one on top the other making stonewall land dividers between the lands they said they owned. Why had the Great White Spirit allowed the white man to destroy his wonderful land?

The day's journey was long and wet. Col. Bennett had journeyed off ahead of the weary convoy. When he returned, he had good news for Chief White Cloud. A white man with a large teepee for his cattle was going to let his people rest for the night inside its walls to keep them from the wet elements outside. It was mid-afternoon when the tribe finally reached the farmer's land.

The farm owners were Mr. and Mrs. Colby where they stopped to rest for the night. Mrs. Colby took an instant liking to young White Eagle. Neither she nor he understood the other verbally, but managed to communicate otherwise. When it was time to milk the cows, Mrs. Colby invited White Eagle to come watch as she stripped the milk out from the cow's teats and into a milking bucket. Watching Mrs. Colby milk the cow fascinated White Eagle. She motioned for him to come to her side and asked him by using hand motions, if he would like to try milking a cow, and he did. He sat on the stool beside the cow as she had. Taken the cow's teats in his hands, and began to pump the nipples up and down as she had. Not one single drop of milk flowed out from the cow's nipples. Mrs. Colby explained to him as best she could by using her hands. She motioned how she took the cow's teat high up next to the milking bag and squeezed her thumb and forefinger tight on the teat as she pulled down and released her grip on it. Then she took the teat in her hand and showed him how the milk flowed out the teat in a stream and into the bucket. He managed to understand her, as she had a lot of patience with him, and was soon milking the cow like an old pro farmer with a wide smile spread wide across his face.

As he milked the cow, his hand encountered a rough patch upon the cow's milk bag. The cow had a small case of cowpox. The cowpox leaked some fluid from the sore, and it entered into a scratch on White Eagle's hand as he was milking. The cowpox fluid from the cow would in turn create a small sore on his hand in the next couple of days. This invasion of the cowpox serum into his young body would vaccinate him from ever developing smallpox later on in his lifetime if ever he was to become exposed to the deadly disease.

Mrs. Colby sat back down on the stool after White Eagle got up to strip the milk out of the cow's milk bag again. In doing so, she squirted some milk from the cow's teat into the open mouth of an awaiting kitten who was sitting next to her on the barn floor in anticipation. She loved animals, and always gave the kitten a treat while she was out in the barn milking. The kitten would sit, meow, and then open its mouth wide. She didn't always get the milk right into the cat's mouth, and would often cover the kitten's face with it. The cat would attempt to lick itself clean and would go through all kinds of antics to rid its fur of the clean milk. White Eagle thought the game of feeding the cat was fun and laughed the first time he witnessed it.

It was midmorning of the next day when White Eagle realized the sun was up and shining down brightly on him from the bright blue sky above. He had been daydreaming like the day before to pass the time away. He daydreamed about the first beaver he had ever seen when he was a baby with his mother down by the lake in the old village. The first village they had to leave before the white man had come, and now was forced to move from yet another one.

He reminisced over the many different things he remembered about the old village and going out into the lake with his mother and father in a canoe. The small lake looked huge to him at first, but realized it to be but a mere puddle in the large world that surrounds him. He recalled the long journey traveling quietly through the woods before arriving at the last village. He loved the different smells, the different colors of the forest, and the many different animals that lived there. He recalled seeing the eagle soaring high over the mountain for the very first time. The mighty creature amazed him with its ability to soar so high above the earth without using its wings flapping rapidly to stay aloft. He enjoyed everything about the woods and the mountains. Now he was forced to move from yet another village he had fallen in love with.

The warm rays of morning sun beating down on him

aroused him from his happy daydreaming. As he looked around, the fields and the gardens of the white man were becoming less and less the further north they went. The forest was getting thicker and thicker ahead of them. Maybe the new village was not going to be too bad after all. It would be another day before the tribe arrived at their new village site. A lone rider on horseback could make the trip easily in two days, but moving such a large number of people and their belongings took a much longer time, but tomorrow they would all be at their new home.

Sitting around the fire that evening out in the open field, White Eagle stared toward the star-lit canopy above. A spectacular shooting star shot high across the heavens leaving a pretty trail of red, white, and orange behind it in its tail. The moon was sitting amongst the brilliant stars a quarter full as bugs of the night started coming out to make their presence known. Knowing their journey was soon coming to an end, his people were singing out in happy nature welcoming the next new day ahead of them.

They all felt their future in the new village would be their last, and a very happy one. A new beginning for all. They thought they would never have to worry about the white man coming into their lives and interfering with them or their village ever again. They would be free to live the way of the Indian on the land of the Great White Spirit the way it was supposed to be. The future was never a sure thing for the poor Indian.

With the sun directly overhead at mid-day the following day, they crossed up over a small ridge in the dirt road. They could see a small valley below supporting a large open field next to a small pond with a stream of water flowing in and out. Behind the meadow stood a large rolling mountain range with plenty of forest for animals to roam freely. This would be their new home.

The layout of the land below was not the way White Eagle had imagined it in his mind's eye when he was having his vision of the new village. The land was not desolate, ugly, or void of forest the way he had seen it in his dream. The new village location looked to be a good place for his people to live, and a sense of good feelings began to fill his heart again. He didn't feel so forced into giving up the old village and having to move now. Nevertheless, why did they have to move in the first place? Why did the white man make them move from one location to another? It just did not make any sense to him.

As the tribe walked onto the reservation, they found a large white man's teepee built to house some cows the white man had provided for them. Inside the big teepee were several small stalls for cattle, a shelter for some pigs, a couple of goats, and a long smaller wooden teepee to collect eggs from the many chickens that were freely walking around the barnyard already.

White Eagle thought the reservation was there for his people only, so why were there several small white man wigwams erected around the reservation? The corn looked planted in a couple of the big gardens, as was two big gardens planted with mixed vegetables for their fall harvest.

Col. Bennett had arranged to have the crops planted for their fall harvest, and a few houses erected for the tribe's people to live in so they might have shelter while they put their new village together. The move from their old village to the new one was too late for them to allow time to prepare the land to plant and have crops for their own stores for their fall harvest.

He had tried to make the move from their old village to the reservation as easily as possible for them. This would be Col. Bennett's last assignment in the region. All the smaller military outposts were now being put out of service, letting the local police and sheriff's departments in the region take over the rule of the land. The men assigned to these once very active outposts were now reassigned to army bases throughout the land.

CHAPTER FOURTEEN

Building the New Village

The hard work of building the new wigwams in the village began the next day. White Eagle's parents had to make a choice; they could either live in a wooden teepee made by the white man or erect their old teepee to live in once again. They chose to erect their old teepee, and live the way of the Indian. They did not want to start living as the white man did in wigwams made from trees harvested from the forest, cut into boards, and held together with metal pins.

White Eagle was so excited about their choice that he started to erect their teepee from the old village all by his lonesome. His father watched as White Eagle eagerly took the many teepee polls from the delivery wagon, laid them out on the ground, and readied them to be reassembled.

Looking to his father for his approval, Red Feathers nodded his head and smiled with great favor in his heart for what his son was attempting to do by himself. He studied each pole carefully as he laid them out with the longer ones first in a circle pointing toward its middle. He formed a circular ring with a rawhide rope and laid it in their middle. He then tied each pull to the rawhide ring. Sweeping all the poles together as one, he tried to lift the bunch up into a standing position. They were just too much for his little frame to lift up all by himself. His father smiled at him for his willing endeavors. Red Feathers and Whispering Winds went to his rescue. The three of them lifted the poles into a standing position, and then spread them out into the circular frame for their teepee. He sudden noticed many changes in his parents' faces that he had not seen before as they helped him lift the poles. His parents were starting to show their age and getting wrinkles like his grandparents used to have before they passed away to their happy hunting grounds. His father had deep wrinkles around his cheekbones, his neck, and around his eyes. Some very scary thoughts about the colorful little ghost spirits dancing around atop the snow-covered land came to him. Oh, how he hated those little ghostlike spirits that took away his grandparents. Shaking his head to clear away the thoughts of them, he began applying furs to the teepee poles for the outer skin wall covering of their home. When he finished helping his parents prepare their teepee, he went about helping other families in the tribe finish theirs.

The next day when he stopped by to help Winonah's family with their teepee, she was down by the pond swimming with a couple of her friends. Most young braves and Indian girls in the village were not as ambitious as White Eagle. They didn't have the urge to go hunting, fishing, or work as hard as he did. He was always ready for a new adventure whether it was for work or just for the fun of it. White Eagle was becoming quite the admired young brave around the village, standing out amongst most the other younger braves.

When the village was complete, he was ready to go on to new adventures in hunting and fishing excursions around the new reservation. He had finally outgrown the bow his father helped him make, so he ventured off into the woods by himself to find another young strong tree to make another bow. He found a nice young maple tree without any visible flaws attached not far away from the village, and brought it back to make his new bow.

For two long days, he tediously sat outside his parents' teepee patiently whittling away on the slender shaft of tree fitting it to him, and thinking he was all grown up now. He then ventured out into the woods again and found some very long straight branches to make some new arrows for his new bow. After he had shaped the arrows the way he wanted them shaped, he set out to cure his new bow and arrows.

His father smiled at him for his endeavors. He carefully dried the small shafts out over the hot fire, tightening the fibers of the wood close together, as he did to his new bow. He treated the wooden shafts with sap he had taken from the pine tree, turning it into a tar base after boiling it down and mixing it with beeswax from the beehive to preserve the quality and life of his hard work. When he was done, he had the tools of a great warrior ready for battle.

His father watched his son make the most perfect bow and arrow set he had ever seen. It was a little thicker in its middle than most bows, even his, but its overall dimensions were perfect. When he was asked why he had made it bigger in its middle, White Eagle's reply was for the strength it would have if ever he was to face a mad bear out in the woods alone. He told him that it would fit him even better when he grew into the bow as he aged.

He was always thinking ahead about how to make things better in life for himself and for his people. When he went out to practice with his new bow and arrows, he had wished he had made everything just a little bit smaller. It was all he could do to string his new bow, and even harder when he tried to load it and pull it back to shoot it. It was much harder than he had imagined it would be.

Day after day for several days, he went out to practice stringing and shooting his bow. After several long days of steady practice, he wrapped the mighty bow up, and put it away for when he grew just a little bit bigger. It was the perfect bow for someone a little older, but not for him at this time.

He again went out into the woods and found a smaller maple sapling to make another bow for his use. Using the same design he used for the first bow, he made it with a thicker middle with slender shafts for its strength. When he finished the bow, he had a bow that was perfect in every way. It was another masterpiece.

His first prize with his new bow was a big jackrabbit flying swiftly across the field as if it had wings instead of feet. When White Eagle whistled, the big jackrabbit made a fatal mistake. It stopped. When it stopped to see where the whistling sound was coming from, White Eagle was already pulling back his bowstring. Just as the rabbit stopped, it fell over dead in its tracks. White Eagle's family had jackrabbit for dinner that evening cooked out over the open fire on a spigot. For the next couple of years, White Eagle became an avid hunter for the tribe. At first, he went out with the older braves to hunt for big moose, deer, and other game animals to help feed his people. He took great pride in his learning the white man's tongue. He paid close attention to how they farmed their land for the very best crops. It looked like he would be the next chief of the tribe to his people as his uncle, the chief, had no more children. He was next in line when his uncle died, or gave up his position as chief to him like his grandfather the old chief had done for his uncle.

One day, when White Eagle went down to the swimming hole to join his friends, it began to rain hard. Winonah and the others came running out from the water seeking cover from the rain. Why he did not know, for there was no lightning accompanying the storm and he thought it quite silly. It struck White Eagle so funny that he burst out in hearty laugher at them all running out of the water. Winonah stopped and asked him why he was laughing so hard. He tried to stop his hearty laughter to tell her why as he looked into her beautiful dark eyes. He could not help himself; he thought it was so funny. She stood in front of him with her nose almost touching his with daggers in her eyes. She was so mad at him that he would not tell her what was so funny. She nor had anyone else had lost any of their clothing in the water, so nothing that funny could have occurred. She demanded to know what was so funny. He chuckled some more before finally composing himself enough to talk calmly to her and explain to her why he was laughing so. "Your name" he said. "It stands for running water does it not?" She said that she knew that it did, as he began to laugh all over again. In between the laughter, he said it was funny for them to be running out of the water and trying to escape the falling rains from the sky. Running water, he laughed, running from falling water trying to avoid the rain. He began to laugh again as Winonah laughed with him as she thought how silly it must have looked to him.

After walking Winonah back to her teepee, her parents tried to persuade White Eagle that she would make him a good wife. All the families in the village would love him to take one of their daughters for his wife, as he was next in line to be chief of the tribe. Her face instantly turned a crimson red with embarrassment. Seeing how shallow she felt from these powerful words, White Eagle told of how lucky any brave in the village would be to have her for his bride. One day in the future, they would both find someone very special to their hearts, would love, and get married.

He excused himself and left their teepee and proceeded back to his own. Deep in his heart, he knew Winonah was the right girl for him, and he would love to marry her. The other young girls around his age were now coming into their womanhood, and some were even more beautiful than she was, but deep down he hoped it would be her in his life forever after.

During the next year, White Eagle made it a point to see her every free chance that he could. He planned to spend every opportune time with her to win over her heart for his. After working the fields all day long, he would take a quick dip in the pond to clean up his dirty sweaty body, and then hurry over to her parent's teepee to see her. If she was not there, he would make it a point to find her.

Sometimes, she would be at the swimming hole with her friends and some of the other braves that were interested in her. It bothered him that these braves were the lazy ones of the tribe, and not worthy of her good company. He took her for long walks around the reservation, and he was always happy when he was with her. He hoped she was as happy as he was when they were together. He enjoyed visiting with her parents and talking about the future of their village. He had many plans for his people when he became chief, and shared a few of his thoughts with her family in lengthy conversations. He was waiting for the right opportune time to arise and pop the question to her about their marriage to one another, but it was slow to come.

Sitting on the beach watching the new spring moon rise high above the village one warm spring evening, White Eagle looked deep into Winonah's joyful dark eyes and asked her to be his bride. A joyful smile brighter than the full moon above broke wide across her happy face as tears welled up in her beautiful eyes. She reached forth with both arms and wrapped them tightly around his neck and gave him an enormous hug. She said she would be proud to be his bride, and had wondered why it had taken him so very long to ask. She was beginning to wonder if he would ever get up enough courage in his heart to ask her.

The walk back to her teepee was giddy, happy, and playful. He explained to her why he seemed so busy during the long cold months of winter and had not been spending as much time with her as he would have liked to. When he was not with her, he was busy preparing for this special occasion. He was gathering furs and special bark from the trees in the forest that they would need for their new teepee he planned to build for them not far from his parent's and Chief White Cloud's wigwams.

He explained to her that if she had not returned a "yes" answer in his special request to her, that he was prepared to leave the tribe, his family, and the reservation to make a life on his own as a hermit out in the wilderness of the mountains. A life without her in it would be worse than death to him. Winonah had waited for this special time to arise as long as White Eagle had. From the time she was very small, she could remember wanting to spend the rest of her life with this boy.

She thought of him at first as her brother when she was small but with a much greater desire than that of an equal peer. He was a magical boy in every respect. When they played together, she would look into his beautiful eyes that appeared greater in strength than those of an alpha wolf, and one who also had a soft smile as soft and gentle as a newborn baby fawn. He always exercised the greatest wisdom, like the one the wise old owl had, when it came to common sense. He was unlike any of the other braves in the tribe. They were the ones who were so envious of her and White Eagle.

The news of Winonah and White Eagle agreeing to marry

one another spread quickly throughout the village like wildfire on a dry tinder day. She, too, would have wanted to die rather than to go through life without him by her side. Hunting parties quickly gathered to make way for the great feast and matrimony.

White Eagle, being one of the best hunters in the village now, led the hunting party into the forest for three separate days and gathered the feast for this special occasion. They took down a couple of white tail deer, a large bull moose, several rabbits, a few turkeys, and several ring-necked pheasants. They caught fish for the medicine man to make the special fertility stew to be eaten with cornbread by the newlyweds to guaranty many children in their future.

CHAPTER FIFTEEN

The Wedding

Drums began to beat out the arrival of the special day early in the morning, filling the air with excitement. The young children of the tribe ran frolicking through the woods gathering beautiful wildflowers to celebrate the special day with splendor. The women of the tribe gathered wild berries just sprouting out with the freshness of spring in them for the festive day. The medicine man was busy preparing his special love potion token with fresh fish stew and corn bread.

The young women friends of Winonah helped her to prepare for the special ceremony. A special bathing ceremony was taking place down by the swimming hole with all the young women in attendance. None of the braves were allowed anywhere near this special event. And if anyone violated the rule, he would be dealt with by the chief of the tribe severely by being shunned by the rest of the village forever. That part of the special ritual was sacred as only women could attend. They took great pride in washing her beautiful long dark hair, and applying special lotion to her naked skin made from sweet smelling wild lilacs growing nearby the water's edge. A couple of her friends took wildflowers and attached them carefully to her hair after they had brushed it to perfection.

While all this was going on, White Eagle sat with his father and talked about fathering a young papoose. He talked about the love he must show his young bride before he was to make them one in union. They talked about being loyal to one another and in love forever. He said there had been braves who mixed their relationships with other brave's wives, destroyed trust among the braves of the tribe, and brought shame to their families in the past.

Red Feathers browbeat his son about the love he must show his young bride. The love she would need, and the tenderness she deserved for being his wife. White Eagle sat with his father listening until the early morning sun rose up high into the morning sky. Being his elder, he listened with attentive ears. White Eagle lived in a very warm and friendly teepee. His father would always embraced his mother with love. Never had he ever seen his father strike his mother or offend her in any way with vicious words, as others in the tribe had done to their women and children in their wigwams.

As he sat listening to his father, he remembered one particular brave in general who once belonged to the tribe. He was banished from the tribe, and was never to step foot back into the village ever again. He had been mean to his young bride. He beat her with his fists, and verbally attacked her with his bad mouth.

Before her father had the chance to kill the young brave, his uncle, Chief White Cloud, expelled the despicable brave from the tribe! Excommunicated from the tribe, the young brave was led out many miles into the wilderness away from the village. He was warned that should he ever return to the village, he would be tied to a stake and burned to death for the dastardly deeds he had done to his poor wife. He had been a good brave and was good to her right up until their firstborn came into the world. He had wanted a son, and instantly turned his feelings against her when she gave birth to a daughter. When she paid more attention to the baby's needs than to his, he thought, he turned physically and verbally abusive toward her. His own family disowned him for who he turned out to be, and they loved their new granddaughter and her mother.

Many hoots and hollers from outside his father's teepee brought White Eagle out of his daydreaming about the awful brave. Several braves gathered outside his father's teepee ready to escort White Eagle to the council ring of the fire for the wedding ceremony. Oh, how handsome a young brave he looked to the others as he emerged out his father's teepee. No wonder Winonah chose him to be her husband over the others. He stood tall and handsome all dressed up in his wedding attire he had collected over the years. He was dressed in soft deerskins his mother had made for him. He wore a vest plate made from the bald eagle's feathers that he had collected over the years from the old village as well as a supreme headdress made from the same. He wore a headdress only a young brave who would be next in line to be chief one day could wear. He looked like a king among kings standing tall and handsome among the younger braves of the village.

His father, now too old to be chief, and his uncle not having any sons, left White Eagle next in line to take over as chief of the tribe. It would not be too long down the line before he would be taking his uncle's place at the council fire as leader of his people. It would become White Eagle's responsibility to take charge over the powwows at the council ring of fire, do the talking with the white man about the laws imposed upon his people, and the future of the tribe running the reservation where they lived.

Much sooner than later would the owners of the paper mills and logging companies in the area become a new thorn in the Indian's side once again as they had been at their old village. The tribe again would have to move to a new reservation a couple hundred miles away in upper state New York. There they would have to share the established reservation with several other tribes of Indians already uprooted from their villages by the greedy white man by taking over the Great White Spirit's land. The white man proved time and time again that he could not be trusted and had no use for the Indian. The white man had no use for the Great White Spirit's wisdom on how to treat his precious land and how not to destroy it.

Venison, bear, rabbit, poultry, moose and fish were all cooking at the many fire pits around the reservation as White Eagle was led to the council ring of fire for the traditional wedding ceremony. Across the village, hooting and hollering echoed around the village from the women gathered around Winonah, as they escorted her to the council ring. As the assembly of women gathered outside the ring, several of the maidens parted way to make an opening for Winonah to enter into the council ring to be with her new husband to be, White Eagle.

As White Eagle stared toward the assembly of girls outside the council ring, he saw Winonah come slowly out from their midst with wildflowers nicely placed in her hair. Her skin looked as soft as clover pedals gently blowing in the breeze across a warm summer's meadow. She held a soft rabbit pelt in her hands covering the softness of her skin and hands. He knew that instant that he was the luckiest brave alive in the entire Great White Spirit's world.

Joyful songbirds flying aloft and on the ground were softly singing their lovely music in forest lullabies in the trees around the village. A gentle breeze was softly blowing across the fields of the village making the tall grass sway back and forth in peaceful waves of beauty. The day had warm rays of sunlight beaming down from the cloudless sky above warming the village land and the ones gathered by the powwow ring of fire for the sacred ceremony.

Saying their special vows in front of the tribe's chief and their family and friends, they partook in the love potion from the cup the medicine man had worked diligently on the night before making for the momentous occasion to seal their providence of marriage. The chief tied the knot securing a hand of each together with a string as a sign of secured commitment between the two forever. The tribe roared with hoots and joyful hollering for the two newlyweds that echoed across the valley. Chief White Cloud held up his staff and hollered out, "Let the feast begin".

Only when the entire village had passed the newlyweds by giving them blessings of good wishes for life, could White Eagle and Winonah untie the twine that bound them tightly together as one. Happily, the chief led them from the council ring to their new teepee, which White Eagle, his father, and Winonah's father had built with the help of their squaws. There they received gifts from the many tribe's members. They received prized furs from the warriors, oil lamps, cooking tools, clothing, blankets, and much more. Never had there been any two individuals loved by the entire village more than these two young people were. The wedding feast lasted long into the late of the warm summer's night with happy times being had by everyone.

The children of the tribe played simple games of rolling round stones toward a stake in the ground to see who could get closest without going past the stake, while the adult men from the tribe threw tomahawks at targets on trees. Many braves shot their bows with accuracy, splitting arrow after arrow, and having a grand time showing off their skills, as White Eagle and Winonah went around throughout the festive day thanking everyone. It was a happy and joyful celebration right up to its end. When the children retired from the celebration for the evening, so did White Eagle and his lovely bride Winonah. The newlyweds were escorted to their new teepee by both sets of parents.

White Eagle took his bearskin from just inside the flap to their new teepee, and spread it out carefully on the ground leading into their new home. The bear represented a symbol of great strength for their marriage. White Eagle wanted to seal their fate with purity and strength. With the bearskin spread wide across the entrance, they entered their new home with confidence of a great life that lay ahead of them. After White Eagle carried his new bride over the bearskin pelt into their new teepee out of sight, Red Feathers and Whispering Winds both smiled with gratitude toward Winonah's parents as the four of them retired for the evening back to their own wigwams.

Gentle as a new mother cat cleaning and caring for her new litter of kittens, so did White Eagle treat his new bride Winonah that first night together. The love they shared for one another grew with great intensity after they became one in union that first night. After becoming one in body and soul, they would never look toward another the rest of their lives, except for a child of their own.

When the sunlight first came up over the horizon, the forest filled with song. White Eagle snuggled up as close as he could to his new bride, hugging her with great intensity, and showing his love for her. She greeted him by slowly opening her beautiful dark eyes to his with a smile filled with love and contentment. They lay there in each other's arms listening to the music of the morning with the mourning doves cooing and all the birds of the forest singing out their early morning song in harmony. The young couple would do this many times in their short time together as husband and wife.

CHAPTER SIXTEEN

A New Life

It seemed the seasons of the years changed more rapidly for White Eagle as he grew in age. Summer passed White Eagle and his lovely wife Winonah by with great speed as it was already time for the fall harvest to begin. The entire tribe took their places in bringing in their crops of summer for the winter food stores.

They dug and plucked the many potatoes by the bushel from the ground, harvested corn left to dry on its stocks in the field for next year's seeds, and winter squash from the gardens by the hundreds. They helped hay the fields for a second time that year for feed for their cows, and stacked corn stocks as well for the cows' winter stores. They placed their harvested crops in holes dug deep into Mother Earth's soil to keep them for the long winter months ahead. There the vegetables would keep fresh, ready to be prepared and eaten when the time came for all. Mother Earth would keep their crops from freezing by storing them in her womb during the long cold winter months ahead. The first cut of hay was stored in the barn's hayloft above the many cattle, goats, and horses so they could eat during the long cold winter.

The tongue of the white man had been easy for White Eagle to learn and comprehend. Learning it made it easier for his people to survive in the new village.

He enjoyed milking the cows, taking care of and milking the goats, as well as gathering the eggs from the henhouse they had built. He enjoyed breeding the cattle and bringing new life into the world for the future use of his people. Especially, he liked making different cheeses using cow's milk and goat's milk for their use. He was becoming a well-versed farmer for his people and would make them a great leader in time if that time came.

Many traditions used by the American Indians were falling rapidly by the wayside. The younger Indians were slowly losing their knowledge of how their people performed different ceremonies accustomed to their beliefs. The Eastern elk were becoming extinct due to the white man shooting them as a game for trophy, and the land around the reservation was dwindling each and every day due to the greed of the white man wanting more land for its timber.

As the first snows of winter were beginning to fall, Winonah began showing signs of bearing a child in her womb; she was pregnant. There was not a happier couple in the world than they were. Winonah remembered the horrible time a young mother had when she delivered a baby girl for their first born. She was scared to death White Eagle might treat her as the young girl's husband had treated his wife. Cuddling up very close to White Eagle one night, she felt the baby kick for the very first time. Placing his hand on her stomach, he too felt the baby kick inside her womb, and White Eagle jumped for joy. A larger than normal size smile covered his happy face with astonishment when it happened. He quickly placed his hand back down on her stomach to see if the child would kick him again and it did. Winonah's face showed a sign of distress, a sign of concern when the baby kicked White Eagle's hand again. "Why do you show such a frown, Winonah?" He asked her as he placed his hand to her stomach again. "Would you not love me if our first born papoose is a girl instead of a boy, White Eagle?" she asked. "Were you not your father's first and only child, Winonah? Did he not love your mother after giving birth to you? Did he not love you the way I would love you if you were to give us a baby girl first? I would love any child you give us. If they are all girls like my cousins, the girls of our chief, I will always love you. My only wish is for us to be happy. If he is a she, or she is a he, I will not love you any less. You should not let such silly things bother you, my love. When you get bigger, there will be more of you to love. Now show me no more frowns. When our papoose comes into our world, there will be two of you for me to love. A happy family smiles, are we not happy?"

Winonah clasped her arms tightly around White Eagle and gave him a mighty squeeze. Her look of concern broke into a smile of delight after hearing those words softly flow from her loving husband's mouth about their child or children to be. Her fears of mistreatment, as the other girl had been in the tribe, vanished forever. As time drew near and Winonah grew bigger, White Eagle waited on her as a servant would his king. He pampered her to the point of driving her nearly crazy with his love. He never wanted her to fear being alone ever or displeasing her ever in any way.

The air of spring felt clean and fresh. Baby birds were beginning to hatch out in their nests, as newborn baby opossums were clinging to their mother's backs riding around the forest nursing their way into existence. Baby deer, elk, moose, and other animals around the forest were being born, also.

The hurtful sudden stomach cramps took Winonah by total surprise. She jumped up from a deep sound sleep grabbing White Eagle by his arm to help herself get up into a sitting position, which frightened him wide awake. "What is the matter, Winonah?" He asked her in a half-sleepy, half-awake stupor. "I was dreaming a horse was kicking me in the stomach and it hurt. That is when I woke up, and tried to get out of the way of the kicking horse. He was getting ready to kick me again."

Then the hurtful cramps suddenly returned. She held onto her hurting stomach and moaned a small whimper. "I think it is time the papoose wants to be born, White Eagle. I am not sure of it, but I think it is time. White Eagle jumped to his feet to fetch Winonah's mother from her teepee, and his mother from her teepee to help his loving wife in the delivery of their first newborn child. Opening the flap to their teepee, the sky was giving up its darkness to a bright new day. The stars were fading quickly away into the light blue haze of the day and cresting up over the forest canopy.

Throwing back the canopy to his parent's teepee, he hollered out to his mother using her name. "Whispering Winds, it is time. Winonah needs your help right away. Please come quickly. Winonah is giving birth." Whispering Winds dressed quickly so she could help with the birth of her first grandson or little Indian princess. It did not matter to her if the child was a boy or a girl as long as the child was a healthy one. That was all anyone could ask of the Great White Spirit.

When White Eagle returned to his teepee, his mother had Winonah surrounded by the softness of rabbit furs and deer skins. She was making her daughter-in-law as comfortable as possible for her first delivery. When Winonah's mother entered the teepee, Whispering Winds sent White Eagle out the flap of the teepee to be with his father and wait patiently in the fresh morning air.

When his mother first asked him to leave the teepee, he at first did not move fast enough for her. With firmness in her voice, she ordered him to leave the teepee so he would not be in the way. He didn't want to leave Winonah, and wanted to be there with her at this very special time. "It is bad luck for you to stay, White Eagle." Whispering Winds and Winonah's mother both blurted out in unison as they told him the story. It will be a baby girl if you stay. Now go with the speed of the wind and go outside. He left out of his teepee flap with his chin dragging on the ground because he wanted so desperately to be with his lovely princess, Winonah, while she gave birth to their first child. He did not care if the baby was a girl he just wanted to be there with her at this special time in their lives. He listened to his elders and left the teepee at once.

As he emerged from the flapped opening, his father along with his father-in-law, Straight Arrow, asked him to sit a spell and wait for his new baby to cry. Straight Arrow told the story of Winonah's birth. He said he had stayed with his wife during the pain and birth of his daughter. It had been bad luck for them, because they had a baby girl first born and not a son.

Straight Arrow chuckled out loud to himself, and then laughed again saying how wonderful it had been. "Straight Arrow happy we have Winonah our first born child." Make Straight Arrow and Ogeechee very proud. Now I have good son-in-law, White Eagle."

Then there came a loud hurtful moaning and groaning from within his teepee. White Eagle jumped to his feet to see what the matter was. Straight Arrow grabbed his arm and pulled him back down to his seat, sitting him down on the log lying as a bench outside the teepee. "Everything is all right inside teepee. Ogeechee and Whispering Winds will help Winonah. No hear papoose cry yet. It is not time to jump. Come sit for a while, and hear how White Eagle born." Red Feathers began to tell about his hunting trip the day his son White Eagle was born when another loud cry came from out of the flap to White Eagle's teepee. Red Feathers talked a little louder and faster as White Eagle turned his attention back toward his father. He explained how he jumped with joy when he first returned to the village still holding onto a full rear quarter of a trophy white tail buck deer when he spotted Whispering Winds holding onto his son, White Eagle.

All three men jumped to their feet when they heard an enormous blood curdling scream come echoing out the teepee, and then there was total silence. A look of fear came over the three men's faces. Never had any of them ever heard such a scream before come from a woman giving birth to a papoose. As White Eagle ran for the flap to his teepee, a papoose began to wail out with a loud cry.

White Eagle's wrinkled up face, with pain written all over it, broke out into a brilliant happy smile. His sudden fear of the worst was over, as he felt all would be well with everyone now. If only White Eagle knew what the next days, months, and years ahead had in store for him!

Opening the flap to the teepee, White Eagle saw his mother holding her newborn grandson. Ogeechee was tending to her very fatigued daughter. Looking at his new son's size, White Eagle was amazed Winonah was able to deliver him. He was so big, and she was so small.

She was lying there still in great pain as White Eagle went to her side to comfort her. "He is a beautiful strong boy, my dear wife, so beautiful." Winonah was still in great pain from delivering such a huge baby. She lay there on the soft deerskins half delirious, half-awake trying to smile toward White Eagle after hearing such wonderful words coming so softly from her husband.

She had had an awful time trying to deliver her son, but to make him happy, she tried smiling, and fought back the growing tears. He grabbed a wet cloth and placed it gently on her forehead as he took her hand in his to comfort her. He was sad seeing his lovely wife in pain this way. He took the warm broth her mother, Ogeechee, had made from herbs for her daughter, to try to ease the pain of birth, and placed it on her lips. It was medicine made from mint leaves and other ingredients taken from the plants out in the forest to help with pain and soothe the nostrils to make someone more at ease with its sweet aroma.

As Whispering Winds lay Winonah's papoose down into her arms, the pain of giving birth seemed to fade away into the fresh morning air. She smiled at her newborn son with a glitter in her eyes for White Eagle, seeing him so happy and so caring about her. Her new papoose looked just like his daddy did when White Eagle was born to she explained to them, as her grandson lay peacefully in his mother's arms.

"We shall call him Little White Eagle," Winonah said with a smile spread across her tired face. White Eagle gleamed with pride hearing Winonah calling her newborn child Little White Eagle. He was more proud than an alpha wolf taking control over his pack of wolves, or the bald eagle might feel when catching the gentle breezes of wind currents, shooting up off a mountain and soaring high above the earth below.

Suddenly flashes of himself entering into the new world from his mother's womb came back to White Eagle. He remembered the pain of traveling down through her birth canal. The very first breath of air he breathed. The chills he experienced from the cool air around him, and the new life that surrounded him as an infant.

He remembered seeing the beaver for the very first time, the squirrels prancing joyfully among the branches in the canopy of the forest above. The sudden thoughts sent chills up and down his quivering spine. How could he or anyone remember such things from the past as that, but they were as real as the air he was breathing and the hair growing on his arms.

White Eagle was more than just tentative to the mother of his newborn son. He was doing all the chores around the teepee for her, including the woman's job of changing their sons soiled garments, and then washing him up for the day before going out to do his own chores. He loved every minute of doing all these things for her and for his newborn son.

He could not wait to teach their new son how to hunt the big moose, the white-tailed deer, the elusive Eastern elk, and how to fish. He wanted to teach him how to farm the land better than the white men could, and do everything else humanly possible. He just could not wait for him to grow up into a young brave.

White Eagle was more like a shadow to Winonah and too Little White Eagle. The only time they had to be by themselves was when White Eagle was out working the land farming and taking care of all the animals with his fellow braves. He would rather be with his wife and child than out throwing tomahawks with his fellow braves or trying to split arrows in a sporting event of archery. As Little White Eagle grew in time, his father had flashbacks and remembered his own past. When his son cried out for his milk from Winonah to fill the hungry void he had in his stomach, White Eagle remembered whining when he was a baby trying to get his mother's attention for milk to fill his own void. He remembered whining louder and louder to get his mother's attention to have her come change his soiled clothing.   It amazed him that he was able to remember these things in such detail for it almost seemed like a dream to him. When White Eagle was small and took his first steps, he remembered the harsh frowns on his parent's faces that quickly turned into bright shining smiles. He could not remember why they were frowning, but remembered quite clearly how it pleased them when he first walked. He remembered tumbling and falling over, making them both laugh until tears filled their joyful eyes with blinding happiness.

It seemed very funny to him that he could remember these things as if they took place for him the day before. The joy of watching his own little son, Little White Eagle, grow up with his wife Winonah would be short-lived. How cruel life would become for him. Why should the pain of loss inside oneself have to last a lifetime?

CHAPTER SEVENTEEN

Return of the Little Ghost Spirits

The late winter snows of spring began to fall early that first part of April. The snow of winter had been slowly melting away as the air around the region was getting warmer with each passing day, and the days began getting longer. The temperature of the day dipped well below the freezing point. White Eagle took his son over to his parent's wooden teepee to show him off, and to show them how well he walked. Two years ago, just before he married Winonah, White Eagle had convinced his parents to move into one of the white man's wooden wigwams that coming fall.

The wooden wigwams were much warmer than a teepee made from deer hide, tree bark, and poles. It surprised him they did because it was the first time they ever really listened to him. After showing them how well Little White Eagle walked, they both returned to their own teepee traipsing slowly through the falling snow. The storm grew with intensity as the temperature outside climbed just short of the freezing mark where the falling snow would have turned to rain. As the temperature outside climbed, the misty-looking snowflakes grew larger until they were the size of small leaves falling from off the trees in late fall. As the dark of night approached the village, the sky above grew clear. Early stars of night began shining down through the parting clouds. When White Eagle sat down beside Winonah, she began making clothing for their son. A loud call for the village people to come quickly out of their wigwams and witness what was taking place on top of the freshly fallen snow of spring. When White Eagle opened the flap to their teepee, he came face to face with the dreaded little ghost spirits all dancing around. He so despised these little spirits floating down from the Aurora Borealis. He hated them dancing among his people and around the reservation as the colorful lights from the heavens flashed wildly across the sky. They flashed in wave after wave of rolling wonder like massive whitecaps on a very stormy and rough sea.

If he never saw the little ghost like spirits again in his lifetime, it would have been too soon for him. He instantly recalled the night he last saw these miserable little creatures dancing around on top of the freshly fallen snow. They came and took away his grandparents' spirits from their village and from him to live in the Great Spirit's land above in the heavens. Stepping outside their teepee with Winonah and Little White Eagle to marvel at the wonder taken place, his worst fears unfolded before him.

The little ghostlike spirits began dancing around his teepee and the ones he loved. Chills instantly began to run up and down his spine as he watched the little colorful puffs of light dance around them. He took Little White Eagle and Winonah in his arms to protect them from the little menacing creatures that scared him half to death just by seeing them in the village.

His roughness in holding them scared his son, and made him cry. He took them instantly back inside their teepee and out of harm's way. He thought as a child would think. If everyone on the reservation would hide inside their wigwams and not be seen by the little ghost spirits, they would be safe from the curse of death they brought with them.

White Eagle instantly put his son to bed, and asked

Winonah to stay inside with him. He shot out of the flap of their teepee and headed toward his parents' wooden teepee. They were both outside on the porch looking out at the little ghost-like spirits dancing around on top of the freshly fallen snow. Who were these little menacing ghost-like spirits after this time, he wondered? He just knew they were there to take someone he loved away to the other side of life to live up in the Great White Spirit's land above.

He told his parents to go inside and stay there until morning when the new day broke over the village. He then ran back to his teepee, taking Winonah in his arms, keeping her safe and away from the menacing little puffs of color dancing wildly around the village that night. In the early morning hours of the next day, his father came quickly into White Eagle's teepee unannounced. He had a sign of loneliness painted wide across his face with welled up teardrops in both eyes. White Eagle knew right then who the little ghostlike spirits had been after, for it was his mother, Whispering Winds.

Going to his father, he threw his arms around him, and the two wept like babies. Oh, how he hated the little ghostlike spirits of the Aurora Borealis. He did not care how many times someone told him they were just reflections of light from the sun, he knew better. Deep down inside, they were the little spirits from the Great White Spirit's land above who had come down for someone from their village. He didn't really know if all these little ghost-like spirits were good ones or bad ones. All he knew was that every time he witnessed them on the freshly fallen snow, someone he loved would leave him to go to the other side of life.

First, it was his loving grandparents, and now his mother. He would never forget the words his father told him that morning, and how his heart and soul felt so terribly empty now. How he loved his only child so much. He did not want to leave him yet, but he could not go on in life with such a broken heart.

He wept upon White Eagle's shoulders for an hour crying like a baby for his departed wife, Whispering Winds. They held each other tight for another hour, draining away their sorrow until their tears dried up for their loved one. For the rest of the day, they comforted each other while the medicine man and a couple of the braves took Whispering Winds' body to the medicine man's teepee, and there prepared her body for the burial ceremony. With Mother Earth still frozen hard below her snow covering, it would be near impossible to bury Whispering Winds in the ground where Red Feathers wanted her buried, and not be cremated.

The medicine man, with the chief's approval, had several braves gather large quantities of firewood and place it over the ground where they would lay Whispering Winds' body to rest in her grave. For four long days, the men of the tribe fed the large fire day and night in order to thaw the ground below the snow. The snows melted away from the grassy land next to the grave for several feet. On the fifth day, they let the fire go out allowing them to dig the grave.

Red Feathers and White Eagle wept together as one, when a few members of the tribe laid Whispering Winds down into the grave dug deep for her final resting place. Now her trapped spirit would be able to ascend to the heavens above and be with her loved ones in the land of the Great White Spirit. After laying his lovely bride to rest in her final resting place, Red Feathers would not eat another bite, as he did not want to live another day. He said he was not hungry enough to eat except for a mouthful once or twice a week. He did not want to go on or live without

Whispering Winds by his side because he had a broken heart.

He would sit for hours and talk to White Eagle about the past. He held Little White Eagle tight on his lap playing with his grandson, but the look of loneliness never left his sad face. One morning White Eagle went to his father's wooden teepee to check on his father for the day, and found his father lying upon the deerskin on his bed that he always shared with his wife. He laid there with a big smile spread wide across his now happy-looking face. His eyes were closed as if he were sleeping, and he looked happy now for the burden of loneliness in his soul had left him. He had passed on to be with his loved ones living on the other side of death in the Great White Spirit's land above. White Eagle had joy and sadness because his father's arms were now wrapped lightly around the love of his life, Whispering Winds. He could not find a lonely tear of sadness anywhere in his hurting heart to shed for his loss, because he knew his father was now happy. The pain of loneliness had passed them both along the way, somehow. Instead of feeling pain in his heart for his father, he felt love and warmth for the man and woman who both had shown him the right way to live his life. He knew he would miss them both very dearly, yet knew they were happy together in a land much better than the one they left behind. They were in a world where the sun never sets, and a place where there are no aggressive warriors to contend with. White Eagle only hoped to be as great of a parent to his son, Little White Eagle, as his parents were to him.

White Eagle's uncle, Chief White Cloud, was getting along in his older years. It would not be very long before White Eagle was to take over as chief of the tribe. How would he be able to be a good husband and father to his son while being chief? Would he be able to make the right choice for his people or was there another brave in the village who would be better fit for the taxing job? As the tribe was lying his father to rest in his grave beside his mother, his father's brother, Chief White Cloud, formed tears in his eyes for him as did White Eagle for his father.

If White Eagle never witnessed another of the little ghost spirits reflected down from the Aurora Borealis ever again in his lifetime, it would be too soon for him. Somewhere deep down in his heart, he felt he would meet up with his loving parents again.

CHAPTER EIGHTEEN

Next in Line to be Chief

How time moves forward and never waits for anyone in its path. An entire year had passed since the death of his father, Red Feathers. Early one morning, Chief White Cloud summoned White Eagle to his house, his wooden teepee. The chief lived in one of the first wooden wigwams made on the reservation for them.

When entering his home, the chief first asked White Eagle to sit with him and the medicine man, and to partake in smoking the ritual peace pipe in a cleansing ceremony.

Sitting there beside the chief was the only medicine man White Eagle had ever known. He must be the oldest brave alive, White Eagle thought to himself. The medicine man took out the peace pipe from its wrappings, and got it ready for them to smoke. Lighting the peace pipe, the medicine man puffed away on it like an iron horse puffing hard while climbing its way up through the river valley. Once lit, the medicine man waved the pipe around in a half-round circle with one arm while chasing away any bad spirits the smoke might possess within it with the other arm. Once prepared, he handed the peace pipe to Chief White Cloud, and then left the room to leave the two of them alone to smoke the peace pipe in quiet solitude.

He exited out the front door to stand guard on the chief's porch so no one would be able to enter his home while they were busy inside discussing tribal ritual. It was always customary after the medicine man chased away any evil spirits, that the chief to take many puffs on the magical pipe first. When he finished puffing on the pipe, he handed it over to White Eagle. White Eagle took the peace pipe and paused. He waited for the chief to nod his head before he took his first of many puffs on the magical mixture inside the bowl of the peace pipe. The chief had only puffed on the pipe enough to keep it lit, but had not inhaled any of the magical smoke it held within it before handing the pipe over to his replacement to be chief, White Eagle.

The magical mixture of tobacco inside it turned to ash as White Eagle inhaled many puffs from its stem. The colorful flames in its bowl suddenly began to fade away. The rushing of the wind filled White Eagle's ears as his inner spirit, the bald eagle, was with him as he smoked the peace pipe. He found himself high above the earth soaring higher and higher with his inner spirit. They dove toward the earth below together, and then caught the gentle rise and wind currents shooting softly skyward as they drifted on them rising higher and higher without having to use their wings for flight.

The bald eagle beside him was his inner spirit watching over him. It was the biggest eagle he had ever seen, majestic in size and extremely beautiful to watch as it soared right along with him. It had the wingspan of ten ordinary eagles. They landed together on a large ledge in the middle of a sheer cliff. Behind him was a large opening to a cave leading into the side of the sheer cliff. Walking up to the cave's entrance, his inner spirit, the bald eagle, let out a horrific screech which echoed all the way down inside the cave as a flash of thunder echoed off his inner mind. Shaking his head vigorously and trying to quiet the loud noise in his ears, he was again sitting beside his uncle, the chief. Flashes and distorted memory of the old village came flickering back to him.

When he and Winonah were small children, he remembered they had pledged to one another that they would return one day to the village to live. The sheer cliff and cave that he and his inner spirit had visited was the mountain behind the old village, and the echoing cave must have been the one where he had found the turkey he had shot with his first bow.

"White Eagle will be chief soon! White Cloud very ready soon, ready to have White Eagle look over our people as their chief. Chief White Cloud is too old to do good job for our people, now White Eagle. Chief White Cloud getting tired. Tribe needs someone young and strong who the people of tribe can look up to." Waving away any evil spirits from within the smoke of the peace pipe the chief had just relit, White Eagle puffed many times again on the peace pipe and found himself back at the old village. He found he was alone, surrounded by all the wild animals of the forest without any of his tribe's people with him.

When he returned back sitting beside the chief from his mind's journey, he was very confident to become the tribe's new chief in the fall. When he returned to his teepee, he confided in Winonah with the good news about becoming the tribe's new chief. He told her about the dreams he had while using the magical peace pipe, but neither knew what to think about the strangeness associated with the dreams. It must have been the strong medicine within the peace pipe making him think such things while trying to find his inner spirit.

CHAPTER NINETEEN

The Deadly Fishing Trip

The white man in charge of the Indian reservation returned to the reservation with good news. He had secured permission for several of the braves to leave the reservation for a one time hunting and fishing trip up north. They were going to be going north to the three Connecticut lakes that were the beginning of the mighty Connecticut River.

They were going to be leaving in five days, and return to the village in two or three weeks with their game when the new moon filled the northern sky. Placing his night roll, food, bow, arrows, and fishing gear upon his horse, White Eagle was ecstatic about leaving the reservation and was allowed to hunt and fish in a territory that he had never seen before.

He had become great friends with the white man in charge of the reservation who was going to lead the expedition north. Mounting his steed, White Eagle waved a happy goodbye to his lovely wife, Winonah, and to his small smiling son, Little White Eagle, who was frantically waving back at his wonderful daddy. White Eagle had never ventured away from the village for longer than a day or two before. He immediately felt a pain of loneliness build up in his longing heart as he rode off with his friends waving goodbye to his loved ones left behind.

Two weeks of leisure in unbelievable hunting and fishing in the wild filled White Eagle with joy. The braves camping out at the second Connecticut Lake were ready to venture north to the third lake for another couple of days of fabulous fishing before heading back to the reservation with their awesome catch that they had smoked over an open fire. They were all pleased with what they had accomplished, and were readily looking forward to another year when they might do it all over again. "Oh, how nice it would be to have the reservation right next to one of these wonderful lakes", White Eagle spoke out.

Mike, the white man in charge of the reservation, spoke to the braves about why that would be impossible. A king from England, across the great sea, gave the land that the reservation was sitting on to a duke relative of his, and he in turn gave it away to his family. They then turned around and sold it all to the paper and logging companies.

White Eagle was as confused as he had always been. How could a single person on any of the Great White Spirit's land that he gave to everyone around the world to use, own any part or all the land in the Great Spirit's world?

Mike agreed with White Eagle, but it was not up to him to decide who owns what. He had to go through many channels to get special permission for the several braves there to leave the reservation, and more finagling to have the paper company allow them to use their lakes for fishing.

As they were discussing who owned what, a lone rider came bounding into their camp. His poor Morgan horse was white with frothing lathered sweat pouring out its sides and from under the saddle. For a warm summer's night, the horse was steaming hot with sweat, and the rider was not looking too good himself.

It was a marshal sent from the reservation with very bad

news about the tribe. The chief was dying, and wanted everyone back to the reservation at once. A severe case of smallpox had broken out among the many villagers and was spreading throughout the families similar to a wildfire burning out of control across a drought stricken forest with high winds pushing it.

Mike explained what smallpox was to White Eagle and to the other braves. It was a highly contagious deadly disease, and they could all die from it if they returned to their village and caught it.

The small group of Indians mounted their horses and rode until the woods became so dark they had to stop for the night. In the early morning, they were on the trail again at the break of daylight. When they finally reached their village, it was very late in the day. Mentally drained, they fell off their horses as if an armored knight of old had leveled them. The deathly sights they saw scattered in and around the village were corpses. Not a one of the group came back to find their families whole the way they were when they had left them for the trip north. A wife, a child, a parent, or a friend had died from the disease that struck the village. The chief had already expired to the disease the day the lone rider came into their camp at the lake.

When White Eagle entered his teepee, he found Winonah soaking wet with sweat holding Little White Eagle close to her bosom where just moments before he had lost his battle to the smallpox disease. Taking her in his arms, she wept profusely in agony for the loss of their child. She had let her husband, White Eagle, down by losing his son to death when he was gone. He asked her how long they had had the fever, and she told him several days.

He laid his beautiful son, Little White Eagle, down on a deerskin fur, and took a wet cloth with water and tried cooling her head down with it. She was burning up with fever and sounded delirious to him when she told him she wanted to go home. She wanted to go home and take Little White Eagle with them, and wanted to bury him there with them.

White Eagle told Winonah that they were home. Winonah took the wet cloth from her forehead, staring deep into his eyes, and said, "I want to go home, White Eagle. You promised me. We promised each other that we would go home someday. I want to go home now where the old village was. You remember the first night we played by the meadow the night before we reached the new village below the first cliff? Remember how beautiful our meadow was? That is where I want to be buried, there in the meadow alongside you and Little White Eagle. Remember we promised each other we would return to the old village someday and live there forever. I want to go home to die. I want to go home now!" "We will. We will when you get better. When you get better, we will go home." "Promise me, we will go home now! I want to go home now!" "I promise, Winonah, I promise! I will take you home now and Little White Eagle, too!"

What was happening? There were no little ghost-like spirits dancing around the village, yet everyone was dying. There were no northern lights that he could see, only the setting of the sun. How could this be happening to them? As he looked toward his lovely bride of only a couple years, she was smiling at him. How could she be this happy when Little White Eagle had just died in her arms? A feeling of power surged from her body into his. Her eyes rolled back as she exhaled her last breath of air, and became limp as cut hay in his arms. He looked at her in disbelief. He knew she was gone, but only two weeks ago both she and Little White Eagle were both so full of life. Tears of agony rolled off his cheeks like a waterfall. He reached over and took his small son, Little White Eagle, from off the soft deerskin that he was lying on. Holding the two of them in his arms, he wept for them. He wanted to go with them to their happy hunting grounds above to be with the Great Spirit.

After hours of crying his eyes out grieving over his lost loved ones, he remembered the promise he had made to Winonah. He knew he was going to die in just a few short days from the dreaded smallpox. He knew he must leave this very night for the old village if he was to make it there before he died trying. His horse was right outside their teepee where he had tied and left her. She was old but strong, and would carry the precious burden of his quite easily.

Carefully wrapping Winonah and Little White Eagle up in soft deerskins, he secured them both to his horse. He took his bow, arrows, and hunting gear with him along with some utensils for cooking, baking, and digging of the graves as well. He would leave his people and the reservation behind as he passed on out of the reservation going by the many wigwams howling with grief. The wooden wigwams had lights aglow in every window that were lit up by oil lanterns and candlepower. Remorseful grieving sounds echoed throughout the village. The checkpoints for passing in and out of the reservation by the guards were abandoned. No one cared who entered or left the reservation now as no one wanted to be around where the smallpox disease was.

White Eagle didn't care if there was anyone at the checkout points or not. He was almost delirious from not wanting to go, but he had made a promise to his lovely bride. He was going to fulfill his promise to her at all costs, even if it killed him. He had made this promise with his heart to Winonah, and he would be careful in his travels so he wouldn't break his promise to her. He didn't want to be stopped along the way by anyone.   His life did not matter to him anymore as he knew he was going to die soon anyway.

The light from the full moon above lit up the roadway ahead of them. He wept mile after mile in his quest to fulfill his lovely Winonah's dream. He walked past the Colby Farm where he had learned how to milk his first cow. He could see the new day cresting the horizon as he made their way toward his destination, a couple of days travel away from where he was. He constantly had his eyes glued to the road ahead of them looking for signs of danger. He didn't want to run into any white man who might want to stop them.

Seeing the light of day rising up over the horizon up ahead of him, he took his mare aside the roadway and into the woods. He had just left the roadway when a big wagon filled to capacity with many pine boards went slowly by them heading northward.

He thought it must be the boards for making the many coffins needed at the reservation for his people. The white man sure had funny ways about burying their dead. Putting their loved ones in pine boxes instead of wrapping them up in soft furs before giving them back to Mother Earth the way they are supposed to be in ceremony.

Resting his horse, and letting her eat and drink, White Eagle dozed off for a couple of hours. He was awakened by the loud whistling sound of an iron horse off in the far distance making its way up along the river valley on its steel tracks. It was daylight with the sun high up in the sky when White Eagle pressed on in his quest. He had to take to the cover of the woods several times, as he headed south toward Lancaster, New Hampshire to avoid the white man. His travels were hard on him during the daylight hours. Passing farm after farm, he would have to take to the fields and into the woods not wanting the white man to observe him.

It was nighttime again when he reached the outskirts of Lancaster. There seemed to be more white man wigwams now than he remembered when they first passed that way heading north not that many years before. He knew he had reached the wooden teepee the white man had built spanning the big river for their road. Another iron horse let out a loud whistle, and he knew it traveled on the steel tracks alongside the river. Avoiding the big city, he headed west toward the sound of the iron horse. The white man had cut down most of the trees to make room for fields to grow hay for their cattle and livestock. His travels were made a little easier by crossing over their fields and darting in and out of the clumped trees still growing wild.

With his mind becoming hazed and foggy from the lack of much needed sleep, White Eagle knew he had to press on. His tiredness led him to believe he was coming down with a bad case of the smallpox.

Another iron horse bellowed out not far from them in the distance. Was it the same iron horse he had heard earlier, or was it a different one? He didn't care. He witnessed its big yellow eye searching the black path of night up ahead of it.

Exhausted, he fell to the ground and was fast asleep almost instantly. His faithful horse stood by him as he slept the hours away. He had a dream that Winonah and Little White Eagle were sitting by the campfire as White Eagle carried a fresh big fish he had just caught up toward them for their evening meal. The screeching of a bald eagle caught their attention. Looking up he saw the largest bald eagle he had never seen, and it was as large as ten bald eagles staring down at them from the cliff above. The eagle was calling down to them. White Eagle took a piece of rabbit from his pouch and held it up in the air for the eagle. The huge bird came zooming down and landed beside them. White Eagle took one of the fresh fish he had just caught out his pouch and handed it to the friendly majestic eagle. It shook the fish, splashing droplets of water off it and onto White Eagle's face. As White Eagle shook his head to rid himself of the smelly droplets of fishy water, he awoke to find it beginning to rain.

It was almost daylight. He could see the big wooden teepee spanning the big river not too far away, and didn't realize how close he was to the bridge when he had fallen fast asleep. With his faithful horse rested, they went off down along the iron horse's path to finish his quest and his promise he made to Winonah.

With no one around, White Eagle led his horse into the long wooden teepee spanning the wide river. He could hear the whistle and clangity clanging of steel wheels on the steel tracks coming through the wooden teepee as an iron horse passed along on the opposite side of the bridge behind them. The iron horse's loud whistle scared his horse as it echoed through the bridge and off the walls around them. He calmed her down just as they reached the other side and exited out of the wooden structure. Several railroad cars and a coach went past the bridge on the other side of the river as White Eagle turned to watch it pass. A feeling of serenity, a piece of mind, filled his lonely heart. He felt that he would be able to keep his promise to Winonah as they were not too far away from where she called home. His feelings of sickness had let up, and he would not die before he had the chance to bury his loved ones. They would all be together again very soon as he knew it was less than a day's journey before he reached the old village. When he could see the great mountain between the two small ones, he knew he would be very close to home.

Passing along the roadway, all the trees growing along the river were gone, and everything was now all fields. He sure hoped the old village was not all fields now. Both sides the road were now planted with crops of corn and hay. It would be nearly impossible to stay on the road any further without a white man seeing them.

Up ahead, a herd of milking cows was being led across the road to an open pasture down by the river to graze. He quickly went down a path to his right between a field of hay and a cornfield trying to escape from sight and capture. He hoped no one had seen him before he left the roadway. The path that he chose was being used by the white man to harvest his maple sap to make his maple syrup. He traveled up through the grove of maple trees and high up on a ridge overlooking the valley below. He could see the two smaller mountain peaks he had to get between in order to be near the old village.

Traveling toward the south, he crossed another road cut into the woods by the white man. The white man had scarred the Great White Spirit's land with field after field and had taken down half of the Great White Spirit's beautiful trees.

Looking toward the east, he could see Mount Washington in the far off distance. He had to be very close now. The day was getting late, and he should have been there by now.

Heading down toward the river, he found himself on the road that led toward Gilman, Vermont. It had taken him most the day to travel the short distance. It would have taken him less time if he could have stayed on the road after leaving the wooden teepee crossing the big river. He was very close now to his destination. Looking up for no apparent reason, White Eagle spotted a bald eagle soaring around in the sky above. She turned and flew in a westerly direction away from the river. Looking toward Mount Washington, he knew he was only a mile or two from home. There were the two small mountains with the majestic mountain evenly divided between the twin peaks. White Eagle followed the flight path the bald eagle took deep into the woods following alongside a small meadow and stream.

Darkness overtook him, and he had to stop to rest. The light of the full moon awakened him in the middle of the night. Compelled in his quest, he drove forward. In the distance, he could see the cliff that stood very tall behind the old village. The horizon was getting brighter as he reached the base of the cliff.

The smallpox disease had not overtaken him yet, as he did not feel sick. Tired, yes, but he didn't feel sick yet. He was lucky that he would be able to lay his loved ones to rest, and commit them back to Mother Earth before he died. Today, he would lay them to rest below the other cliff in its beautiful meadow where they had played when they were small. It was not far away from the old village site where his promise to her would be fulfilled.

After stopping to rest and eat a small morsel of food, he was off again. By midmorning, he had crossed over the white man's road dug deep into the land and not far away from the meadow. When he reached the burial site at the meadow, White Eagle fell to his knees and thanked the Great White Spirit above for helping him find his way through the wilderness. He asked him for the strength he needed to dig up the three graves he would need in order to bury them all together. After praying to the Great

White Spirit above, White Eagle began the rigorous task of digging and preparing the gravesites for his family. Hour after strenuous long hour, he labored at Mother Earth's firm soil thanking her every time he took a spade full of earth from her body. When he was finished digging two of the three graves, tears of sadness filled his eyes. White Eagle, with great tenderness, lowered his beloved princess, Winonah, down into her gravesite, and then lowered his little son, Little White Eagle, down into his own grave that was set close beside his mother's gravesite. He then went about building the ritual fire, and began the mighty task of the spiritual dance to commit them both back to Mother Earth and her care. He danced with great pride in his heart so Mother Earth might release their souls and let them both ascend to the heavens above to be with their other loved ones in the Great White Spirit's land.

Sitting by his campfire late that evening, he witnessed two shooting stars simultaneously shooting across the heavens above, one large and one very small one in size that refreshed his inner soul. He thanked the Great White Spirit for accepting his loved ones home to his care.

Finding rest in accomplishing the promise he had made to his lovely Winonah, he fell fast asleep atop the soft grasses of the meadow beside his campfire. He rested into late morning the next day until the warm sun's rays broke through the early morning fog laying thick over the Connecticut Valley and warmed him awake. He had been too tired to dream last night. He was exhausted from making the long journey south, and the hard emotionally draining task he had undertaking in digging up and preparing the two gravesites. He had slept this night away in peace.

Lying rested, he stared up into the bright blue sky as the morning fog vanished into the dry mountain air. He didn't feel the slightest degree of getting sick yet, so he wondered why. How long would it be before the evil fever set in and he would not be able to move from where he was?

He knew he had to prepare himself for death very soon, or it would be too late. He went to work digging and preparing a third grave for himself before the deadly sickness would overtake his strength. When his gravesite was finished, he placed himself down inside to make sure he would fit into the space. The soil of the earth was nice and cool, yet the air around him was very hot. He then knew why the wolves and other wild animals of the forest dug dens in Mother Earth's rich soils to keep themselves cool from the hot summer heat, and warm from the cold chilling winds of winter.

Looking up from his new dug gravesite, he stared at the top of the high ridge behind and above him in the meadow. He wondered if he might see the sheer cliff of the old village mountain from its height. Climbing a path made by many animals ascending the mountain to its peak, he spotted a small opening between two large rocks. Behind the rocks lay a small cave just big enough for him to escape the elements of the weather.

When he entered the small cave, he scared out a whole bunch of tiny sleeping bat's that were making the small cave their home. The bats startled him as they all flew by him in droves out into the bright sunlight. The floor of the little cave was covered and filthy with bat dung, so he turned and left the cave to the fleeing bats. Outside the bats' cave, he could see the top of the sheer cliff by the old village. He felt safe and at home being in this area of the forest. How little did White Eagle know for how long he would call this region of Mother Earth his new Home? Thirsty, he descended the trail to the meadow below and went to a nearby stream to quench his thirst. There he plucked out some roots from a berry bush growing by the stream's shoreline and took the roots back to his campsite by the graves and boiled them down into a tea for him to drink.

Little did White Eagle know, but he had become vaccinated against the deadly smallpox disease by a cow, the cow infected with cowpox, as he was taught how to milk by Mrs. Colby.

After several long days of not coming down with smallpox, he decided to clean out the small cave filled with the bats as protection for him from the elements. He never knew why he did not get sick and die, and was almost disappointed that he didn't. His loneliness was most unpleasant, and he felt that he had run out and abandoned his people back at the reservation that were in need of his direction. He had been the chosen one by his uncle, Chief White Cloud, to be their new chief. Who would the tribe choose now to be their new chief? He felt deeply sad with himself for deserting them. White Eagle wondered if any of his people were still alive back at the reservation, or did they all die from the smallpox disease. He did not die, so why were all the others in the tribe dying? If only he could talk to the Great White Spirit above to get answers to so many questions. He was even mad at him. No, he was as mad as hell at him and did not quite know why. Should he go back to the reservation, or stay with his wife Winonah and their small son, Little White Eagle. Would he make this area his new home? With winter coming in not too many more moons, he had to make up his mind very soon.

Suddenly a thought about the big cave on the mountain above the old village came to mind. The cry of an eagle came echoing through his mind as he thought about his future. How big was the cave inside the mountain rock?

Would it be big enough for him to live in year round, and what would he do with his horse?

He had not prepared for his horse to stay with him for the winter. The grass of the meadow was good for the time being, but when the winter comes, there would be no more food for her to eat. What was he to do with her? Swinging his leg up over his horses back, he would travel back to the old village and check out the cave above. He had many things to think about now, and would have to make some very difficult decisions very soon.

At first, his horse became jumpy when he mounted her. She quickly settled down, and they were off through the woods to check out the old cave above the old village.

CHAPTER TWENTY

The Great Cave

The time passed by quickly for White Eagle and his horse as they arrived at the site of the old village below the cliff. When he was small, it seemed to have taken forever to arrive at the village from the meadow. Just a few weeks ago, it seemed to have taken forever to travel and bury his loved ones. Then he was tired with a fuzzy mind leading his horse through the woods carrying the heavy load. It had not been more than an hour or so in travel time from the meadow to the sheer cliff this time. Why did the white man have their village moved in the first place? The trees around the old village were the same, only older and bigger now. The council fire ring of stone was still in its place. Nothing in the area around the old village had changed all the time he was away.

Staring up above the sheer cliff, he saw an eagle flying. She was soaring higher and higher on the heated air currents rising up off the warming mountains without using her wings. Soon she turned into a tiny speck and disappeared into the bright blue of sky. Letting his horse graze on the grassy vegetation growing near the cliff, White Eagle climbed the old trail next to the cliff in hopes that he would be able to find the cave again. He was trying to pinpoint its hidden opening from memory when he was a younger brave descending the mountain trail from the lookout post above. He remembered it was near a thicket of spruce trees. No, alders near by a big rock that hung out over them. There it was, hanging out over some alders just the way he remembered it was. Looking beneath the massive rock overhang, he found nothing but solid ledge.

He had been sure this was the place, but it was not. Where on the mountain then was the great cave? He knew he had chased the turkey quite some distance before finding it. Now he found himself standing on top of the mountain in the lookout post where his friend had died from a gunshot fired by the rogue soldier who also died. He could see for hundreds of miles around with the sky so clear from up there. He spotted the iron horse climbing up the side of Mount Washington. He could see it puffing out its black and white puffs of smoke as it climbed up the mountain pulling two cars behind it. He heard its whistle making its way up through the river valley below, leaving its telltale sign of smoke trailing high in the air behind it. Finding his way back down from the lookout post, he looked carefully for a clue that might lead him to the cave. Finding another ledge sticking out over some alders, he felt he had found the cave at last, but again it was solid rock. Where had he been when he shot the turkey? Was it closer to the base of the mountain or higher up on the rocky trail where he first spotted the fowl? No, it was down further.

He slowly proceeded down the trail looking for the spot where he first saw the bird. He remembered it was a flat area that he had come to on the trail when he took aim and shot the turkey. From there the turkey had scampered off, and he had to follow it in order to retrieve it from the cave.

More than half way down the trail, he suddenly turned around and went back up the trail toward the top again. He remembered the flat spot was near a narrow ledge beside the trail. When he came to it, it looked a little familiar, but everything had grown up around it. He searched the area and found a thick grove of hemlock hiding the overhanging slab of rock. Beneath it, he found the opening leading into the side of the mountain and into the cave.

He remembered what his father had told him, and crawled into the cave very carefully. He didn't want to be attacked by any wild animal that might have been living in there at the time, but found it was as empty as he last remembered it.

In the dim light, it looked as big if not bigger than the old council teepee was inside. He crawled back out of the cave's opening, and brought in some firewood with him to light a fire to have a good look at what was inside the massive cave.

The big cave had several small tunnels leading off into the rock of the mountain in several directions. The smoke from the fire found its way up into a crack in the ceiling of the cave. The smoke must be rising up to the top of the mountain somewhere, he thought. He would look later to see where it was escaping.

Amazingly, there were no signs of any bats, bears, wolves, mountain lions, or any other forest creatures in this natural cavern. For such a beautiful cave, he thought it was very funny that nothing had ever made it their home before now. Was there a wild boar or other ferocious animal lurking in one of the several tunnels leading out of the main cave that he could not see?

The faint sound of an eagle calling out came echoing down the shaft of one lof the several tunnels. Making a torch from one of the lit pieces of firewood, White Eagle ventured forth down the cave to the right wondering what he might find at its end, if it had an end.

Slowly, with caution flowing in his veins, he ventured forth stepping quietly flatfooted and not making a sound in case he found unhappy inhabitants in the cave that didn't want him there.

Coming around a curve in the tunnel, he saw a sliver of light come shining down the shaft. Rounding a second curve, he found the source of light. It looked like an opening to the sky above him, and he saw nothing but blue sky everywhere out of its opening. He still pondered over why no mountain lion, bear, or other wild animal had not used the cave before, and then he found them. There were skeletal remains of rabbits, fish bones, squirrel bones, and other smaller animals' remains at the end of the cave.

Ahead of him out the opening of the cave was a large ledge jutting out from the side of the sheer cliff. Off in the distance, he could see Mount Washington standing taller than any other mountain around. Stepping out onto the ledge, he found himself above his old village, and he knew he had been right. For all these years, he wondered if there could perhaps be a tunnel connecting the ledge to the big cliff on the mountain.

As he looked down to where the old village had been, he began to cry. His eyes instantly filled up with big tears, and he wept like a baby. How beautiful it would have been to live here with Winonah and Little White Eagle. Why had he not taken them away from the reservation before the smallpox disease struck and took them away from him? The cave in the mountain would have made a wonderful home for the three of them to live in forever. Standing out on the sheer cliff, White Eagle made up his mind. He would make this cave his home until the Great White Spirit above called him home to be with the ones he loved.

Heading back down the tunnel to the great cave was hard on him without the aid of a torch to light up the way. He stumbled on many loose stones a few times while he guided his hands carefully down along the sidewalls of the tunnel to help him find his way back down in the dark. The light from his fire in the great cave lit up the rest of the way back through the cave's tunnel. If he had waited much longer before returning, the fire he had made would have burnt itself out. He could have been lost forever in one of the many caves if he had taken a wrong turn and lost his way without ever finding his way out.

He would never venture inside the mountain again without sufficient light to guide his way. He'd mark the tunnels in the future so he would always know where he was when inside the mountain's vast cavity.

CHAPTER TWENTY-ONE

Filling In His Grave

He wept all the while he stood filling in his gravesite in the meadow until there were no more tears left to shed. How could he been spared the wrath of death from the smallpox disease? What did the Great White Spirit have in store for him to do now?

When he finished, he knelt down beside his wife and son's grave to make a pledge to them. He would return to their grave sites as many times as he could to weed away stray grasses and other weeds that would steal the life from the flowers he had planted there for them. He told Winonah with heartfelt tears in his eyes, that they were home now, and he would stay there the way they had promised each other they would when they were children.

When White Eagle felt sick and ready to die, he would dig up his gravesite beside theirs again and lay his sick body down in mother earth to die, and join them above in heaven if he could.

He didn't know who would light the ritual fire for him, or who would do the sacred Indian's dance for his soul's release from Mother Earth allowing his soul to ascend to the Great White Spirit's land above to be with them. He only hoped Mother Earth and the Great White Spirit would find it in their mercy to let his soul ascend to be with theirs. In the meantime, he would have to live hidden away in the forest from the white man. He knew if he was found living in the area, he would be sent right back to the reservation.

There, he would be found to be an outcast amongst his people for having left them without a chief that they so desperately needed in their time of crisis.

His decision to stay was a hard one for him to make. If he went back now, they would probably welcome him back with open arms due to the severe circumstances surrounding why he had left. If he stayed away from the reservation any longer, he would never be able to return and hold his head up high.

Then he had another trying thought enter into his head. What if he returned to the reservation and died there. The white man would never allow him brought back to the meadow for burial. He would rather die an old lonely hermit on the mountain without friends than leave the beautiful land where he buried his loved ones.

He made many decisions while kneeling down praying beside the graves of his loved ones in the meadow. He talked to them as if they were alive and with him in a teepee, as he was just getting ready to fall fast asleep for the night. He would never leave them there alone, and he would never return to the reservation. Winter would soon be upon him and his horse. He had no extra food for his horse to live on during the long cold winter months, and she would die a horrible death of starvation if he didn't do something for her real soon.

He would have to leave her off at a white man's farm for the farmer's family to adopt her and take care of her for the rest of her life. There they would put her in their big wooden teepee with their other animals during the long cold winter months. He knew she would be better off away from him than to stay.

Gathering up his belongings from the small cave on

the mountain trail above the meadow beside the burial ground, White Eagle returned to the big cave above the old village. He had not once seen the white man anywhere near the old village ever since he returned to the mountain. Whenever he crossed over a white man's road, he would always dismount his horse and cover up their tracks if they were to leave any. If he never came across a white man ever again in the wilderness before he died, it would be too soon for him as far as he was concerned.

CHAPTER TWENTY-TWO

Fixing Up the Cave

It was almost fun for White Eagle to fix up the big cave for his new home. No one in his tribe had ever had a stone teepee before, he thought, and thinking about it made him laugh. He took great pride in his work fixing it up. He selected stones from the forest floor to make his fire pit inside the cave, and hung pelts of animals on the walls as he caught and dressed them out for his food. A good food supply for him was important now that it was so late in the season, and he was not able to plant vegetable crops for a fall harvest. His winter stores of food would be nil if not any at all.

He ventured out to where the tribe had planted potatoes, corn, and squash for their fall harvest crops long ago. He was with a little luck, as some of the seed of the earlier plants had replanted themselves. He found several squash plants growing scattered about with squash almost ready to harvest. He found very few corn stalks, so he would have to save the several ears of corn he found to dry and plant seeds the following year. He found several potato plants growing wild with potatoes half the size they should be due to the lack of care they received. He would eat only a few of the smaller potatoes, and save the bigger ones to plant the following year for a better crop.

He knew the winter months ahead for him would be lean and rough, and would have to eat very lean this next winter in order to have a plentiful crop for the following year. Hunting game to eat would freeze solid, and the meat would not spoil from too many warm days of bright sun. He hoped any of the bears around would go into hibernation earlier in the fall, and none would decide on his cave for their winter hibernating home. He decided to keep a fire going inside the cave all the time to keep out any wild animals that had an inkling to take over his cave for themselves.

Now the important matter was concerning the welfare of his faithful horse. He had to find her a new home, and not be seen by the white man in this duty and obligation to her. She had been his friend through thick and thin. She would always listen to him when he was feeling down and out, and in need of someone to talk to. She would look at him when he was talking to her like she really cared and understood what he was saying. She always listened faithfully in his time of need. He could count on her to be there for him always, and now it was time for him to be there for her and say goodbye to an old friend.

In the morning, when the sun comes up and the foggy mist of the air lifts up out of the valley, they would be off. He would find her a new home with a family that he'd choose for her. It would have to be a white man who looked kind, treated his animals with dignity, and had a big wooden teepee for his animals to stay warm in.

The night had been a long one for White Eagle as he laid wide awake thinking how he was going to find the right home for his horse. As the sun rose high, he flung himself up on her back, and they were off through the woods. They headed east toward the Connecticut River and the town of Gilman, Vermont, and traveled along the edge of the big swamp. With the water low, the beavers were busy chewing at trunks of trees, trying to harvest them for food, and build damns to hold back whatever water they possibly could.

After a couple hours of travel, a whistle blew from an iron horse heading north up the river valley. They were not very far away from its tracks, and White Eagle knew they were close to the road that he had traveled on to get back to the village. There in the woods just up ahead of them, White Eagle saw the house of a white man that he had seen from the ledge on the high cliff while looking out the cave. He carefully dismounted his horse, and watched as a young man plowed his fields getting them ready for a crop of winter rye. He stood watching the young man for the longest time as he used his horse. White Eagle stood there with his hand over his horse's muzzle so she would not make any noise to let the young man know they were there hiding in the woods watching him. When he was comfortable with the way the young man treated his horse, White Eagle led his faithful old mare out to the edge of the field, and slapped her on her rump to get her to run out into the field to be with the young man and his horse.

She whinnied softly when he slapped her, shot off out into the field, and left him behind to watch. White Eagle crouched down behind a fallen timber and watched what would happen next. He looked up as the young man walked up to his horse that had come to a stop just before reaching them, and led her up to the farmhouse. Calling out to his wife, she came running out to see what the matter was.

Feeling quite confident in the choice he had made for his horse with this family, he turned back toward the woods, and disappeared into the underbrush of the swamp to return to his home. The swamp would cover over any of his tracks if he made any. He stepped carefully on top of roots just barely visible atop the water's surface and on those roots that were just below the water's surface to cover his tracks as he went.

The trip through the swamp was the shortest distance between where he left the horse and his new home in the cave. Crossing over small islands in the swamp on his way back home, gave him a good idea for his next year's vegetable crops. He would not be able to plant them in the forest the way his people had done before. He'd have to plant his assorted vegetable crops of corn, potatoes, and squash on many different little islands located within the protection of the big swamp. This way he would have his crops hidden out of sight from the white man and not in plain sight. The swamp would also protect his crops from most wild animals eating them with its natural moat already built around them.

He was surprised by the short time it took for him to travel through the swamp. It was less than three hours from the white man's farm to the bottom of the cliff according to the position of the sun above. He had taken his time and stopped to look around at the different islands in the swamp as well.

Not having to go around saved him a whole lot of time in his travels. He stayed awake most the night again worrying about his faithful friend in her new home. He questioned his judgment in leaving her with the first white family he came to. The hope in his heart was that he had made the right choice for her. He went up to the high ledge through the mountain's tunnel to see if he might see his faithful horse.

With the night air chilled, he went down to the cave for some firewood and returned to the ledge to make a fire. He built a small one to take the chill of the cool night air off him, but most of all it was a signal fire for his horse to see from far below so that she might know he was always thinking of her. He had to give it great thought before he lit the signal fire. No one in the valley below would ever be able to find his fire pit on the high ledge, unless one was capable to fly like an eagle. Seeing no man could possibly fly, he lit the signaling fire for his horse. Seeing he had a hard time finding the cave's opening and knowing it existed, he was very sure no white man would ever find it unless they followed him to it, and he was not about to let that happen.

He had carefully concealed the cave's only opening by hanging a deerskin inside out covered with ash to make it look like the stone of the mountain over the inside of its opening, blocking in any light that might be seen by the continuous fire he kept burning inside the cave.

CHAPTER TWENTY-THREE

White Eagle Got His Wish

The winter was cold and long the way White Eagle had wished for it to be. The meat he hung in the cold air outside became frozen until he thawed it out to cook it over his fire. He had prepared well for the long winter in the short time he had before the first snows began to fall. He gathered his firewood from the fallen trees that had given up their branches from the previous year's bad storms from off the forest floor. He stacked most the fallen wood in the many cave openings of the tunnels in his new home and out of sight of the white man. He blocked up all the openings inside the main cave to keep his smaller living quarters of the cave warm. The good skills in hunting with makeshift snares came in handy for his survival during the long hard dark days of winter. He was glad he had listened well to his father and the other clever braves of the tribe when it came time to set the snares he had put together with branches of trees and rawhide made from deer pelts.

His skillful manner in finding paths used repeatedly by small animals came in handy for him. He would set his snares in ways these animals would not see them, and when they passed over or through the straps, they became his source of survival. He was not always lucky at catching small animals, and would sometimes go to sleep at night hungry with a gnawing of emptiness in the pit of his stomach during the long cold winter.

When the cold outside the cave dipped well below

freezing, White Eagle stocked a large white tailed deer for his food supply. He could not take down a large animal with his bow before the waters outside over the swamp froze solid. This way he would be able to preserve the animal's meat by having Mother Nature freeze and store his food for him.

He only hunted to survive, never wasting any part of the animal he slew for his food. He would use the animal's bones for tools after heating them in the fire to rid them of any animal fat and bone moisture. He used their hides for his clothing and their meat to eat for his survival. His vivid imagination and knowledge of the forest served him well.

Paying particular attention to the ways of his elders when he was young paid off for him. Even some of the ideas he learned from the white man helped in his survival. The way the white man took ice from the lakes, rivers, and ponds to store food with during the warm summer months came in handy for him during the heat of summer. It preserved food that he would have otherwise had to throw away if he had not stored a larger amount of ice for the summer.

White Eagle had a plan. An abundance of ice would be taken from the swamp. Lighting a torch he had made from leaves and grass he had rolled up in pine pitch, White Eagle went in search of the best tunnel for the ice storage. Taking the tunnel to the far left, he found himself descending a long narrow corridor to a large hollowed-out area in its base. There were many small openings in the cave's outer stone face wall leading out to the outside world the size of arrow shafts. It looked like someone had used the side of the mountain for shooting practice with their bows and arrows. This tunnel would not do. He needed a tunnel that he could stack layer after layer of ice layered between leaves and grass to keep it cold. It needed to be away from the heat, and where it would not melt real fast.

He returned to the main cave and took the next tunnel to his left. He became a little nervous with himself this time. Why had he not checked out all the cave's tunnels before he moved into the main cave to live? He didn't want to find any surprises in them or surprised by anything lurking in the darkness. Carefully, he made his way down the shaft of the tunnel. This one was short in length with a small natural hole in its floor at its end. This would allow waters from the ice to run out of the cave when some it melted.

When he returned to the main cave, he entered yet another tunnel, all the while shaking in his moccasins at what he might find down the next passageway. In his searching, he found that none of the tunnels had any connection to the outside world. The only two entrances to the main cave were the one leading up to the ledge where the eagles fly, and the other one well hidden beneath the alder grove covering the slab where the main entrance was.

The many different caverns within would become support rooms for him. Large closets to keep his stores in. One of the tunnels had a very small stream flowing through it. The bubbling water scared him at first as he thought he had heard an animal scurrying around at the end of the shaft. It was his pure determination that pushed him forward into the shaft to see what was making the sound. The water was bubbling out of a small crack in the sidewall and exiting out into a big crack in the floor of the cave at its end.

He wished he had known about this water supply earlier. He had been carrying his water from the spring that helped feed the big swamp back to the cave which was strenuous work for him. This new water supply would make his life inside the cave a whole lot better and easier on him.

White Eagle wondered what other strange things he might find in the other caverns leading out from the main cave. Seeing the water on the floor of the cave brought back memories of his childhood. He recalled when he and two of his fellow friends were out exploring the forest, and they came upon a cleft of rocks sticking high up out of the ground. He remembered going in between the jagged rocks to help his friend that had fallen down between them. His friend had fallen to his death, but the water in the cave brought back what he saw between the cleft of rocks. It was a wide, long watering hole in between the massive rocks where a huge fish had jumped up out the water while catching a dragonfly to eat. Had he dreamed it after carrying his friend's dead lifeless body back to the village, or was there really a spring or hidden body of water below the ground between the cleft of rocks? It must have been a dream as no fish can live underground, but he would check it out just in case when springtime broke out over the mountains.

Now he had a chore to do. He would gather ice for the hot summer days ahead. In the morning, he went to the swamp and broke out large chunks with his tomahawk, and became extremely tired after chopping all morning long. On his way back to the cave carrying the ice, he devised a better way in his mind how he would go about harvesting more ice. He cut some branches from a pine tree and laid them crisscrossed in and atop the water after he had broken the ice from the top of the swamp's surface. These patterns of wooden branches spread atop the water, he hoped would allow him to strip the ice out from the swamp and using less strength. When he went back the following day, his trick worked better than he could have imagined it would. Harvesting his ice became much easier for him after that.

Every day he would go to the swamp and make one or two trips back and forth to his cave with his special backpack filled with ice. It took almost three full moons' time to carry ice back and forth to the cave a few times per week to fill his storage cave for the summer months ahead. His tunnel was full of ice. So full that it would probably carry him half way through the next winter season before he needed any more to keep his food fresh.

Between checking his snares for his food supply, gathering his ice, cleaning and preparing the furs of the animals he caught, and keeping his vigil fire burning in the main cave, White Eagle had little time to think about anything else. One night while sitting out on the ledge of the sheer cliff, an overhanging of snow fell down upon him from off of the cliff above. It instantly extinguished his fire, and covered him in wet sticky snow. If he had been standing on the other side of his fire as he sometimes usually did, looking out over the beautiful valley below, he would have been doomed. The snow would have pushed him off the ledged shelf and down to his death.

After every snow storm from then on, he would make it a point to climb to the top of the mountain, and knock away any snow that may have accumulated above the shear cliff's ledge. He never wanted to be surprised by any snow falling down on him ever again. As spring approached, he was sick and tired of eating rabbit for his main course. He had saved most of the potatoes for planting his crop that spring. His supply of assorted squash had been very limited, and he was very careful in saving every seed he could salvage from the fruit he ate as well. He didn't eat any of the corn he found the previous fall, anticipating a good harvest the following year.

The winter had been lean for him, and he had lost some weight from fighting the hunger that surrounded him half of the winter. If only spring would arrive sooner than later, fresh wild berries would be a delightful change for him to eat. He would search the forest floor over for roots of plants safe to eat to satisfy him other than rabbit. There were many plants around the mountain forest that he had found to eat just to stay alive that first winter. They didn't taste very enjoyable, but ate them anyway.

He could not wait for the ice covering the swamp to melt away so he could go fishing and have some fresh fish to eat. He tried to fish down through the ice covering the swamp during the long winter months, but was unable to find a suitable fishing hole therein to catch anything.

He would have to wait for the ice to melt away so he could look down into the water to see where the larger pools of water were that would support life for fish during the winter months.

With the snows of winter almost all melted away, he wondered about the fish he had seen in the cleft of rocks. Had it been a dream when he was a little boy or had he actually seen a huge fish jump up out of the water hole in Mother Earth's ground of rock? He took some fishing line he had made from stripping the fibers out of some reeds he found growing near the swamp. Making a fishing hook from one of the copper broad heads he used for hunting his game, he took a small piece of intestine from the last rabbit he had caught in his snare for bait. He wished it was a live earthworm or a grub, but the intestine that looked like a worm would have to do. He would wiggle and jiggle it in the water hole to make it look alive for the fish to see. He was now ready to go fishing and tried to remember where the cleft of rocks was located that pointed toward the heavens above. He had only been there once and that was when he had to carry his dead friend back to the village. He headed east southeasterly away from the old village.

The rocks were not as far away as he remembered. Then the rocks seemed to have been many miles away. They were closer than the sheer cliff was tall, and stood tree-top tall or just a little bit higher. They seemed taller to him when he was a young boy. He wondered if he would still be able to fit in between the small openings in the rocks now that he was older and all grown up. He was right about one thing, the opening between the rocks was small, and he had to squeeze in between them to fit. He turned one way and then another dragging his hind end on one side, and his belly on the other. It was still early spring, and he had on his winter furs. If he had taken his heavy garments off, he would have fit quite comfortably through the small openings.

The circular interior between the rocks was what he remembered it to be. In its center was the huge well-sized hole. To his right was another opening leading down a rough shaft lined with stalactites hanging down from its ceiling and stalagmites pointing skyward from its floor. While walking around the big hole in its center, he looked down and remembered his friend lying in a heap on the rocky ground not far away. Carefully, he descended the narrow passageway avoiding the sharp pointed stalagmites and stalactites but holding onto them as he made his way to the bottom of the maze. He walked carefully over to the large waterhole in the ground. It looked like about four feet wide and about ten or twelve feet in length. It had ripples on its surface as if there was moving water beneath the surface of the earth. He almost put his hand into the water to see if it was really moving, but instead he baited up his hook and dropped it in. The strong current of water pulled his hook and bait beneath the rock. He stood there for the longest time wondering if he was wasting his time, and if anything in the hole would ever bite. He stood there wondering about the fish he thought he might have seen. His imagination could have been playing mean tricks on him back then. Maybe it had been a piece of rock from above falling into the hole that his friend had loosened and dislodged or a rock he had kicked into the water when he came down quickly into the opening. He would give it another few minutes before he pulled in the line, baited his hook, and head back toward home in the big cave. To his surprise, he had a big tug on his line and tore out through his fingertips and hands at an incredible speed. He applied pressure to it so the fishing line flowing out his hands wouldn't all be gone in an instant. He was trying to slow it down as it burnt his flesh with friction, the line speedily disappearing below the rock in the water.

Just before running out of fish line, the speeding line slowed to a stop. Hand over fist, he began to draw the line back in toward himself laying it in a smooth round circle on the ground.

He wondered what could be on the other end of the line. A big fish, an eel, an otter? He just couldn't imagine what it might be. With most the line pulled back in, it shot out from his hands once again. Repeatedly, he would pull in the escaping fishing line just to have it shoot back out through his burning hands and disappear again beneath the water. Finally, he saw what it was, a large lake trout, bigger than any he had ever seen before in his lifetime. He had caught a couple of very large lake trout when he and the other braves had gone on the fishing trip up to the Connecticut lakes, but had never seen one this size.

He wondered how any trout, never mind one this size, could possibly be living beneath the ground. How big, how deep was this body of water in Mother Earth's stomach?

Someday he would take a long tree branch and find out how deep the water hole was when he had the chance.

White Eagle was tired, and figured the trout was tired, too, but he was mistaken. The large trout fought him several times more before he was able to bring the huge fish up alongside the opening in the ground. He reached down and took hold by its gills and heaved it out onto the rock floor beside him. It felt like it was the weight of a small deer. He was just plain tired out from fighting the big fish for so long. It was much larger than any the big salmon the tribe had caught in the swamp. When the salmon were spawning in from the big river and ocean, they smoked and dried them for food for the long winter months. This big fish would feed him for several meals. He was finished fishing for a while.

With curiosity getting the best of him, he left the big fish on the ground beside the hole tied to a rock, and went to get a long slender pole to see how deep the water really was.

When he returned, he slowly pushed the tall pole down deep into the water to find its bottom. The current in the water made it difficult for him to hold the pole straight, but he managed. To his surprise, there seemed to be no bottom in reach of the tall pole that was treetop tall. He poked it out of the way to find the area below the rock in front of him, but the space was hollow except for a straight flat wall beneath his feet. It almost scared him half to death to think there was a large lake beneath the earth's surface. He was determined to find the bottom to this hidden pool. He went out again and secured yet another tall thin pole, and tied the two together using the fishing line to secure them tight. Still there was no bottom when he pushed the two poles straight down into the hole. Pulling the two poles up out the water, they stood taller than the cleft of rocks. With his curiosity unfulfilled, he returned to his cave to feast on the trout. What a joy it was, and his mouth and taste buds watered profusely from the taste of fresh fish.

Oh, how he wished he had a piece of fresh corn bread to go along with the fish. He would have to wait until the fall of the year before he might have any cornbread, squash, or potatoes for his meals. He would have to be satisfied with eating the roots from the different plants growing wild in the forest that he could safely get for now. He hated the idea of having to go through the summer season without any cornbread, so he tried to make some bread by using acorns from the great oak trees when they shed their seeds.

He would try just about anything now after having rabbit for most of his meals since fall fell upon the land. He could not wait until the fiddlehead ferns began to grow or the dandelion plants of spring shot up from Mother Earth to give him something different to eat.

In the fall when his crops come up for harvest, he would make sure never to go another day being hungry ever again. He would use all the different techniques he had learned from his tribe's elders and the white man to preserve his food for the winter. He would make it a point to find wild honeybee hives for his sugar needs. He would make up tight pouches from hides to preserve his wild berries and store his maple sugar syrup. Whatever it took, he wouldn't go hungry ever again in his life like he had during this last long winter in the cave alone.

If he had only known he was not going to die from the smallpox when he returned to bury his loved ones, he would have planned better for his food supply. Now he had a special fishing hole, he hoped, as long as the fish he just took out of it wasn't the only one in the entire hole. He would be able to use the hole if it doesn't freeze over when the water in the swamp and the beaver dams all freeze over.

White Eagle was not well equipped for collecting the sap from the maple trees in spring for making his maple sugar syrup and sugar candy. He used several pouches that he had cured and made from small animals. He took a lower branch on the maple tree, broke the branch off, and placed the pouch over the broken branch. It didn't take long before the several pouches were filled with the sweet sap and ready to boil down into maple syrup.

He collected the sap for several weeks. He boiled it down daily until the sap in the trees stopped filling the pouches. By the end of the sugaring season, White Eagle had made several gallons of maple syrup and a few containers of maple sugar candy for his winter and summer stores. He placed the maple syrup in airtight pouches he had made from thick dear hide, and sealed them up with pine pitch. Than he placed the sugary makings of his labors down in the ice bin tunnel beneath some ice to keep it fresh.

White Eagle was quite pleased with himself for doing such a fine job. It was a good start to his new life of being a hermit. He hoped his life would be a happy one filled with new pleasures that he'd make for himself. He felt very sad that he could not share the happiness he had with Winonah and Little White Eagle.

Having a sudden urge for more fresh fish to eat, White Eagle returned to the fishing hole down between the cleft of rocks. Looking down into the water hole, he saw a handsome Indian reflecting back out at him without a smile. The Indian looked very sad. A sudden drop of rain fell into the water, and caused a ripple to spread from one side of the pool to the other, but it was not a raindrop. It was a huge sad teardrop falling from the eyes of a very sad face looking down into the water. The sad Indian thought how all alone he looked standing there all by himself. In the reflection, he saw his lovely Winonah and his little boy Little White Eagle standing there beside him in the cavern. He turned his head quickly from side to side to see if it was true, but it was not. When he turned back toward the reflection of his loved ones, the reflections of them were gone.

He would never look into another body of water reflecting back his image ever again if possible. He never wanted to miss his loved ones the way the reflections had just made him feel. His subconscious mind would automatically block out all memory of happy times that he had in his life up until the death of his loved ones. He was determined to forget the past, and he would until a later time in his older life.

Dropping his baited hook down into the water caused an instant explosion. Water suddenly burst out of the fishing hole like someone was throwing water at him with cupped hands. A large fish came to the surface to snag the baited hook before it hit the water's surface. Without warning, White Eagle lost his balance and was sucked down beneath the cold water of the fishing hole between the cleft of rocks. He didn't remember falling or slipping into the water, but there he was. He had enough instinct before he submerged below the surface to catch a full breath of fresh air into his lungs.

The shocking hurtfulness of the ice-cold water made him want to scream out in pain. The light from the fishing hole behind him was slipping rapidly away when he suddenly stopped. His vest had snagged on a sharp shard of rock sticking out from the sidewall of the hole where he was stuck. He found it was impossible to swim against the swift current as he tried to release his vest from the rock. He grabbed frantically at everything he possibly could in order to get back to the light of the open hole in the ceiling of rock behind him. Hand over hand, he pulled himself toward the hole, but he was getting ready to pass out from the lack of oxygen that he so desperately needed. He poked his head up out of the water hole and gasped for a breath of fresh air. It did not come easy to him as he tried holding onto the stone without passing out. Finally, the blackness that had overtaken his eyesight turned back to daylight again. He must have passed out for a short period, but his hands did not let go of the rocky edge where they were clinging tight. He was so weak he almost could not climb up out of the hole from the cold water. With one last push, he slowly climbed up and out of the water hole and lay on the ground panting for air.

While lying on the ground and letting the sun warm his cold body, he began to think. Why had he not just let the cold painful water from the hole take him away to the other side of life? Why did he fight so hard for life, when it could have all been over for him a short time ago? There would have been no more pain of missing his loved ones ever again. Would the Great White Spirit above receive him if no one had done the ceremonial burial dance for him to release his soul from Mother Earth to his land above? Would his soul be a prisoner inside the waters of earth trapped beneath the stone floor forever? If it was true, he would never be able to be with his lovely wife Winonah or their wonderful son Little White Eagle ever again.

Not wanting to think about its outcome anymore, he picked himself up off the stone surface and went back to the cave to warm up and put on a change of dry clothing. Back there, he pondered over the thought of his soul being trapped inside his body forever when he died.

The very thought of it made him bitterly mad and sad all at the same time. In the morning, he would travel not too far away to where he buried his loved ones in the meadow. Once there, he would beautify the lands around their place of rest.

The morning brought a gentle breeze with the smell of spring to the mountain air. With loving care in his heart and not wanting the white man to capture him, White Eagle ventured forth out across the forest floor and took in all the beauty of nature she had to offer him. With an attentive eye for danger, he watched as the early morning squirrels played in the canopy above the forest floor. He watched as rabbits hopped across the path in front of him, and laughed when he surprised two deer pawing at the leaves beneath their feet looking for fresh shoots of grass. His quiet movement through the forest caught many wild animals off guard as he stepped oh so softly on the dew-covered leaves and pine needles beneath his moccasins.

A red-tail fox ran from him as he rounded a large pine tree. A blue jay scolded him from above for being in her woods, as he made his way to the meadow in the quiet of the fresh morning air.

With a good part of the morning gone, he came to the white man's road made in the forest. He heard the sounds of a horse's hooves and the swishing sound a wagon made on the dirt road coming his way.

He laid down quietly beside the road in the thick of brush as a buckboard with a family of three passed him by. He laughed to himself seeing their funny looking dress. The man holding the reins had on black clothes and a funny tall black cap. His woman wore a big funny dress, and on her head she supported a big round headdress with flowers sticking out its ends. In the back of the buckboard, sat a small boy dressed similar to his father. He was wearing a black vest over a white shirt, and his pants looked cut off just below his knees. Sitting beside the boy in the back seat of the buckboard, sat a big black dog. It began to bark and bark after they passed White Eagle lying hidden down beside the road. The dog had picked up White Eagle's scent, and its fur stood up high on its back when it began to bark and growl at something in the woods the others in the wagon couldn't see. White Eagle was relieved when the wagon passed from his sight. He quickly crossed over the roadway without leaving a sign that he had been there.

Entering the meadow below the small cliff, he observed wildflowers getting ready to bloom on the edge of the field near the forest. He would keep them in his mind for later use as he journeyed pass the gravesites to the small cave on the hill. Again, he had to chase the bats out as they had returned to take back their den from him. He had to clear the bat dung from off of the cave's floor before he could use it for his own use.

How dare they return and mess up his second home away from the main cave. He lit a fire to discourage them from returning again as he went about throwing brush all over the floor to burn it clean a second time. He wanted to get the cave ready for when he returned during the summer months to visit his loved ones. He would devise a covering for over the cave's entrance to discourage any bats from returning again. Getting the cave clean again was a disgusting smelly job.

He went about taking great care in digging up the many different wildflowers growing near the outskirts around the meadow. He chose them by how tall he thought they would grow, and by the assorted color they would present when they were finished blooming. He then went about planting them in mixed rows around the three gravesites. It took him two long work-filled weeks at the small meadow to fix up the grounds the way he wanted them to look for his loved ones.

It was time to venture back home to the big cave. He had enjoyed watching the deer nibble on the grass at dusk in the meadow below as he watched them from the cave on the hill. He laughed after he scared away the porcupine that tried to steal his acorn bread while he was sitting watching the deer. He enjoyed watching a moose meander by as he watching White Eagle plant the many wildflowers. The fox that sat on the edge of the meadow day after day wondered what this creature was doing with all the flowers and rocks he was playing with. It had been an enjoyable hard-working two weeks, but it was time to leave now.

Half way back to the main cave, White Eagle noticed a clump of swarming honeybees clinging to a low branch of a tree. He had watched how the white man made beehives to house the honeybees for the collection of honey for its sugar and beeswax. He sat and thought a while about how he would keep the honeybees for his own use as he needed their honey to add to his food supply. It never hurt to have honeybees around except if one might sting you when collecting their sweet nectar. As he was sitting there watching the swarming bees, suddenly a thought about the tiny holes perforated in the tunnel of the cave came to him. Inside the main cave, the tunnel would make a perfect place for a collection of beehives for his personal use and a good place to leave them all year long. They would be able to come and go through the tiny holes in the wall of the mountain, and he would be able to have several of them there all at the same time, if he could possibly find more of them to fill the hives he didn't have yet.

He took his deerskin sleeping roll from his back and carefully tied it around the cluster of honeybees. While holding the branch they were on with one hand, he took his tomahawk with the other hand. With one mighty hard swing, he took the branch off the tree. The sudden weight of the swarming bees in his left hand almost took him to his knees so he hurried back home to the cave. Leaving the swarm of bees all wrapped up in his sleeping role outside, White Eagle hurried inside and grabbed some maple syrup from his supply and quickly took it back outside to the honeybees. He wanted to keep them busy gathering the sweet sugar from it while he made them a beehive. His only hope of the day was that they would still be out here when he returned to get them.

After taking some dry firewood into the cave, he split the wood into many thin strips with his tomahawk. He then hurriedly wove the thin strips together into one large square basket. Next, he quickly made a cover for the hive and some honeycomb racks to put down inside. Using small slats, he supported the honeycomb racks one on top of the other and made a small hole in the base of the basket for the bees to go in and out. His new beehive didn't look as nice as the white man's beehives did back at the reservation that were made from smooth wooden boards, but it would have to do. He poured some maple sugar over the inside of the beehive, and quickly took a torch and lit it before carrying the heavy hive down the tunnel. To keep it up off the stone floor, he put it on some firewood that he had carried down with him.

When he went outside the cave to retrieve his sleeping role with the swarming bees inside, he found his sleeping role still all covered with honeybees. He didn't know if he dared to pick it up or not. Grabbing ahold of the branch which they had attached themselves to, he carefully picked up the swarm and took them down the long tunnel to their new home.

He carefully opened up the sleeping role, trying not to get stung, as he gently dumped the buzzing honeybees carefully into the new hive. He gently shook his sleeping roll out over the hive, hoping the queen bee, who had caused the swarm in the first place, would still be in the massive clump of honeybees. He then put the woven cover he had made on top of the hive. He left his sticky sleeping roll covered with the remaining honeybees on the stone floor of the cave, and hurried up the tunnel to the main cave. He was amazed that he didn't get stung once. He felt exhausted from the events of the day, but still had built-up energy to burn. He went about making a bee smoker to use when he went back down the tunnel to check on his new hive. The smoke from the smoker would make the bees calm down before he opened up their hive to see how well they had adjusted to their new home. He only hoped they would still all be there when he went down to check on them.

In the next week, he went about making several more beehives. This time he took his time in making them, unlike the first one he had made in a rush. He didn't want them to go outside and put them next to the first one. To his amazement, the honeybees were busy coming and going from the hive. This was a good sign.

They had not deserted the hive, and his idea of getting more bees to fill the other hives was not just a dream. It was time to plant his crops for his winter stores. He had wasted time beautifying the meadow for his loved ones and making his beehives, but he should have planted his vegetable gardens by now. He took the several seeds he had carefully plucked from the couple of squash he had gathered and the few kernels of corn he took from the ears he had found in the old gardens from his storage pouches, and was off to the swamp to plant his first crops.

The water in the swamp was very high due to the large amount of snowfall they had had during the long cold winter months. As the snow melted, the thinning snowcap filled the swamp with water beyond its capacity. The once big islands in the swamp were much smaller now than they had been in the fall, and the little islands once there were now non-existent. He would have to change his strategy in planting.

His feet became soaked while trying to walk on the roots of plants just barely under the water when going from island to island trying not to make a trail leading to his crops. Once on dry land on the island, he tilled the soil ready and placed a small fish that he had caught at the bottom of each hole as fertilizer, giving the nourishment to the seeds to be planted. He covered each seed lightly with soil into the earth to let the seed sprout easily from the ground.

For the next couple of weeks he worked diligently hard on planting his crops of corn, potatoes, and squash. Maybe later on in the summer he would venture out to the white man's garden to collect the seeds of other plants that he'd like to plant for the following year. It would be a chancy move on his part, and probably not worth the risk. The more he thought about it though, it would be nice to have a variety of vegetables to eat during the years ahead instead of just squash, corn, and potato.

After having planted his crops successfully, he went back to the swamp on a daily basis to gather the dark grayish blue clay he found accidentally one day while out planting his crops. He carried vast amounts of this clay back to the cave to make into pots, cooking wear, and containers to store the food he would dry out from his crops for his winter stores.

He would sit for hours at the fire pit in the cave taking the raw blue clay and turning it into slender rope. Then he would take the rope clay, lay the strands one on top the other, and formed his pottery. Once the pots and containers formed into the many shapes he wanted, he let them dry for several days. Then he would take more clay and smooth the insides and outer sidewalls and edges. Once they were dry again, he put them gently into the hot embers of the glowing red fire pit, and covered them up with more hot embers to heat them into solid watertight vessels. After his jugs and pottery were finished hardening in the fire, he took more raw clay and formed covers to fit each individual jug and pottery separately. When finished, they became airtight and bug proof.

If a jug was to break in the process of making it, he knew he did something wrong, and proceeded to make another. Maybe he had spun the clay too thin or had gotten some dirt into the clay he used to make the jug when it broke. Whatever the reason, he pushed for perfection in doing everything he could to make his life as pleasant as possible.

During the rest of the summer, if he was not out hunting or making one of his several tunnels inside the big cave ready for his winter stores, he was over at the meadow tending to the flowers and grass around the gravesites keeping them trimmed and weed free. On his way home from the meadow a second time, he found another honeybee's nest swarming and clinging to another branch real close to the ground. Again, he covered it up with his sleeping role as he had the first time, and took it home with him. He placed it into one of the extra beehives and put it down in the tunnel next to the active beehive. Taking the smoker he had made a second time from clay, he looked into the first beehive to see how well they were doing. Taking some hot embers from his fire, he put some wet moss and dry maple leaves over the hot coals, and blew the smoke into the hole of the first hive. After a few minutes, he did it again. Then he lifted the hive's top up a little and puffed some of the smoke into the hive, and placed the lid back down over it. After several long minutes, he took the top right off the hive. The hive was thriving and almost filled to its capacity with honeycombs, honey, and honeybees. Then he carefully took a couple of the honeycomb sections out of the hive and placed them into a third new hive.

Unbeknownst to him, the old queen was ready to swarm on the cone he had taken and placed into the new hive. Now he had three active hives.

CHAPTER TWENTY-FOUR

The Injured Eagle

Going out to check on one of his snare traps one morning going down along the path leading to the bottom of the mountain, White Eagle heard an alarming screech come echoing up from the bottom of the sheer cliff where the old village had once been. Repeatedly he heard the horrendous cry. In checking it out, he found an eagle with a broken wing down below. She was a small bald eagle who couldn't fly and was trying to protect herself from a hungry fox that was circling around her and trying to snag her by the head with his salivate snapping jaws. The fox was swinging its head back and forth trying to catch hold of the eluding small eagle, and trying hard not to be bitten by her very sharp beak.

The fox was trying to get behind the injured bird, but she was quick. She turned and struck out at the fox like a coiled up timber rattler. Before White Eagle had a chance to intervene, the eagle had taken the fox by its nose. She took half of his nose off his face as he tried to get away from her. The fox turned and cried out in pain as it disappeared off into the woods.

The small bald eagle let out another horrendous screech as White Eagle approached her. She was trying desperately to defend herself against him as well while dragging her broken wing along beside her. She still showed that she was full of fight and ready to take on the world in defending herself against anything. White Eagle knew it would not be long before another predator would come along and take full advantage of her dire situation. She would also starve to death if he didn't do something for her.

"You are a great one, aren't you my friend," he said. "I have come to try to help you if you will let me." The eagle screeched out another bellow of alarm at him as he neared. "I come to help you and all you can do is scream and strike out at me. You are a great one, are you not? You will be called Great One. How is that for a name, my friend?" The eagle screeched out another warning to White Eagle, as she had the fox, and tried to scare him off as well. White Eagle crossed his legs beneath him as he sat down on the ground a short distance from her. He began singing her an old Indian lullaby that his mother had taught him when he was a child about friendship to calm the eagle down. It had a soft melody to it, and was about two people who meet each other in a lonely lost world. It fit the situation for the two of them at the time, bringing back memories of his sweet mother. He loved having her sing him to sleep at night like she so often did when he was a child. Seeing White Eagle was not going to harm her, the eagle settled down after a short time. She laid her broken wing down so it didn't hurt her as much as she rested on the ground.

When White Eagle got up from his sitting position, the eagle let out a loud warning screech toward him. Her loud cry almost deafened him and made his head spin. She was letting him know that she tolerated him sitting there, but that was all. He was not to approach her in any way as she would defend herself to the end. He would have to wrap the eagle up in his game sack in order to help her and not get wounded by her pointed beak or be torn to shreds from her razor-sharp dangerous talons.

He took a dead rabbit out of his game sack that he had

just taken from one of his many snares, and tossed her a piece of the rabbit. It landed just in front of her by her feet. She just looked down at it for a few seconds. Slowly, with caution in her eyes, she bent down to take a bite of it while still watching every move White Eagle made. She was hungry, but she was also cautious.

White Eagle took the rest of the rabbit and tossed it to her. It landed just out of her reach, behind her where he wanted it to land.

She had a very fast head. She would look toward the rabbit and then back toward White Eagle with lightning speed. She was hungry, but still very watchful of the beast who just tossed her the food. White Eagle was ready for her if she went for the food. He had his game sack ready to go over her head the second she made a move for the rabbit. Back and forth, she moved her head rapidly. White Eagle had stopped singing the lullaby shortly after throwing the rabbit behind her. If he had to move fast, he knew she would instantly detect the change in his voice when he jumped toward her. It would have been futile, so he stopped his singing.

Like a cougar ready to pounce, White Eagle held his game sack up in front of him waiting for the precise moment when it would be safe for him to move quickly. Suddenly, diving forward with the speed of an eagle diving off a cliff toward the earth below in pursuit of prey, the eagle had turned taking one step toward the dead rabbit. With its head turned for the split second, White Eagle made his move toward it with the accuracy of an arrow striking a target's bullseye. The game sack went down over the eagle's head. She reached out with her talons to protect herself, but White Eagle was not as quick as she was, and she took him in the arm. He began to bleed. It was only a mere scratch to his skin, but it still hurt like the dickens. She was just barely old enough to leave the nest, he figured. With the game sack securely tied down over her head, she began to calm down. Taking his vest off, he was careful in wrapping up the baby eagle and didn't want to hurt her any more than she already was.

Inside the cave, he tied her two feet together with a short loose line. Tight enough so she couldn't strike out at him with her talons again, but loose enough so she would be able to walk a short distance without getting into any trouble. He next took his vest off her. She didn't move a muscle as long as the game sack over her head was securely tied. Carefully, he spread her good wing out that was not broken. She resisted at first, but then let him finish it out after he started to sing her the lullaby about friendship again. With her good wing spread wide open, he wanted to know what her broken wing was supposed to look like before he set it for her.

The wing was broken in several places and not only a simple break. He figured she must have slammed it into the ledge, a tree, or a big branch in flight while chasing something to eat before hitting the ground. The wing was a mess. Taking very small twigs and string, White Eagle meticulously made a wooden splinter for the young bird by tying it around the shaft and over her broken wing bones. Similar to a tailor making delicate clothing, he carefully threaded the smallest twine he had in and around her many feathers. The twine would help her to mend in time. When he was finished putting the restraints around her broken wing, he took the game sack off of her head. He held up the rabbit that he had tricked her with, and within seconds of her eyes adjusting to the dim light of the cave, she tried striking out at it, not to eat it, but to defend herself. She also tried striking out at White Eagle with her talons as he sat there, but fell flat on her back.

White Eagle burst out in jolly laughter at her. How funny she looked trying to defend herself while being all wrapped up like an Egyptian mummy. Lying flat on the floor, she was not able to get herself back up to her feet. White Eagle began singing the soft melody to her once again. He had sung to her most of the night while trying to help fix her broken wing. The song kept her calm in the meantime. He picked her up off the floor and placed her down at the outreach of the string tied to her feet. She tried repeatedly to strike out at him with her talons as her wings were confined to the wraps he had placed carefully around her body.

She was frightened at first with her new surroundings, not knowing what was going on around her, or what was about to happen to her. He had a funny feeling. It seemed like he was talking to her without talking aloud. He thought he saw something deep in her heart through her eyes that said thank you. Thank you for scaring away the hungry fox and fixing my broken wing so I might fly again. The eagle reached out and took some rabbit meat from his hand a couple of times while staring deep into his eyes. She pinched his fingers a couple of times while trying to take the meat without looking. White Eagle did not flinch, but instead repositioned his fingers without taking his eyes off her so she could eat her fill. They were bonding as friends.

In the morning, White Eagle bolted from his night roll to the screeching sound of Great One mimicking the sound of an iron horse blowing off its loud whistle in his ear. He awoke with a start and was disoriented for a short time.

He wasn't accustomed to awaken in such a loud way, especially by an eagle's loud screech echoing off the inner walls of the big cave. There she was on the other side of the fire just staring over at him. She screeched again. Going to his icebox, he took out a piece of venison. It was the last piece of the leftover meat he had from winter. Great One did not hesitate one minute or even one second and took the meat immediately from his hand and began nibbling at it. He brought out a wooden bowl he had been whittling all winter long, and gave her a drink of water from it.

After eating a piece of acorn bread for himself for breakfast, he was out of the cave to go check on his snares again. What a pleasant surprise he had waiting for him in one of them. He had caught a turkey in one that was made for a rabbit. It had poked its head down and had entangled it in the snare. It was trying its hardest to free its head. With a quick swipe of his tomahawk, White Eagle took off the turkey's head. Its body went flapping off into the air trying to find its head, he thought. The snarl of a hungry mountain lion came echoing down from off the mountaintop. White Eagle didn't reset the rabbit snare because he didn't want to make it easy for the mountain lion to stay around the area and feast on the game he caught in his snares.

He knew mountain lions were clever creatures, and never showed themselves prior to their attack. White Eagle knew she probably had young kittens with her and didn't want to get in between them and their mother. Big cats are as bad as bears are when it came to coming between them and their young. They become ferocious and do not care what the size the animal is between them and their offspring. They would attack the intruder strictly out of instinct to protect their kittens. It was bad enough the turkey was flopping and flipping around and spreading the blood oozing out its neck all over the top of the ground. Finally, it calmed down and stopped its flopping. He quickly scooped up the dead turkey's head from off the ground, and took it along with the big tom turkey back to the cave to clean.

He didn't see or hear the cats again on his hurried trip back up to the main cave. As he entered the cave, he jumped back with a start. Great One let out a tremendous screech scaring White Eagle half to death when she heard the flap to the cave open. He fell over backwards and rapped his head against the ledge of stone overhang behind him. It was not serious to him, but it hurt like hell. Rubbing it to ease the pain, he told Great One to be quieter especially when he comes back into the cave.

He sat by the fire and plucked the feathers from the big bird, giving the turkey's innards to the eagle. Great One ate it with pleasure, as White Eagle put the bird's cleaned carcass on a spigot over the cave fire and cooked it. A fresh turkey would be a nice change in diet occasionally, he thought, if one was to get itself caught in one of the several snare traps he had placed in the forest. He would have to study how this big turkey entangled itself in the first place and purposely set a trap or two for turkeys in the future. He would purposely stay hidden in the cave for the next few days, and let the big cat pass. If it didn't move on, he would deal with it then.

He was very careful when plucking the feathers from the big turkey. He would set them aside to dry and use the feathers later on to make ceremonial headdresses, vests, bracelets, and anklets.

He'd store them with all the other feathers he was saving to make his big collection from ever since he moved into the cave. Every feather he found in the forest during his travels, no matter what size, would be brought back to the cave with him. Some of the special strong medicine feathers from the eagle would be used when he scared away any evil spirits from the peace pipe's smoke when he lit it. The pipe was made from clay when he was making his pottery.

With the big cats gone from the area, it was time to go check on the crops he had planted throughout the swamp. He crossed over the receding swamp waters with ease this time, and stepped carefully on top of the plant roots growing just below the water's surface.

As he was stepping down onto a submerged stump's root, he spotted a salmon spawning. He could not believe his eyes. Where did she come from? As his curiosity mounted, he forgot all about his crops, and journeyed off to the beginning of the swamp where the beaver had made their dams and beaver lodges. As he made his way across the swamp, he spotted a female salmon in the water laying her eggs, and the male salmon fertilizing them. Smoked salmon for the long winter months, he thought. That would be nice. He hadn't been back to the fishing hole between the cleft of rocks since he almost drowned there. While crossing over the beaver's dam, he found the waters below it busy with salmon lazing around and making their way up the stream and into the swamp to spawn. He quickly cut the branch from a tree with a fork in it, and cut a couple of barbs in each end of the forked ends and used it as a spear. In no time at all, he had tossed a dozen or more salmon out of the water and onto the bank of the brook ready for him to clean and smoke.

He looked at the salmon swimming and continued tossing them up out the water and onto the bank. Now he had fifty of them out on the bank. He had to stop. He had no idea how long the salmon would stay spawning in the swamp. In order to catch enough fish for the winter months ahead, he would have to prepare a smoker and make a salmon trap to catch a large number of fish.

After hurrying back to the cave as fast as he could with the cleaned salmon on his back, he was exhausted when he reached the flap to the cave. He placed one of the big salmon down in front of Great One. She tore into it as if it was candy and she was starving, but she was not. He put the rest of them on ice, and would tend to them later. He went to the next plateau above the cave and cut down many small saplings for the fish traps, and put all the shafts of saplings into the cave to work on them after it became dark.

He next busied himself by making a smoker for the fish he had just caught, and started smoking them over the cave's fire inside. He put wet hickory shavings that he had cut with his tomahawk onto the fire to make it smoke. When the wood dried and the fire flared up, he would then add more water to the wood shavings, making them smoke even more. As a boy, he had watched his mother smoke the fish the braves had caught for their winter stores.

Working late into the evening hours, White Eagle made a couple of large fish traps ready to be set into the stream of the swamp the next day. Early the next morning before sunrise, he fed Great One and headed out the flap to go and set his fish traps. Crossing over the swamp became almost second nature to White Eagle as he didn't have to look down for his next footing of roots. His feet became like magnets to the plant roots growing beneath the water's surface. Excited to see all the fish, he placed his first fish trap in the stream. They would be able to swim one way up through the fish trap, but the trap would not allow them to swim back downstream through it. He went downstream into the water and herded the fish up the stream as a farmer does to their cattle. Using a three-foot spear he had made with barbs on its end, he would occasionally spear a fish and heave it out of the stream. By day's end, he had all the fish he could carry back to the cave. Returning to the cave with his catch of the day, he laid them out and covered them with ice. For the next entire week, he caught fish and placed them on the ice, but his stores of ice that he had put in the cave over the winter were quickly disappearing.

For three long days and consecutive nights, he worked hard on smoking the fish he was able to land and drying them out and ready for winter. When he returned to his fishing traps the following day, he found them destroyed. They looked like a bear had found them and had been picking its fill of fresh fish out of them. The bear had destroyed them all at the very same time it was eating. He was lucky to have speared another dozen stragglers left behind by the bear. The spawning season for the salmon run was over, it had come to its end. He would have a better plan for catching more salmon the following season.

Returning to the big cave, he gave Great One a couple of the last two big fish he had with him. He loosened the cloth belt he had tied around Great One to keep her from hurting herself, allowing her to grow a little. She looked bigger to him from eating so many fish. He then cleaned her area of her excrements, keeping the cave clean, and not having to smell her unlikable odor.

Tomorrow he would tend to his crops. He hoped the animals had not destroyed any of them the way they had his fishing traps. If he did not tend to them soon, he wouldn't have any food for his next winter stores. He sure didn't want to eat rabbit and venison for his mainstay as he had to do this past winter. He had at least caught some fish this year for the winter.

From island to island throughout the swamp, White Eagle went weeding his crops of corn, squash, and potatoes. In his travels, he would come across an herb plant he would need to make some of his ancestors' medicines. Traveling throughout the forest, he threw different herb after herb into his pouch. Before the end of the summer, he would have enough herbs and special roots of plants to make up any kind of medicinal potion he might need to survive and make his life a little easier for him. At least he knew how to make the potions. The aspirin root for pain relief medicine, the tar root for getting deep splinters out of his flesh that he could not get out any other way, and other medicines for taking care of infections, dysentery, and for other causes of discomfort.

Weeding and sorting out his gardens paid off for him in the end. His harvest in the fall was fantastic. He had plenty of fresh corn to eat right away and much more to dry to make his corn meal. It looked like he was going to be eating well this next winter. He dried and stored away many more seeds this time for a bigger crop the following year.

Things for him were looking up. He was able to harvest some wild wheat growing alongside the swamp. When he was done, he had several of his large clay pots filled to their tops with wheat flour ready for mixing with corn flour or used by itself in his cooking.

He couldn't see it, but the constant frown he had developed upon his face out of loneliness was slowly turning into a smile. All the potatoes in his potato crops were small, but fair in size. He would plant nearer the mountain next spring so the soil would be not quite as damp, and they would stand a better chance to grow bigger and firmer for him.

His squash crop was fair as well. There had been excessive water around the plants on the small islands that he used, he thought, and would do with them what he planned to do with the potatoes the next spring. Before the bitter winds of winter came to the region, White Eagle gathered as much fallen firewood as he could from the forest floor. He filled a couple of the empty tunnels in the main cave up with his firewood, and when he was done, he had enough dry firewood in the cave to last the entire winter.

He would not have to go outside for anything except to rid the cave of his and Great One's excrements. His ice stores were almost gone. White Eagle was glad in a way to see the cold winter months come to the region so the ponds and water in the swamp would freeze over. It would be springtime before he would be ready to return to the meadow where he had buried his loved ones.

Taking care of Great One turned out to be a bigger job than he had expected. He had to feed her every night and in the morning by hand. She was like an automatic alarm clock before sun up, and would screech and scare him every morning. It bothered the heck out of him, as he never could adjust to the loudness of her piercing screech.

Her wing was so badly damaged that White Eagle chose to keep it tied up in his makeshift cast for four long moons. When the first snow of winter came, White Eagle chose to untie Great One's wing. She had all the faith in the world in him by this time, and was gentle with him when he hand fed her meals. When she got the least bit nervous, he would sing or hum the soothing lullaby to her, and it would calm her right down. He would sit for hours beside her in the cave. At first, she was afraid of it, but after a few weeks, it didn't bother her at all.

She seemed very content with him as he was the one who fed her and sang to her when she was nervous. Great One didn't know what to think when White Eagle unwrapped his special wrapping from her wings that had been coupled around her body for such a long time. He had loosened the ties around her body to allow her to grow several times, but this time he removed the wrappings altogether. She was free to do whatever she wanted to do. She tried stretching her wings out, but was unable to because they had been bound for such a long time. She was stiff and her joints started to lock themselves together. If White Eagle had waited one more moon, she may have never been able to move them again due to calcification build up in her wing and shoulder joints.

One day after another she would attempt to stretch her wings, and then let them relax back down to her sides. She exercised daily, and one day she really exercised as White Eagle was sitting next to the fire. The wind created by flapping her wings caused such a draft it blew hot embers out of the fire pit and onto a couple of his prize furs. White Eagle was furious in his voice, but kind in his actions. He moved Great One back into the cave and away from the fire pit. Unhappy with her move, she screeched in reprisal at him, and didn't want to be that far away from him.

Lifting up the flap to the cave, the sun was glistening down upon the snow. White Eagle lit a torch, and led Great One to the ledge on the sheer cliff. She just stood inside the cave's entrance and looked out at the snow. She had never seen the likes of it before as everything was pure white and very bright. It took a few minutes for her eyes to adjust after being inside the cave's dingy light for so long. The last time she had seen any daylight was when White Eagle had found her below the sheer cliff with her broken wing.

"Go ahead Great One, fly." White Eagle yelled to her. He started flapping his arms up and down pretending they were his wings and he was about to fly. Several times in a row, he flapped his arms until he was tired of it. Suddenly Great One mimicked him and flapped her wings. Several times she would flap her wings, and immediately stopped when White Eagle stopped flapping his arms. After several hours of trying to get her to fly on her own, White Eagle returned down the tunnel to the main cave with Great One following along behind him like his little shadow.

"All in time." White Eagle said to Great One. "Maybe tomorrow you will fly." Day after day for a week, White Eagle took Great One to the opening of the cave on the sheer cliff, but to no avail. She would stand on the ledge, flap her wings vigorously, but not fly. Once she raised herself up off the shelf of the ledge an inch or two, but she wouldn't commit to flying. White Eagle woke up real early one morning after having a good night's sleep without Great One around. He quickly poked his head out the flap, but did not see any fresh tracks in the snow outside the cave's entrance. She must have gone up to the cave's opening alone and tried to fly.

Grabbing a torch, he headed for the tunnel leading out to the cliff. Going around the corner, he saw her standing there. She was on the edge of the ledge flapping her wings vigorously, and then she stopped. White Eagle yelled out at her to go fly. "Go, go fly Great One. Go and show White Eagle you can fly. You can do it Great One. Go fly."

As if she had been standing there all the while practicing and waiting for him to come and give her permission to fly, she spread her beautiful large wings to the air and dove straight downward. Suddenly a lump came up into White Eagle's throat. He hurried to the edge of the ledge to look down off the cliff, and saw her hit the air currents of the mountain and sore skyward. Oh, what a relief it was to not see her dead on the ground below. Soon she was above him soaring higher and higher up into the early morning sky.

At first, he had thought she had forgotten how to fly. Like a new mother, he was afraid for her, but now he was proud. Oh, what a beautiful child of nature he had saved, and marveled at her beauty as she soared skyward. White Eagle called out to Great One by making a sound he thought she could relate to.

"KI-EEE, KI-EEE" he called out to her. She didn't know the meaning of KI-EEE, KI-EEE when she heard it for the very first time, and could not relate to it. Over the next several years, he thought she would learn its meaning well. For hours, she flew high above the mountains, eastward toward Mount Washington out of his site, and then back again. To White Eagle, she looked quite happy flying around, and wondered if she would ever return to him in the cave. After hours, it seemed that she was gone. He returned down the tunnel to the main cave to get something to eat, and thought he had probably lost the friend he had saved. She had turned out to be bigger than most bald eagles he had ever seen in the wild. Maybe it was because he had fed her so much fish and rabbit throughout her developing growth.

After a couple more hours, he felt she would never return to him. She was strong now, and he had accomplished a job well done in returning her to the wild. He felt good for his good deed, but sad that he had probably lost her forever. He sat by the fire pit and reminisced over his loss. What a beautiful creature she had been, he thought. She had a wingspan that spread out two bow lengths wide. Wider then he was and two times his height. She was truly a great one, and was one of a kind.

Suddenly a most horrendous screech from behind him took him up off his seat by the fire pit in total surprise. It scared the feathers right out of him as he had been daydreaming about Great One. She had not screeched like that in a real long time. He turned as white as a ghost as her cry echoed off the inner sidewalls of the cave. She was standing behind the bearskin pelt that he had covering the entrance to the tunnel leading up to the cliff's ledge with only her head poking through the opening. She stood taller than a short man did tall, and was a magnificent creature. He was mad at her for scaring him so, but very glad she had returned.

She came past the bearskin strolled up to stand in front of him. For many minutes, she stood staring and glaring into his eyes with deep compassion flowing out from her mind to his, as he stood staring back into her eyes. What was it she was trying to tell him? In her eyes, he could see the paths she had been presently flying over in her travels. The brilliance of the snow cover over the valley below and on top of the mountains. The smoke from the fires of the several logging camps in the region swirling up from the forest and into the bright blue sky above. Lumberjacks busy at work in the woods cutting down tall timbers, and then an iron horse steaming its way up the steel path through the river valley below.

How wonderful it would be to fly, thought White Eagle. For a split second, White Eagle wished Great One would fly over the reservation and his old village. He was curious to see how everything would look below, and she could return and show him how his people were doing. He shook his head vibrantly, ridding himself of the thought. He really didn't want to know because of the grief he had witnessed and the pain everyone was going through when he left. His brother, sisters, his brother braves, and his brother's children from the tribe were all dying from the smallpox. He had witnessed enough grief in his life already. The only grief that he wanted to see now was taking animals for his food. It saddened him every time he had to shoot an animal or catch one in a trap for his food, but that was survival for him. He felt bad for all the animals' families, because he knew how much they were going to miss them.

After her first flight, Great One took many flights from the cave to the skies over the mountains and valley. She would be gone for hours at a time, but would always return for something to eat. White Eagle could not believe how much she ate these days. He wished she would soon start providing her own food instead of relying on him for all her meals. He was afraid he had taken that part of nature away from her, the ability to provide for herself.

One day she came strolling in from out behind the bearskin rug carrying a huge snowshoe rabbit in her beak. It was so big she could barely carry the animal. White Eagle realized she would have generally carried the rabbit back to her nest with her talons and dropped it there, and not used her beak to carry it. The abnormal feat of hers amazed him. It must have been hard for her to carry the big rabbit all the way down the long tunnel of the cave, but she had brought the rabbit back for them to share.

The snow of winter had finally melted away, and spring had finally come to the mountains. White Eagle ventured forth to the burial grounds several miles away that he hadn't ventured to ever since Great One came into his life. The eagle required much of his time to enable him to return to the meadow before winter set in. He knew by this time, the area around the gravesites would require a lot of special care when he arrived. Little patches of snow remained beneath small ledges and vales where the sun didn't shine on it. The sun was high in the sky when White Eagle approached the meadow where the burial grounds were. He easily spotted the three graves with the many stones he had used to decorate them, and saw the remains of the colorful flowers resting flat on the ground beside the rocks. By the looks of all the dead flowers, the meadow must have been a beautiful sight in the fall when all the leaves in the trees surrounding the meadow turned their beautiful colors. It must have been beautiful, just the way his wife, Winonah, would have wanted it to be for her and their small son, Little White Eagle. White Eagle was pleased with what he saw. It would take a lot of work to weed and take out any of the old plants that had died, but was pleased the hard winter had not destroyed the area.

The small cave on the hill above the meadow was another story. The bats had returned to it and had taken back the cave for their home once again. He wondered if it was fair to the bats by his always taking the cave for his own use. They were small creatures and could easily find a place of refuge in small crevices of trees and rocks. If he didn't take it over, he would have to build a shelter and expose himself to the elements and the white man.

He built a big fire inside the cave to drive the bats out and dry it out once again for his own use. He would stick around for the next couple of weeks and work on the flower gardens surrounding the gravesite. While the fire burned inside the cave, he started the work on the gardens. Looking up, he noticed the smoke had finally stopped billowing out of the cave. When he returned, he hung another animal pelt supported by a pole to block out any bats that wanted to return. He coated the ceiling of the cave with wet sand and mud; this way if a bat tried to cling to it, the sand would break loose from the rock, and the bat would fall to the floor. That should work, he thought. He devised something to keep them out of his second home away from home, he hoped. He would probably find out the next time he returned to the area to sleep in the small cave for the night.

In the far off distance, White Eagle could see Great One flying high over the mountain above the sheer cliff. He had left a fresh rabbit high up on the ledge of the sheer cliff for Great One to eat. He had blocked off the tunnel leading out to the cliff's ledge so she couldn't come back down through it and into the main cave. He figured she would destroy the place if he was not there to supervise her, and knew she would not starve to death in his absence. She had provided them with a couple of big horseshoe rabbits during the long winter months. Now that spring had arrived, she brought back a couple of field mice, a gray squirrel, and a couple of unlucky chipmunks. He knew she could very well fend for herself, and would be all right without him around for a while.

By the end of the second week, the shrubberies White Eagle had foraged and taken from the forest, made the area around the gravesites look wonderful. It would enhance the splendor of the flowers he had planted before. They formed a natural external boundary line around the graves and flowers. He figured it would take at least one more week to complete his task in the meadow, so he stayed for another week to finish. When he was done, he sat down beside the small cave and marveled at the beauty below. His family would be very happy with him when they looked down on the meadow from the Great White Spirit's land above.

Returning to his cave on the mountain, White Eagle found everything was still intact. Everything was the way he had left it, and not even a mouse or squirrel had entered into it. He lit a fire in his fire pit to take away any of the moisture from its inner walls. He next went down the tunnel to his store of ice to fill his homemade icebox. He had built his icebox on top of a naturally hollowed out stone shelf inside the main cave. He used double-blind deerskin pelts filled with leaves as an insulator to keep the ice from melting too fast and to keep his food fresh inside. In the bottom of the hollowed out rock was a small crack that kept it from filling up with water as the ice melted, and drained it out through the wall of the cave.

Taking the heavy branches and pelts away that he had placed in front of the tunnel's opening, White Eagle ventured through the tunnel to the ledge on the sheer cliff. He called out to Great One. "KI-EEE" he called out. From high on an adjoining cliff, Great One answered by calling back down to him. She had made a nest on a stone platform that stuck out from an adjoining cliff and had a mate standing there on the edge of the nest with her. She flew down to the ledge, leaving her mate behind high on the nest, to be with White Eagle.

She looked different to White Eagle now. How only a few short weeks can bring change to one's life, he thought. He knew he had lost her to one of her own kind, another male that she could better relate to. In White Eagle's heart, he hoped she would never forget him. She stayed with him for only a few moments, and then she was gone. She left the ledge to be with her mate at their nest and raise a family of her own, he hoped. For a split moment, White Eagle's mind drifted back to his lovely Winonah and their ceremonial wedding night. He remembered holding her tight in his arms before they made love. Suddenly his subconscious mind took hold of his memory and blanked it out, protecting him from his pain.

Another full summer would soon be upon him, and it would be time to plant his crops throughout the swamp and in the forest for his fall harvest.

Little flashbacks came to him about Great One as he ventured back down the tunnel to the main cave. Sadness filled his heart as he thought about the many hard and funny things he went through to help her survive. Was she gone forever this time, he wondered? Would she ever come to him if he called out to her from the ledge? He would have to wait and see.

Looking into the fire pit in the main cave, a sudden warmth filled his heart. He felt the presence of his inner spirit, the bald eagle. His inner spirit told him that Great One would return to him when he called out to her. He was her father, brother, sister, and mother all in one. His inner spirit told him Great One would return to him many times and bring her offspring for him to see. In a time of turmoil and danger, would her fondest memories remain in his heart forever? How soon would this uniting take place, and under what conditions would it be?

CHAPTER TWENTY-FIVE

The Nightly Vigil Fire

Sitting out on the ledge of the sheer cliff, White Eagle lit his nightly vigil fire. Squatting down beside it, he wondered if his horse could see him in her heart. Oh, how he missed the long talks he had with her. She was such a good listener, especially in all the times he needed a friend. He hoped she was happy in her new surroundings. A shooting star flashed above in the heavens, breaking his train of thought, as it shot brilliantly across the sky. It followed a path directly toward the mountain from the north where the reservation was located. He wondered who had passed away to their happy hunting ground this time. No matter how hard he tried to block out his past, little flickers of his memory would shoot through his mind. Like the clotting of blood on an open wound, his subconscious mind would take hold of these memories that were trying to invade his mind and solidify them into nothingness before he had the time to think about them.

His horse had been his only outlet to the past. She alone knew his people. She had known Winonah, Little White Eagle, the chief of the tribe, and the others. Without her around to talk to about the past, it seemed his inner happiness would soon be lost forever. He had no one else to help keep his internal fire of life's happiness remain burning. For his survival in life, White Eagle found his worldly happiness in the many birds of flight, the assortment of different animals, and wildlife that surrounded him in the forest.

On a rare occasion, Great One would bring a different one of her two chicks to the ledge for White Eagle to see. During the long cold winter months, she returned to the cave with him, only she never ventured any deeper than the opening to the main cave from on the sheer cliff. She formed some coldness toward him, or was it an instinct of survival that she formed about another creature in her midst. Occasionally she would talk to him, and he to her. White Eagle asked Great One about her flying. He wanted to know how beautiful the land looked while he was looking down on it from up there soaring. They talked about the present and never about times gone by before had they met, and maybe that was why Great One seemed so cold to him. White Eagle really needed a way to talk about the past, to vent out all the hurtful feelings and sorrows he held deep inside himself. The pressure of sadness in one's lonely heart could drive a person mad.

How bitter the bite of death would be on a sad lonely heart. As the years and seasons passed him by, White Eagle looked forward to seeing the aurora borealis appear out of the northern sky. Maybe the little ghostlike spirits that accompanied the great northern lights every once in a great while would come for him, and he would be able to join his loved ones once again. He could not wait to see Winonah, Little White Eagle, his families, and friends again in the Great White Spirit's land above.

Sitting up on the ledge of the sheer cliff in the dead of winter, White Eagle would gaze up into the northern night sky letting the heavy snowflakes from the winter storm fall and melt upon his nose. He liked letting the large ones melt up against his warm flesh as he looked forward to seeing the little ghostlike spirits of light, but they never came for him. He danced many ceremonial dances trying to please the Great White Spirit. He made one up and asked him many times if he would bring him home to be with his lost loved ones above. He made special sacred potions to please the Great White Spirit, and smoked the peace pipe, trying to please him in rituals, but to no avail.

For some reason the Great White Spirit never heard his pleas, and never called him home. One night in the dead of winter while sitting out on the ledge, White Eagle lit up the sacred peace pipe to appease the Great White Spirit. Great One was sitting just inside the cave not very far away from White Eagle. White Eagle waved away the evil spirits with the first few puffs of smoke like the medicine man of his tribe had done. Smoke entered the cave and caused Great One to let out a horrendous screech. The loud response from her took White Eagle by total surprise. She only screeched the one time, but it made chills run up and down his skin. After he had only taken a few puffs of smoke, his inner spirit the bald eagle appeared before him. In his glory, White Eagle went soaring with her. It was springtime in the mountains, and another smaller eagle was out soaring right along with them.

His inner spirit led them out over and across the Connecticut River Valley. She showed them how the eagle fished, and how they hunted for their meals by spotting their prey below from high above. White Eagle wondered why the little eagle went tagging along with them. His inner spirit told him to watch over this small eagle, and to teach it the ways of the eagle. He wondered why he should be the responsible one watching over this small eagle. Suddenly, he was back sitting at the fire on the ledge beside Great One. What was this message all about?   Who was the little eagle who soared so high with them?   White Eagle was confused. Maybe next time his inner spirit would be a little clearer as to what she was trying to say to him.

Walking slowly past Great One, White Eagle stopped and slowly turned with concern written all over his face.

He looked back toward the majestic eagle, and asked her a few questions. "What did my inner spirit mean, Great One? Who was that other smaller eagle with us, was it you? White Eagle cared for you when you were injured. White Eagle fed you your meals. White Eagle helped you when you needed help. What was that all about?" She did not flinch or move a muscle; she just stood there in the cave watching him ask her the questions. She did not know what had transpired with White Eagle and his inner spirit. If she did, she wouldn't have been able to tell him anyway.

Springtime came again to the region. The winter snow melting in the warm spring air smelled enjoyable. It gave freshness to the area along with the crackling sounds of dry oak leaves snapping while still hanging onto the branches after the hard winter.

The music of springtime birds singing, returning to the mountain, never put a smile back on White Eagle's stern face. His face was as stern as petrified wood like the Old Man in the Mountain that was made of solid granite. It was his phase of life in existence without meaning. The only wrinkles White Eagle ever saw now were the wrinkles on the backs of his hands. He had not seen his own face in years. He had made a vow when he was a young brave never to see the reflection of his self-image ever again in any body of water. He didn't care if it was just a mere mud puddle, he made himself look away from any reflective water wherever he was. Even when he took a drink of water from the terra-cotta cup he made from the clay from the swamp, he would shake it to make ripples in the liquid, and never look into it.

He only knew his hair was getting grayish white because of its long length. He stopped keeping track of his age many moons before.

He had not seen the tiny wrinkles forming beneath his eyes or his nose and cheekbones that were slightly changing shape due to age. His body was starting to tell him that his internal seasons were changing right along with the changing of time. He had only recently started feeling the little pains in his joints, back, and along with his legs tiring more quickly now as he hiked through the mountains. He was beginning to experience shortness of breath. Time waits for no one, and age is never forgiving toward its host.

The sounds of a white man talking to a young white boy caught White Eagle's attention as he slowly crossed above them on his trail home from visiting the meadow gravesites. He had spent the last two weeks clearing and cleaning up after the long winter, making the meadow beautiful again for his loved ones.

The bats had made a small hole in the bear pelt he had put up over the cave's entrance to keep them out. It didn't work as well over the spring as it had over the last decade, and the cave was a mess again when he arrived. The bats had not visited the cave in many years. It took him two long days just to clean it up.

He was returning to the main mountain after spending two weeks of beautiful weather at the meadow. The sky had only spat light rain once, and that was during the late-night hours. The air of spring was warm, and the plants were popping up very early this spring. When he tired from plucking out the old plants from the garden soil, he laid back on the new spring shoots of bright green grass and listened to the music of the meadow and forest drifting on air.

The birds chirping, the squirrels running through the canopy above the forest, and the other animals of nature making their music in the forest a pleasant one. It was so soothing that it almost put White Eagle to sleep. The meadow had been alive with forest music for the entire two lovely weeks he was there, and now this sound of a white man's voice floating on the air spoiled everything about the forest music. The white man's talking was disturbing and almost frightening. White Eagle had not heard the sound of a white man talking since he left his old friend, his horse, off at a white man's farm years ago.

He stopped instantly in his footsteps, so he wouldn't make a sound on the forest floor and give himself away. If he made any kind of a crackling sound of a twig breaking beneath his feet, they would know he was there with them.

How many more white men were there down below? He had not seen any white men in these woods ever since moving back here. He was sure if he did make a sound, they would send him back to the reservation without ever returning to the cave or this part of the forest.

His mind was going in circles faster than a mountain lion could possibly run. How many men were down there, he wondered. Have they found the cave yet; and if they had, how many men were lying in wait to ambush him when he returned there. He felt sick to his stomach from being so nervous about going back to the reservation to live out his life. Would they send him back in shackles and chains? The more he thought about it, the more it made him feel sick. He didn't dare vomit from fear of being heard.

What would the rest of the tribe think of him back at the reservation now? Once a mighty warrior who was very strong and ready to be their chief who had deserted them in their desperate time of need, turned out to be a loser, they would think. They'd shun him into non-existence, and he would no longer be a part of the tribe. They would probably tar and feather him, and then make the white man move him to another reservation where they would not know him. His people wouldn't understand the promises he had made to Winonah, and would probably only think about their own wants and needs.

The voices from down below the ridge were not moving. White Eagle crept closer to have a better look. Pushing his head up carefully between two fallen trees, White Eagle saw a middle-age white man and a young white boy busy starting a campfire for the night. The boy was busier than a beaver trying to stop a leak in one of its dams. He was running from fallen tree branch to fallen tree branch collecting firewood for the campfire. The white man was busy starting to cook something over the fire. The boy would drop an arm full of firewood next the fire, and returned to the forest floor to pick up more. He hurried around like a little whirlwind picking up firewood and carrying armful after armful back to the fire. He had enough firewood stacked by the fire for a week's worth before White Eagle stopped watching him.

White Eagle was curious as to what the two of them were up to out there in his forest. He would not make it home this night because he wanted to follow them and see what they were going to do in the morning.

The smell of the beans and salt pork the white man was cooking in his pan filled the evening air with a most delightful aroma. It made White Eagle's mouth water, but he would find a couple of wild chestnuts to satisfy his hunger for the night if he was lucky enough, and the squirrels of the forest had not already picked the forest floor clean of them. He had used up the last of his food rations at the meadow, and was not going to eat again until he returned home to the cave that night, but things had changed. He would eat some roots from plants he knew he could fill his empty stomach. Tomorrow after he found out what the two white people below were up to, he would go home to eat a good meal at the cave.

Without losing sound of their voices, White Eagle ventured out to find his food. The squirrels had cleaned the forest floor of chestnuts and acorns, and there was not a single nut of any kind left on the ground anywhere. He would have to settle for a fiddlehead fern that grew near the ledge overhang next to the ridge where the two white men were. The ferns would have been much better tasting if they were cooked, but eating them raw and filling his empty stomach was okay, too. He sat eating his fill as he watched and listened to the two of them talk.

It had been a long while since he last heard the white man's voice, and was having a hard time understanding what they were saying. They were talking about the heavens and the stars above. Something about a fallen baby star lost on the mountaintop. All the stars above should be able to look down and see it they said. He was having a hard time understanding them talking about the little star. White man is not very smart anyway, White Eagle thought to himself as he listened to the conversation below. He thought about how the white man thinks he owns the Great White Spirit's land, and he does not. Someday, they will all pay for the way they treat the Great White Spirit's land by the wrath of an Arch Spirit from above. The Great White Spirit will take back the land the white man has taken away from the Indian.

Suddenly a great-horned owl dove down in front of the white man's fire, and picked up a mouse that was nibbling on a piece of bean that one of them must have dropped. It landed on a big branch of a tree by the fire and not far from them. They could see the owl regurgitating up a hairball from its previous meal, and dumping it down onto the ground below. As the owl lifted the dead mouse up with its beak above its head ready to inhale it, the young white boy ran over and picked up what the owl had just spit from its mouth. He then ran back to the fire with it cupped in his hand. The boy constantly looked off into the darkness of the forest toward where White Eagle lay hidden. He felt safely hidden in the bush out of sight, but a strange feeling came over him as he lay there hidden down in the brush.

He envisioned the little white boy as the eagle had been flying with him and his inner spirit. The vision instantly faded away into the darkness. What could his vision on the cliff have meant to him? Was it this lad a white boy or was he not? White Eagle sensed something very special and different about this young boy. He was inquisitive, energetic, and laughed with music in his voice. A quick remembrance of his son, Little White Eagle, flashed before him in front of his eyes, and then it was instantly gone. The willpower White Eagle had in holding out and hiding away the pleasant memories from his past didn't want to remember was very strong.

In the morning, White Eagle followed the two trespassers on the Great White Spirit's land, the land he had allowed himself to call his own for the past years. No one except for the animals of the wild was supposed to trespass on his mountain range, and no one was going to take the land away from him now. He would stand up and fight as he was his own chief without anyone else to worry about. It was only him this time around, and he was ready to fight. He had made up his mind. He would not return to the reservation or be made to leave the wonderful land of his. He would take up residency in the small cave by the meadow if need be or die fighting. Looking down at his wrinkled up hands, he knew it would have to be a war of wit. He had no strength left to fight any longer for his age was against him now.

Throughout the morning, White Eagle followed the two intruders once they came within feet of the main entrance to the mountain's cave. When they continued up and over the top of the mountain, White Eagle snuck into the mountain's cave beneath the slab overhang.

Cautiously he pushed back the heavy pelt flap covering the main entrance to it, and found the cave filled in total darkness. This was a good sign, he thought, as no one had been in there.

He flipped the gray-colored pelt up from the entrance. Then he uncovered the tunnel leading up to the ledge shelf of the sheer cliff. Once at the outer entrance to the cave's tunnel, he could hear voices drifting down from above the cliff. He stayed hidden safely inside the great cave, and didn't want one of them to see him. If someone was to lay out over the sheer rock and look straight down at the ledge below, they might see the fire pit in the middle of the ledge.

White Eagle sat patiently just inside the cave like a deer hunter would in a tree stand waiting for a deer to come prancing by for the kill. Suddenly, he heard a commotion of voices yelling, and then some pebbles came crashing down along with someone's pocketknife. It landed just outside the cave within arm's reach for him to grab. A trap he thought. They wanted him to go and retrieve the pocketknife, and then they would have him. White Eagle sat there quietly until darkness overtook the day. As the moon rose up into the sky above, he got up from sitting, and picked up the pocketknife from the ledge.

The brightness of the half-moon shining down on the blade of the pocketknife made it glisten in the light. Off in the distance, he saw a small campfire all aglow against the darkness. Carefully White Eagle left the safety of his cave, and from above slowly approached the campfire. Again, the boy sat looking off into the darkness of the night as if looking for something. White Eagle had a strange feeling that he knew this small boy somehow. He didn't know how or why, he just felt it in his inner spirit of love. It was a feeling of closeness he chose not to want any more in his lifetime.

It was the little boy's pocketknife that he had lost that White Eagle picked up off the ledge that had been a gift to him from his Uncle Bill, the man whom the boy was sitting with at the fire. White Eagle's English was poor from the lack of using it, but good enough to know they were not out there to harm him. The small boy continued looking off into the darkness as if he was looking for something. He told his uncle that he felt eyes of the night watching over them.

White Eagle had a flashback to the middle of the winter when he was smoking the peace pipe. The little eagle, he thought, was the little boy sitting there beside his uncle at the campfire. A twig beneath White Eagle's foot snapped as he slipped down on some wet leaves covering some damp moss. The boy by the fire jumped to his feet, staring in White Eagle's direction. Did the boy see him or not? He closed his eyes halfway with the darkness of the night to cover the whiteness of his eyeballs. When the boy sat back down, White Eagle snuck off to the quietness of his cave.

Looking out over the valley from his sheltered ledge, White Eagle could see the lights of night shining out of the wooden teepee windows around the valley. He could see the intruders' campfire a short distance from his cave shining toward him through the trees. The farms across the valley had lanterns shining brightly in their animals' wooden wigwams. The sparse lights that scattered below in the valley, looked as if someone had sprinkled a few stars from the heavens above all out over the countryside. If he could see them, they more than likely could see him and his fire burning bright at night up on the cliff's ledge. For the next few weeks, White Eagle was more than cautious, and was very vigilant in everything he did. Someone had violated his land, and if others were as curious as the last two were by peeking down over the cliff to see his fire pit, others would come and follow them there. He not only acted like a man who was being pursued, but like a wild deer would be followed by an aggressive hunter. Every move he made in the forest was slow and steady. He moved every hanging branch aside in his way that looked loose or went around them in order to not break them off or bend them, possibly leaving a trail that an Indian scout or military man could follow. He always walked flatfooted every step he took, and not to leave any sign of a trail. He took great care in the way in which he lived, always on the lookout now for trouble. He felt he had been too lax over the years by the way he was living, and now would be more cautious. Finding the campsite again that the boy and man had left in the woods had excited White Eagle. The young boy had stockpiled enough wood for a week or more worth of campfires.

It was late and White Eagle decided to make camp there for the night. Using a little of the wood from the stockpile, he would replenish the wood in future travels. White Eagle was returning to the great cave after being gone for a week working on the meadow. He was going to use the ready-made campsite once again.

He heard a dog barking off in the distance that caught his immediate attention. The young boy was back with a dog and not his uncle this time. He took great care in approaching the campsite this time, and carefully crouched down behind a bush to hide, enabling him to watch over the boy's campfire.

He, like his uncle before, was cooking something over the hot fire. When he finished cooking whatever it was, he tried to feed it to his dog. He watched as the dog refused to eat it. The boy became upset with his dog for not wanting to eat what he had prepared. When the young boy tried a bite of his own cooking, he spat it out. He reached down, and patted his dog's head to tell him he was a good boy for not eating it.

When the two of them were fast asleep, White Eagle carefully approached the campsite. He put the boy's pocketknife he had taken from the cliff's shelf, and put it into the young boy's sleeping roll. Cheerfully, he crept away so he wouldn't wake either of them, and returned to his cave to get some much-needed rest and food for his hunger.

CHAPTER TWENTY-SIX

The Blinding Rainstorm

The summer had turned out to be extremely dry. The rains of the changing seasons didn't visit the valley the way they usually did in spring and summer. The forest was turning tinder dry from the lack of rain. The leaves on the forest trees were turning brown in the middle of the summer. The corn crops in the valley below produced short corn stocks, and its fruit was not worth the picking.

The nightly fires on the cliff were kept very small, as White Eagle didn't want to start a forest fire by a spark from drifting embers. The crops he had planted in the swamp were doing just fine, but the ones he had planted in the forest had not flourished in the beginning. His crops of corn, potatoes, and squash would have been very lean for his winter's supply of food if he didn't do something drastic to help them. He filled water skin after water skin from the spring in the swamp, and carried them to his crops in the forest. If Mother Nature would not do her job as she had in the past, he would help do it for her. His crops began to grow as they had in the past. He would have a fine crop again in the fall of the season for his winter's harvest.

When the salmon of summer began to spawn, he was ready for them. He had his fresh new fishing traps made ready and lying on the ground beside the streams. He would position them in the channels of water that the fish would use when they swam up the stream and into the swamp to spawn.

In his travels, he again spotted the little boy and the white man he had seen in the forest by his mountain. This time they were far across the swamp on top of a second beaver dam downstream from their first dam. He watched as the two white people ran quickly away from the dam, and then it exploded. It sent sticks, mud, and water high up into the air. The waters from it started to flow downstream toward the big river. What right did these white men have to come into his forest and disturb his friend the beaver? It had worked so hard assembling the dam to make the swamp's pond bigger for their own growing family. White Eagle was mad, but it didn't last long. He made his way back home carrying what salmon he had caught from his traps to his cave in the mountain.

Maybe it was a good thing they had blown up the second beaver dam downstream. When he returned the next day to his traps, they were overflowing with the fish that swam up the stream the white man had made by blowing up the second beaver dam.

Day after hard-working day, White Eagle caught and carried his huge loads of fresh caught salmon back to the cave to be smoked. After a couple days of catching them, he would smoke them, and start the ritual of catching them all over again the next day. His stores of fresh fish for the next winter would be his treasure for the long cold winter months ahead. When finished catching and smoking his fish for his winter's stores, he set out for the meadow lands where he had buried his loved ones. He knew the flowers there would be in desperate need of water, if they were not already dead from the lack of rain. He figured the weeds that stripped the water from the ground beside the flowers had probably taken over his precious garden, and the quick growing weeds were now probably taller than the flowers.

It had been a long time since he was last there to water the flowers and take out the invading weeds from the gardens. He was right when he first got there. The weeds had taken over the garden as he had suspected. He spent the day taking care of the ones that almost choked his beautiful flowers to death as they were wilting and shriveling away. After plucking and clearing them from the garden, he began the rigorous task of carrying water to feed them from a stream a long ways away back to the garden. Carrying the water to the meadow was hard work. After a couple of days of making several trips a day back and forth from the stream, the flower garden was back in full bloom and made the gravesites a sight of beauty. It was a garden made for a princess, his princess Winonah, and for their noble prince son, Little White Eagle.

Looking out across the valley, White Eagle watched as Great One flew industriously carrying fish after fish from the big river back to her nest on the plateau. He thought it was very strange to see her doing this the way she was. She wasn't taking her usual time as she frequently did to stop and feed the fish to her young. He watched her drop the fish from her talons in midflight over her nest and return to the big river immediately for more fish. Maybe she had always done it this way, but it didn't look right to him.

Even the squirrels of the forest were acting differently. It seemed to him that they were extremely busy carrying extra branches to their nests, and sticking them in all around their nests. The friendly music of the forest had come to a quick stop, and the birds had stopped their harmonic chirping and friendly singing. The sky looked clear enough, but something was definitely amiss. He had to get back to the main cave in the morning because he knew a storm was brewing somewhere in close proximity. Only when the forest around the mountain becomes as quiet as a church mouse does the weather concern him, as that is when Mother Nature produces her trying storms, the quiet before the storm.

He awoke very early the next morning to a world without sound except for the squirrels scurrying through the forest canopy still busily working on their nests. The quietness of the air made him feel uneasy. Without a doubt, something very wrong was brewing.

Closing up the small cave quickly, White Eagle headed swiftly off for home to the big cave on the mountain. Almost running through the woods, White Eagle felt a presence he had never felt before. Anxiety filled him as he hurried along the trail wondering what was happening in his world. The air around him felt as though it was squeezing at him as well as the air he was breathing had a different texture to it as it entered into his lungs. Something definitely different was happening in his world, but he could not put his finger on it. The faster he traveled the more anxiety he felt. He had never seen the forest quite this quiet ever before, and it was scary to him. Even the scorning blue jays up in the forest canopy were quiet, and there was not a single squirrel running or chattering anywhere above. Something was very wrong in the forest. It was as if the doom of evil was lurking everywhere around him, and he needed to get back to the cave as soon as possible.

The strange feelings caused by the air around his body made him feel nauseated. He felt as if there were hot flames shooting out at him from a fire in all directions pushing him onward toward home before they could engulf him.

His mind began running wild with thoughts about warriors shooting arrows at him, and the little white ghost spirits of the aurora borealis dancing wildly around small eagles in nests. These thoughts scared the feathers out of him. He had to shake his head to clear up his thinking before he wandered off his trail leading him back home. The evil forces of daydreaming had been blurring his vision. He had drifted up higher on the trail leading him back home, and now it would take him longer to reach the cave.

Suddenly, he stopped dead in his tracks and looked out over the river valley out toward Mount Washington. A curtain of pure blackness stood behind the mountain with lightning flashing above. The black rolling clouds engulfed the huge mountain as if an avalanche of black snow was to cover a small twig on the ground beneath a mountain. Mount Washington disappeared before him. With the winds picking up, White Eagle wondered if he would make it to the cover of the cave in time before the destructiveness of the deadly clouds and lightening overtook him.

High on the adjourning plateau opposite White Eagle's sheer cliff ledge, Great One was attempting to make her two young baby chicks fly. She wanted to persuade them to fly down to the cave on the sheer cliff for their own protection. She wanted them to be with the one who had saved her life from harm's way when she was small. Her baby chicks were not quite old enough to fly on their own yet. They needed a few more days, but they didn't have any more time left to grow and develop their strength. It was either they flew now or never would because when the storm struck, they would be swept from their nest by the high winds and die.

Somehow, Great One knew the storm was coming and attempted to get them stronger with force-feeding them with as much fish as they could hold, but it had not worked the way she had hoped. She forced the first one out of her nest. The chick did not spread its wings until almost at the bottom of the cliff and crashed in a heap on the floor of the forest just below the sheer cliff. Once out the nest, the second chick had instant control over its wings once it hit the rough air. Great One joined her chick in midflight and guided her down to the ledge by the fire pit just outside the cave entrance on the mountain. The baby chick landing behind her took a tumble as it landed on the ledge. It was shaken up a bit, but it was all right. Quickly Great One led her baby chick inside to the safety of the cave. She and her lucky chick looked out over the valley and scanned the menacing clouds as they came thundering in across the valley floor toward them from New Hampshire.

White Eagle made it to the mountain cave just before the storm hit. He went directly up the tunnel to the ledge on the sheer cliff. He wanted to check on Great One and her two baby chicks on the high cliff next to his. Knowing he could not do anything for them, he wondered what Great One would do with the two to protect them. As White Eagle rounded the last curve in the tunnel, the baby chick along with her mother let out an ear-piercing screech. Its sound scared White Eagle half to death, as he jumped back not knowing what had just made the noise. On hearing her baby cry out, Great One jumped right out in front of White Eagle, stopping him dead in his tracks. It was as if to say leave her baby alone.

Quickly White Eagle began chanting the lullaby he had sung to her when she was a small eagle herself. It worked like a charm as it had before. She calmed down right away, and let him pass out through the opening to the ledge just outside the cave. White Eagle wondered where her other chick was. He saw more than just the baby eagle lying down on the ground below. He spotted the little white boy trying to pick up and save the baby eagle.

A flashback from the past came quickly to him about the day he had saved Great One from the fox. At first, the baby eagle tried to scurry away from the white boy, but stopped and let him help. The boy didn't have to stop and save the baby eagle either, but he was trying his best to help. He could have just as well been taking cover from the storm beneath the cliff's overhang, but instead took the wrath from the rain and the hail the horrifying storm was pelting down on him and tried to help the injured baby eagle.

White Eagle watched as the boy carefully wrapped the injured baby eagle up in some sort of cloth. His mind drifted back to when he was with his inner spirit, and his inner spirit told him to watch over this boy, this baby eagle. He was to take care of him, and to guide him in life.

What about the reservation, he thought. For a split second, the thought of it kept going repeatedly over in his mind. Would he go back to the reservation for helping the small white boy, and there shunned by the ones who once looked up to him to become their chief? He wondered if they knew if he was still alive or dead, but in their eyes he would be dead anyway.

Looking down, he wondered where the boy was going. White Eagle could see the boy was climbing up the wrong path that led to nowhere. In the hard driving rain, he could possibly slip or step off into space out over the sheer cliff to his death. He had no choice, as he had to warn the boy that he was heading toward death. He yelled out to the boy, but to no avail! The strong ruthless winds produced by the storm pushed his voice skyward away from the boy's ears as the young boy climbed to his death. He yelled again at the top of his voice, but still again to no avail, and his voice fell upon deaf ears below. As fast as his aging feet could possibly go, White Eagle descended down the tunnel and back down to the main cave. Stumbling over himself several times on the way, he fumbled out the animal pelt covering to the cave and went in a flash.

The howling winds outside were nothing he had ever experienced before in all of his lifetime. The mammoth rains pelted down on him like a waterfall and felt more like angry stinging bees with its sleet mixed in with the rain. He could not see two feet in front of himself. There was no wonder in his mind why the young boy could not hear him yelling. The sound of the rain and sleet in the trees was making so much noise that he could barely think himself.

As quick as lightning, as if being guided by his inner spirit, the bald eagle, White Eagle raced stumbling his way down the path toward the boy and the baby eagle. The hard rain and sleet on his face felt like it was burning its way into his pores and stinging him like angered bees all at the same time. Why was he out in this horrendous storm doing this? He should be safe inside the mountain's cave riding out the storm by the warm fire pit. If he saves the boy, he is going to lose in the end. Then again, if he doesn't save the young lad's life, he is going to lose his inner pride and not be able to live with his conscience for another day.

Mixed feelings of joy and pain ran rampart within his mind as he reached the path of no return on the mountain. The boy was about to step from the sheer cliff into the space of nothingness, a time of no return from a certain death was at hand. With the boy about to take his uncertain step into thin air, a helping guiding hand from behind reached out and saved the two of them from death.

No one ever knows what to do at all times in their lifetime. To be right is to be wrong, and to be wrong is to be right all at the very same time. If we can live with a clear conscience, we can live with its results and consequences that it has in store for us for the rest of our lives.

THE END

THE BEGINNING
FIRST OF THE SERIES
OF CHIEF WHITE EAGLE

BY L.S.WOOD

www.ingramcontent.com/pod-product-compliance
Lightning Source LLC
Chambersburg PA
CBHW071754190726
48292CB00003B/973